Praise for *Midnight Bowling*

Midnight Bowling is a brimming, brilliant, deeply American novel rooted in family secrets, young love, and the dark legacy of war. Dalton unlocks long-held, closely guarded family secrets in multi-layered love stories that play out over generations while revealing the beauty of lifelong devotion set against the backdrop of small-town American life. Dalton's writing is genius, and, with this novel, she's proven to be a true literary force of nature.

—Julianna Baggott, author of the *New York Times* Notables *Pure Trilogy* and *Harriet Wolf's Seventh Book of Wonders*

Quinn Dalton gives us fascinating insights about bowling in this excellent novel, but she knows just as much about love's complexities, particularly between fathers and their children. *Midnight Bowling* rings true as a perfect strike.

—Ron Rash, author of the *New York Times* bestseller *Serena* and *The World Made Straight*

Midnight Bowling is a terrific novel, not only a page turner, but a substantial piece of love-work. The characters are persons, not characters. The place is place, not setting. The story is convincing, sometimes scary, and often heartwarming. But it is bowling that holds the narrative together. When I felt the power of the sport take hold of me, I knew the book was a solid triumph.

—Fred Chappell, author of *I Am One of You Forever* and *Familiars*

MIDNIGHT BOWLING

Midnight Bowling

A NOVEL

QUINN DALTON

CAROLINA WREN PRESS

*The mission of Carolina Wren Press is to seek out, nurture,
and promote literary work by new and underrepresented writers,
including women and writers of color.*

This publication was made possible by Michael Bakwin's generous
establishment of the Bakwin Award for Writing by a Woman and the continued
support of Carolina Wren Press by the extended Bakwin family. We gratefully
acknowledge the ongoing support of general operations by the Durham Arts
Council's United Arts Fund and the North Carolina Arts Council.

Library of Congress Cataloging-in-Publication Data
Names: Dalton, Quinn, author.
Title: Midnight bowling / Quinn Dalton.
Description: Durham, NC : Carolina Wren Press, [2016]
Identifiers: LCCN 2016003012 | ISBN 9780932112828 (alk. paper)
Classification: LCC PS3604.A436 M53 2016 | DDC 813/.6—dc23

For David, Avery, and Alia

Part One

Tess Wycheski

✳ 1 ✳

TWO MILLION PEOPLE watched that day in January 1963 when my father choked at the pro bowling championship at the Showboat in Las Vegas. Everybody he knew had seen it, and he had plenty of time to think about that on the drive home to Sandusky. He was in the car his coach Leo Florida had left him before he skipped town. Leo had also left him some cash, but he was gone, and my father was alone, and only seventeen years old, and before that he hadn't been as far as Cincinnati on his own. Since then, not a word from Leo for a decade. No one, including Leo's own family, knew where he'd gone, though there were plenty of theories—he was back on the hustling circuit, he'd become a Communist spy, he'd gone to jail, he was dead—the last two lines gaining ground when he didn't show up for his own mother's funeral.

I didn't know about any of this when my father took me to the Galaxy Lanes for the first time. It was my ninth birthday, November 8, 1973, and he'd just gotten a promotion at Engineered Fittings, so he said we had a lot to look forward to. And not only that, he said, Leo Florida was back in Sandusky. There was of course no way for me to know what this meant to him even if he'd tried to explain it: who he'd been before I was born, what he'd hoped and dreamed for, and how I figured into any of it.

For me, the big event that year had been that my best friend, Chelsea, who'd lived across the street for as long as we both could remember, had moved at the beginning of the school year to a large split-level built on a former cornfield at the edge of town. Though the development was only a mile or so away, not far on bike, neither of us was allowed to cross any streets with traffic lights. She might as well have moved to China, was how we felt. We'd long believed we were actually sisters, and it was just an oddity that we lived in separate houses. So we cried and hugged as the movers loaded the truck, even promised we'd write a letter a week, though we knew we'd see each other at school, and our mothers had promised to take turns having us over every weekend.

My mother and Mrs. Vickham had spent hours in each other's kitchens, and I'd thought they were best friends, just as Chelsea and I were. I can see them now—my small-framed mother in a T-shirt and shorts, sipping on a Tab, brown hair in twiggy ponytail, wide-set brown eyes lit with laughter at something Mrs. Vickham had just said. And Mrs. Vickham—willowy, blond, perfectly pressed and coordinated—nodding appreciatively at her own wry humor. She was at least ten years older than my mother, college educated, and a businesswoman—a top Mary Kay sales lady in the area. At the time I couldn't have known how their different backgrounds might have affected their friendship, such as it was. I imagined our mothers telling secrets under a lace-edged comforter in Chelsea's room, though of course that was Chelsea and myself, not my mother and Mrs. Vickham.

But our mothers weren't actually friends, as it turned out. They had just been neighbors. The distinction had escaped me before, and apparently it had escaped my mother as well. In the two months since the move, Mrs. Vickham hadn't been over once, and my mother and I hadn't been invited to their new house, though my mother had even called to ask when she could bring their house-warming gift (a casserole dish—in case Mrs. Vickham didn't already have one? To bring casserole baking to the outer reaches of Sandusky? It wasn't clear to me). Chelsea and I had our own routine—at home, we were inseparable, but at school she tended to hang out with girls she took tennis lessons with at the Plum Brook Country Club, which her family had joined after her father had gotten the job at Kemper Golf. And I was in Mrs. Turner's advanced class, so we often didn't even have the same recess. If we noticed the lack of communication between our mothers, I don't remember us discussing it—we were still young enough to view the mysteries of adult behavior as unsolvable and beyond our concern.

But my mother was furious. "I guess they're better than us now," she said at dinner one night, after she'd managed to catch Mrs. Vickham on the phone only to be promised a call back shortly, which hadn't happened. My father laughed. "His last job was selling toilet parts!" he said of Mr. Vickham, while my mother stared at him as if he'd suddenly lifted off the ground.

My father, for his part, had maintained a hello-and-nod relationship with Mr. Vickham for all the years they'd been neighbors, which had seemed completely satisfying for him, and not worth pining for in its absence. Topics of discussion, if our fathers happened to be retrieving their papers or doing yard work at the same time, were limited to matters of upcoming or in-progress home repairs, the Cleveland Browns, and fishing conditions. Our street dead-ended into Lake Erie, and the houses had been built as summer cottages, so they were small and poorly insulated, and owners had over the years added back rooms or second floors, as was the case with our house, and had shored them up as well as they could. Pink insulation puffed from door frames like cotton candy, plastic billowed over windows, including over the roof of Mr. Ontero's house two doors down. Every November he would tether huge tarps to his gutters, which flapped like sails in the wind off the lake. They probably did little good, but Chelsea and I loved seeing them appear each year, just as we loved his pair of meticulously trimmed round bushes, which looked like ass cheeks.

The lake, and what weather it might bring, was another source of brief but serious exchanges between my father and Mr. Vickham, providing a note of continuity when the Browns weren't playing or neither man had been fishing recently. Mr. Vickham was given to grunting if it could convey his point as well as actual words, and my father had mused in front of me once about whether Mr. Vickham could string together a full sentence if money was on the table. But after the Vickhams moved, and it began to dawn on my mother that her friendship with Mrs. Vickham had been one of convenience rather than true attachment, my father professed to miss the Vickhams greatly, which only provoked my mother more. I knew not to so much as mention Chelsea's name at home unless I wanted to hear about the Vickhams' general lack of propriety, along with the specifics of how they were ruining Chelsea.

"I know her mother lets her wear makeup," my mother said out of the blue one time while pouring my cereal before school. But Chelsea and I often played with the Mary Kay samples Chelsea's mother gave us, which my mother knew, and I saw no gain in pointing this out.

Chelsea and I had worked out my birthday plan at school, not trusting logistics to our mothers. Chelsea would come with us to dinner at Frisch's Big Boy and then to a movie, and then spend the night. Since I knew my mother would refuse to drive to Chelsea's house herself without a formal invite from Mrs. Vickham—probably at that point it would've had to have been engraved—I'd enlisted my father to handle transportation.

So on that morning of my birthday, I sat in the living room watching cartoons, waiting for the day to pass, wondering what news Chelsea would have for me when afternoon finally came. Our games at that time involved pretending we lived in a New York apartment, or in a spaceship, or in college—nowhere specifically, more like College, a destination in and of itself. Anyway, there was a travel theme. She had already made it clear that she would be leaving Sandusky the day after we graduated from high school, and that she would take me with her if I wanted. Where we were going was not a detail I remember us discussing—it was the fact of leaving that mattered. I pretended to be excited about the idea, but I couldn't seem to make myself care either way, maybe because we still had a good eight years—another lifetime, almost—before any of these decisions would be available to us. And perhaps also because I had begun to suspect, even at just-turned-nine, that the world held nothing of great interest for me. The world had presented itself, and seemed not too hard to get along in, but nothing had claimed my heart yet, and maybe nothing would. Chelsea allowed me to drift along in her schemes and obsessions, and that was as close as I figured I would get to real excitement.

So when my father came into the living room from the garage that morning, walking briskly and wearing a jacket, I thought he was going to suggest picking up Chelsea early, and I sat up from the couch and began looking around for my shoes.

"How do you know we're going somewhere?"

"You're jingling your keys," I said.

My father laughed, pulled his hand from his pocket. In his other hand he held an odd-shaped leather bag. I'd seen it in the garage hunched like an animal on the metal shelves behind jugs of anti-freeze, the zippered, curved spine furred with a greasy dust. It had never occurred to me to ask about that bag or to look inside it; I imagined it held something dormant, better left alone. But that day, even in the gray light, I could see the leather had been cleaned. It smelled of shoe polish and car exhaust.

"You want to come with me?" my father asked.

I was happy to go anywhere, just to get out for a while. I turned off the TV and found my sneakers in the kitchen and sat down to put them on as he told me about the Galaxy Lanes and Leo Florida— names and places that meant nothing to me—and all that we had ahead of us. He was so tall to me then, his wrist bones poking past the edges of his sleeves, his shoulders curling inward as if he might be about to crouch down and cover his head, as we'd been taught to do in school tornado drills. He had red hair, gray eyes, high cheek-bones and a largish nose, and a smile that took over his face. He was only twenty-eight years old—my parents were nineteen when I was born—and pictures of them from my early years show them as the full-grown children they were, skinny, big-eyed, grinning. But he was my father, and thus ageless to me then.

He reminded me to get my jacket as I got to my feet. He seemed in a bit of a hurry as we headed out, closing the front door quietly so as not to wake my mother, and I wondered if he might be worried that she would stop us. Later I thought it more likely he was worried he would change his mind.

"Leo," my father said when we were in the car and on our way. He might have been starting to tell me something about him, or prac-ticing how he would greet him. I kept my eyes on the view over the dashboard; I already knew you could pick up a lot if you seemed not to be listening. My father turned on First Street, then Ogontz, then Cleveland Road, and then into the gravel lot of the Galaxy Lanes, a place I had been driven past for all the years of my life without inci-dent or comment, a place that had no mark on the map of my world until that day. It was only a few minutes by car from our house.

We coasted toward the aluminum arches of the Galaxy Lanes, which I guess had been designed to look space-aged but by then seemed as sweetly corny to me as the *Star Trek* reruns I watched after school. The lot wasn't crowded but my father parked way off to one side, half on the grass. He cut the engine and looked up at himself in the rearview mirror. "Stay close to me," he said as we got out, which thrilled me, though I had no intention of doing anything but.

I should point out that my father had never so much as mentioned bowling before. He'd never turned the television dial to ABC during PBA nationals, and we'd never watched "Make that Spare" or "Bowling for Dollars" while those shows still aired. My experience of sports of any kind had come through Chelsea, who, like her mother and older brothers, played tennis, while her father played golf—pastimes which seemed to involve a lot of green and hot sun and seemed to be as much about what you wore as what you did. My parents did not play any sports, and never had, to my knowledge. My father didn't even own a pair of sneakers—he did chores in his paint-splattered jeans and fishing boots. His idea of fun—and mine, too—was a day fishing in Put-in-Bay with a stop off at the Bait Barn for a bottled cold Vernors for me and beer for him, or bird-watching at Crane State Park, or ghost hunting on Johnson Island, where the last Civil War POWs were said to drift like smoke to the beaches in the evening, trapped by Lake Erie's dark water. My mother rarely came on these expeditions, not being a fan of fishing, birds, or the outdoors in general. She shooed us out the door with bagged lunches. This was fine by me because I was my father's daughter, eager to know what he loved—a promise that something hidden would be revealed, that I might be the only witness.

And that was how I felt that day, on the way to the Galaxy Lanes, until we stepped inside and stopped on a stretch of worn red carpet. The red looked to have been cut in to replace the spaceship-patterned stuff—which, I noticed as my eyes adjusted to the dimmer light, covered the rest of the place from the floors to midway up the walls. There were body-sized bleached streaks at our feet from the salt people had tracked in.

"Place has seen better years," my father said, and I had to agree. It didn't look to me like anything space-aged had happened in that place for a long time, if ever.

Ahead of us were the lanes. A father with some kids at one end. To our right, a few old men hanging by their elbows at the bar, cigarette smoke thick above their heads. There seemed to be no women around. I pointed to the row of red, shiny, rounded objects that looked like the fenders of old cars—one at the top of each lane. "The ball returns," my father said. He pulled me along with him toward the counter, and I bounced at the end of his hand like a netted fish, already itching to leave. I was thinking of what I would say to Chelsea about this odd little errand, how run-down and dark and, well, suspicious the place looked, when we stopped beside a small wooden swinging door. Beyond that, there was a doorway through which I could see shelves lined with wilted-looking red and white shoes.

We stood there a moment, and I felt my father's impatience coursing from his fingers into mine. He tapped the fingers of his free hand on the counter, turned his head left and right.

"You got anything to put your hair back with?" he asked me. I dug in my jeans pockets, turned up nothing. Behind us, the pins clattered every few seconds, and I cringed at the noise. Just as he stepped back from the counter, ready to leave—I hoped—a dark-haired, big-chested man came through the doorway. He had a pair of shoes in one hand and a can of aerosol spray in the other. He gave my father a nod like he'd just seen him yesterday, put the can down, and reached out his hand.

They shook. "Leo," my father said, just as he'd said in the car on the way over. Maybe he had been practicing.

Leo put the shoes on the counter, at just about eye-level in front of me. "Saw you coming," he said. "These should fit you." He winked at me and I stared back. I wondered why he hadn't gotten out a pair of the red-and-white shoes for my father, too. But later, I understood that this would've been an insult between pros—or former ones, at least—and of course my father still had his own shoes, custom-made Linds, shined as freshly as the bag he'd pulled them from.

The pair Leo got out for me fit just right, and it was hard to figure how he'd managed that at a glance, when at Zleigman's, where my mother took me to buy school shoes, you had to step on those cold metal measuring trays every time. But that was Leo, I learned soon enough. He'd seen us coming. There were, as it turned out, only a few things in his life he hadn't seen coming.

My father reached for his wallet, but Leo shook him off. He pushed through the small swinging door, saying something about the royal treatment, and led us to Lane 3, which I learned that day was my father's lucky lane, and which also became our lane. There was nobody to our left, and several lanes to the right were empty, too.

Leo wanted to know if there was anything else he could do for us. My father set his bag on a bench and straightened up. "We're fine, thanks," he said.

Leo shoved his big hands in his pockets. He cleared his throat, nodded. He seemed to want to talk more, but my father leaned back to his bag, unzipping it and rummaging until Leo turned and headed back to the counter.

"Let's get you a ball," my father said then. He led me over to the racks of balls, all of them black, looking like bombs straight out of *Looney Tunes* cartoons. He made me lift ball after ball, the kid sizes, until he thought the finger holes were spaced right and the weight was something I could work with. They were all too heavy as far as I was concerned. "This one," he said finally, and then he led me over to the Lustre King polishing machine and let me put a dime in the slot and told me to push the button, which I was happy to do because I loved lighted buttons as much as any other kid. The machine swallowed the ball and kicked on, and the ball rolled out of the slot again a minute or so later looking like it had never before been touched. He held it up, inspected it. It seemed as light as a balloon in his hand. He pursed his lips, looked down at me, narrowed his eyes. After a moment he said okay, and then told me to follow him.

"Watch what I'm doing," he said when we got back to Lane 3. He squatted at the top of the lane, kept his balance with his fingertips as he leaned even farther forward, chin jutted, squinting. No one else was doing this, I noted as I looked to my right at all the other bowlers. They were just rolling the ball, their arms swinging forward as smooth as pendulums.

Finally he got to his feet. "Not one change in the lay of the land there," he said. I had no idea what he meant, and he didn't explain. He retrieved his ball from his bag and held it up like an exhibit. It was a deep red with a low sparkle in the finish that reminded me of the tall red plastic cups I drank sodas from at Harry's when we went for sandwiches on Saturday afternoons. "Now. I roll a Amflite Magic Circle because it's springier on these lanes," my father said. "Leo, he probably still rolls a bleeder." He must've read my confused expression because then he shrugged. "They soak up the oil, you have to wipe them off all the time." He gestured toward the front counter.

"His dad rolled with the Sandusky Icebreakers, you know, which—well, they were a name for a while." My father stopped, looked at me. He seemed to have so many things to say and show me that it was a physical struggle to figure out where to begin. The effort to decide played out on his face—the fast blinking, the pressed lips. Even then, I understood. Sometimes my head hummed with things I wanted to say, and I couldn't choose and so I said nothing. My mother seemed to think we were both keeping our respective secrets, and that may have been true of my father, but for me, much of what was going on in my mind was a mystery to me. I could look at him and see myself.

My father set his ball in the return next to mine. "Let's walk to the line." He showed me how to back up four-and-a-half steps. "That's your point of origin. Not just where you start, but where your roll starts."

Then he said we should practice our approach. "We're going to teach you everything just the way it should be done," he said. "Watch me." He backed up and then slide-stepped to the line, his feet barely lifting, stopping with the tip of his left shoe even with the line, his right hand reaching, as if he might be trying to catch something falling through the air. "It's like dancing," he said. "Try it."

It wasn't like any kind of dancing I'd seen. I looked around. I felt foolish, pantomiming, but no one seemed to notice what we were doing, busy as they were actually bowling. Every few seconds the pins crashed in the boxes at the ends of the lanes and were swept away. I backed up and glided forward, or tried to. As I backed up, I felt my father's fingers on my wrists. "You don't keep your hands at your sides. You use your free arm to propel you, and your body to propel your rolling arm," he said. I had the feeling he'd be willing to practice this particular move with me all day, until I had it right. The prospect wasn't exactly appealing.

"Back up, let's try again," my father said, and I said okay, and we stood at our points of origin again, mine slightly forward because my stride was smaller, preparing for my next phantom roll.

"Why don't you just let her give it a try?"

We both turned to find Leo leaning on the return a few feet behind us, one hand resting on it, a cigarette burning in his other hand.

"Well, now, that's a thought, coach," my father said, his eyebrows raised but no smile on his face. I didn't think he liked Leo, so why come here? There were other bowling places around.

"That's all it is," Leo said. He took a drag off his cigarette and looked across the lanes as if he had other things to keep an eye on. But he didn't seem to be in a hurry to leave us, either.

"Any other words of wisdom?" There was a pained tone in my father's voice, which I'd heard before, sometimes late at night if I happened to wake up and hear my parents talking. I couldn't catch the words, even through our thin walls, but it always seemed my mother wanted something, and my father wanted to understand what it was.

"If you're wondering where I went, it was nowhere good," Leo said. He tapped his cigarette on the tray attached to the console, took another drag. "Hey kid," he said. "You see your father over there? You know he went pro, right?" Leo pointed to the wall next to the counter, where there were rows and rows of black-and-white photos, some head shots, some team shots. I took a few steps closer. And there was my father with his slicked-back hair and pointy-collared shirt, a big goofy smile. He didn't look much older than the sixth-grade safety patrol kids in my school.

"You know he had the record for the most perfect games in one season in his age group," Leo said. He really was trying. I looked back at my father, who was studying his glossed shoes as if he wondered how they'd gotten on his feet. Leo looked like he had about given up on any kind conversation. Behind me, pins crashed two lanes over, and I shivered at the noise. Leo saw this and grinned—I'd given him something else to talk about.

"That's nothing, kid. I used to be a pin boy down at the State. There was an alley down there, in the basement. Did you know that?"

I shook my head. What a question—why would I know? The State Theatre was a downtown landmark, but it was closed by then, its windows dark. Of course I didn't know there'd been a bowling alley there. My father rolled his eyes, but Leo ignored him. "Okay, well, there used to be a little bench between the pin boxes every two lanes, and that's where you'd perch." He pointed at the space between the end of our lane and Lane 4, and then looked at me to see whether I'd grasped the risks of doing such a thing. My father was standing beside me now, hands in his pockets, making a show of listening. I had a sense that anything Leo said was going to upset him. This kept my attention.

"So there was a board on each side called a side kick that was supposed to keep the pins contained. You'd sit up there—" he stood in a crouch, feet spread, knees bent, looking almost like a jockey on a horse, "and when a box was done, you'd jump into the pit, put the ball on the return and roll it to the bowler, and scoop the pins. There was a pedal back there, too. You'd step on it to raise these rods so you could place the pins. Then you'd drop the pedal and hop back up on the bench and pray the pins wouldn't fly up and hit you when some guy cranked it back down the lane. And you're doing this on two sides, mind you."

Leo acted all this out, and my father watched. I couldn't read his expression. "Anyway," Leo said, straightening up, "if you were good, you could set without the rods. But most people wanted you to use them, so you couldn't crowd the pins and do someone a favor for a cut."

He winked as he said this last part. He was what my mother called a flirt, the way he made it seem all of this was just between us. I liked him, I decided, even though I understood that whatever was between him and my father had nothing to do with joking around.

"Because there was always betting. Wasn't there, Leo?" my father said. He rested a hand on my shoulder. "You should tell her about that. Tell her all you know about that."

Leo looked down at the ball return, patted it like a dog's head. "Sure thing," he said. He stubbed out his cigarette, gazed out over the lanes again. "I'll leave you to it."

My father watched Leo walk away until he was almost to the bar. He turned back to Lane 3, surveyed it again as if considering a great distance. He got his ball from the return and carried it to the top of the lane, cradled it against his chest as if he were praying. Then he said he might roll a few just to get warmed up.

Of course, I didn't know how it must've felt for him, stepping back from the foul line after so long. I didn't know then that the last time he'd done that, more people than lived in the entire state of Ohio had watched him bomb on national television. He probably felt he was being watched again by everyone there, and he was probably right.

He glided forward. And he did look like a man dancing, or skating on glass as he approached the line, his arm swinging in front of him smooth as a trapeze artist, reaching through the air, his chin uptilted in a way that looked both confident and fearful. He expected nothing, that's what I think now. He had given up, and come back humble. But he'd chosen to take me with him. That's what I felt—as if I'd been let in on a secret, one I wasn't even sure I could express to Chelsea, to whom I told everything—and that this place, the Galaxy Lanes, was a room in our house which had been kept locked until that day. My father, who always seemed rushed and nervous, now looked to be swimming, his movement graceful and measured, though the ball appeared to shoot from his fingers, slowing only to curve into the pins. I thought of school films about the astronauts landing on the moon and the lower gravity there—*imagine moving through water*, our teacher had told us—and I could imagine it, watching him.

My father rolled nine strikes before he missed a pin. When he made the ninth, he turned around and said to me, "And here's your wish for next year, sweetheart."

Then he rolled again and dropped them all but the ten pin, but that was okay. My pulse felt big in my throat. I had seen something of him that I hadn't known before, and it seemed to me for the first time that there was a world of things I didn't know.

"I want to try," I said—actually, I didn't realize that I'd said anything, but my father had heard me. He put down his ball, retrieved mine, and ushered me to the top of the line. He tapped my thigh to remind me of the four-and-a-half steps back. He showed me how to position the ball at my chest, and he pulled my shoulders back so that the weight of the ball wouldn't throw me off balance. At some point, I knew it was time to move, and so I tried to glide forward as he had. But while he'd seemed to be floating, I felt only weight—in my arm, in my legs, and the soles of my feet. The ball dragged me forward, left my fingers too late. It slammed into the floor rather than sailed; it meandered to the pins. A few tipped lazily as if agreeing to lie down just to humor me for trying. I was dumbfounded—my father had made it look so natural.

The pins rolled and stilled, and I turned back to my father, expecting him to be disappointed. Instead, he had the same look as game show contestants when they'd won the grand prize. There was a sudden gleam at the edges of him, as if he'd found something that no one else in the world knew existed.

I walked back to him and he turned me around, gave me some more direction about the optimal bend in the legs, about letting the ball go a heartbeat earlier. I tried again with more power though not more accuracy. I rolled a few in the gutter, but my father was only happier with each roll, his words clipped when he leaned in to explain this or that adjustment.

Eventually, I got a strike. I whirled back to face him, threw my hands over my head, jumped up and down, expecting him to do the same. Instead he looked no different than before—just smiling at me and nodding to himself at some calculation he'd tried and confirmed. "Fine, good," he said, same as he'd said when I'd rolled a gutter ball a moment before.

I turned back to look at the lane. The evidence of my first triumph was already being swept away, the next frame set. I had the sense that those pins in particular, not to mention the place itself, had been waiting for me. There was a pressure in my chest, almost the same feeling as when I was about to cry, which I hated to do. But this was more powerful. I felt as if I'd expanded somehow, filled myself more fully. I couldn't have explained this to anyone, not even Chelsea, maybe especially not Chelsea. But I did know I wanted to roll again.

I walked back to where my father stood waiting for me. He looked at me with concern, as if he could see what was happening to me. "How's your arm?"

"Fine," I said. I wanted to get on with it, and he could see this, too. "How's your wrist?"

I said fine again, and shook both hands to demonstrate. "You should watch your wrists," he said. "Your mother has weak wrists."

This was not a detail I remembered either of my parents mentioning. My mother, overall, was not known for weak points. She had moments when nothing could satisfy her, when she found doom in every misplaced spoon, and during those times, if my father was not at work, we went on one of our various expeditions, or just for ice cream downtown, or to the marina to watch the boats—which was only steps away from where we stood now, eyeing each other. My father, I knew, was sizing me up, and I was trying to decipher what he thought he was seeing.

"Did you see that—what I did?" I said, since I didn't yet know the word for strike.

"Yes, I did," he said. "And it was great. But let's not overdo it."

"I want to go again."

My father tilted his head to one side, and the smile in the wrinkles around his eyes told me he loved me—that part of his expression I recognized. But there was something else, a watchfulness, as if he was seeing me in some new way. And he was; he told me later. He understood what I wanted, even though, as was typical for me then, I couldn't put a word to it. Mastery—that was the desire pushing against my ribs.

By the time we left—hours later, it turned out—my father tipping an imaginary hat to Leo at the counter as if he'd beaten him fair and square at something, I had fallen in love with bowling the way you love a food and can't remember what life was like before you tasted it. I loved it for the way the ball curved—hooked, my father explained—magically into the pins. But, no, he said; it wasn't magic. A hook took years to get right; it was a fingerprint, the full expression of a bowler's movement, traced across the boards. I closed my eyes and listened—I loved the way he sounded, explaining everything to me, and I believed he had come back to bowling not just to see Leo Florida again, but because of me, because of us.

After that, at the Galaxy Lanes, we were the Wycheskis. My father might have only been pro for one day back in 1963, and he might have choked on national television in front of millions of people, but he was still a pro. No one else there except Leo Florida could say that.

We were the Wycheskis, and we had a plan. By the time I'd rolled my first 200 game, I'd known what to do, because my father had explained it. Get going with Youth American Bowling Association, learn the competition through that and scratch matches. Start after school at the Galaxy when I got old enough, working the counter and scoring matches. Letter in high school, keep up with league play and tourneys until I was ready for the PBA qualifiers. It was a path. It had been my father's path, in fact, and while it hadn't gone exactly right for him, he was prepared to show me the way. He would teach me how to be weightless on the glide forward; he would teach me the timing of the release. The game was, after all, about position and timing, and he would help me absorb this truth into my very cells.

My father warned me that some people wouldn't understand this level of focus—he didn't name Chelsea and her set specifically, but I got his point. Bowling wasn't exactly glamorous—not anymore at least, though the framed black-and-white photos on Leo's Hall of Fame wall made me wish that men still wore suits and women tight-waisted, full-skirted dresses, sitting in neat rows to watch the home-town matches. My father said it didn't matter that those days were gone; it didn't matter that the Galaxy wasn't a showplace anymore, or that the unions were on their backs in our town and across the Mid-west while the good jobs blew away, or that thousands of men, some of them scarcely a decade older than me, had streamed from the jungles of Vietnam to the Veterans Home on Columbus Avenue, many of them missing this or that part, some of them still seeming to be on the lookout for them. What mattered was that perfection could still be had in the form of a ball curving with just the right spin toward its target. Correct action could prevail. "Don't let Leo make you think the *how* doesn't matter," my father said to me over and over again. Maybe he worried from the beginning that Leo would ruin me like he'd nearly ruined him. Anyway, I didn't care—I believed my father when he said the past didn't matter. The important thing was that he was my coach, and we were the perfect combination: natural-born talent and experience. All we needed was each other—we knew this the way we knew the order of pinfall in a perfect strike, left-handed or right-handed, or the number of boards a ball had to hook across to make that strike.

What we didn't know was the number of years and months and days we had left together, which were seven, five, and two, respectively. That math, simple and final as it turned out to be, was beyond us.

2

THE FACT THAT Leo Florida left my seventeen-year-old father in Las Vegas the night he froze at the foul line at the Showboat was reported in *Bowling News*, *Ohio Bowler*, and the *Sandusky Register*. Only one article, the one slightly sympathetic to Leo with a nod to his high scores—"semi-pro material"—mentioned that Leo had at least been kind enough to leave "the young Joseph Wycheski" his car, in which they'd driven out there together. The question was where Leo went and why. My father had always believed that Leo had taken off, and stayed away for years, because he was so embarrassed by my father's failure. And this was the reason my father had sworn off bowling. He never said this to me, but I knew, and knew just as well not to ask him about it.

It wasn't that he hadn't rolled well. He didn't roll at all. There is probably still footage coiled up in a can somewhere, and you could play it over and over again: my father standing at the top of the lane at the Showboat, four-and-a-half steps back, ball cradled like an egg, perfect form. He advanced to the line, shuffling forward. And stopped. Shook his head. Went back to his point of origin. Advanced and stopped again. Did this a couple more times. Sat down at the line and bowed his head, clutching his ball between his knees until Leo came onto the floor and led him away.

My father, an only child born late to his parents, hardly left their house that spring after he returned from Vegas until his father, a

nonbowling quarry worker—thirty-five years in the pits off Milan
Road—demanded he get a job. So at the beginning of that summer
after his famous failure, my father was onboard as a deckhand on the
Neuman ferry line, which runs back and forth to Kelleys Island, and
that was how he met my mother, who was on vacation with her family. He found her on the upper deck, face turned to the sun. She was
small and beautiful, her brown hair tinged with blond. He was sun-
sick at the time, his skin burned and peeling, but he knocked off the
patches of dead skin the best he could and introduced himself to my
mother, asked her to meet him that night. Just like that. Whenever
my father told that story, I couldn't imagine any boy my age having
that much courage. But then, my father had gone from rolling lines
on national television to tossing rope coils, so maybe he thought he
had nothing to lose.

After the last ferry run of the day back to Marblehead, he took
his father's bass boat and made the four-mile return trip to Kelleys
Island. My mother was waiting for him outside the Hoezvelt cottages. They took two of the bikes her family had rented for the week
and rode by moonlight to the glacial grooves, which looked like frozen water, petrified crests and troughs of waves. They sat on a beach
nearby, and he went swimming out to a buoy and back in the black
water to impress her. When he sat dripping beside her and tried to
kiss her, she'd slapped him on the ear. I know, because she told me
later, that the reason she'd slapped him was because it was the first
time she'd thought she might be in love and she was scared.

As for my father—maybe he'd used up his fear for a while. He told
her he wanted to drive down to Centerville and take her out on a date
that Saturday night, and she said her father was a preacher. He said
in that case he'd come on Sunday, when her father was at work. And
this made her laugh. My mother had grown up in a family of devout,

nonconversational Methodists, and she wasn't used to humor. She, too, had been born late to her parents, though she had two siblings, a twin brother and sister, twenty years older than she, who lived together all of their lives and never married, a family detail she chose to say very little about. She and my father agreed that if they ever became parents (on this first date, I imagine they were speaking about their own distinct futures, not yet seeing them as intertwined—or maybe this moment was their earliest inkling) they wouldn't wait so long to have kids; they didn't want to look like grandparents at their children's high school graduations, as her own father had, who was seventy-two when she'd gotten her diploma the previous spring.

Whenever my mother told stories about her childhood, which wasn't often, I imagined it in black and white, like the first part of *The Wizard of Oz*. Mostly she talked about being bored, about wanting to run away, about moneymaking schemes to fund a bus or train ticket to New York, Chicago, or at least Columbus. She had considered careers in dance, acting, and fashion design—and maybe when she and my father met, those dreams were still clinging to her, a gauzy hope that lit her cheeks and eyes and made him fall in love with her.

After that first date, my mother didn't get caught sneaking back in her cottage, and my father sped across the glass-gray dawn water in his father's bass boat and made it to work on time. They got married that Christmas in 1963, and I was born the following November.

My father never said he was unhappy with my mother. Once he said to me he wished she'd slapped him harder, brought him to his senses. But that was after she started working at the Emmanuel, a store-front church that had moved in after Zleigman's Shoes closed, and she started bringing home slippery little pamphlets with pictures of a blue-eyed Jesus looking sadly down from the mount, or from a cross, with what I later recognized as just a hint of sex in his eyes—

something I knew better than to mention. Another time, when my father replaced the roof of our house himself, he told me to keep in mind that the root of "mortgage" was old French for dead. Many, many times he told me that, when it came to marriage, I should wait. The reasons, whatever the specifics, always had to do with keeping the Wycheski Plan on track.

He didn't have to worry. I couldn't think about anything else. There were notes home from my teacher Mrs. Turner about my loss of focus, but she had it all wrong. My focus had simply shifted.

My mother felt it, too. Of course we talked about our days at dinner the way we'd always done, but she was no longer in the same orbit with my father and me. It never occurred to me to think about how this felt for her.

For my father, and so also for me, what mattered was bowling a perfect game. Leo teased us about it. "Perfection is a nice side-effect of winning," he said whenever he heard us talking about it, how we'd come close, or where we'd fallen short. My father ignored him, and told me to do likewise. But by then things had eased between them. They seemed to me like the old men at the bar when they came back from fishing, telling different stories about the same catch—calling each other liars but laughing it off just the same.

Maybe my father's quest mattered even more to us both when the first wedges of pain forced their way into his knees, then his shoulders, and then all his joints. The year I turned eleven, he was diagnosed with rheumatoid arthritis. His doctor warned him that there may be only a few years, given his young age at the time of diagnosis, before a wheelchair claimed him. Over the years, he slept less and less. He woke me up many nights once I started high school, nudging my shoulder with the toe end of his sliding shoe, his bag in his other hand. "C'mon," he'd whisper, and I'd pull on sweatpants and follow his slow progress downstairs and out to the car. Sometimes Leo was just closing up, but he'd let us in anyway, and there we'd be on Lane 3, with the whole town asleep. Most nights, Leo's nephew, Donny, would be there, too, and I wondered if he'd even gone home for dinner. Of course, I never asked. I was there because my father wanted me there, and that was enough for me. Sometimes, with everything dark and just the lights along the lanes glowing against the spaceship-dotted carpeting, I felt as if we were sailing, the whole place a ship skimming over the lake.

During those late-night practices, my father taught me the roll was in the release. The perfect strike lived in the grip, in the swing of my arm, in the lift off my fingers, in the letting go. He talked about how good I was, and how I could do anything I wanted with an arm like mine. By that time I was almost as tall as he was, and though I had my mother's coloring (my brown hair tinged blond in the summers, just like hers), I was broad shouldered and skinny like him. When I looked at my arms and wrists and hands, I could see a smaller version of my father's same lines, and sometimes I wondered if the pain he was enduring was lurking in my own joints.

And for all he did to hide it, he suffered more and more as the years passed. It didn't matter how many tournaments I won, how many trophies he placed in our window, which I would quietly take down and hide in my room so as not to seem to be boasting to the neighbors. It didn't matter that I lettered as a freshman at Sandusky High. That was the year he started taking so many prescriptions that he needed a special box to keep them straight—different ones to help him sleep, to control nausea, to give him a steadier hand at Engineered Fittings ("A job is a job, isn't it?" he'd say when I asked him how was work). His body was freezing up as surely as it had at the Showboat in Vegas, and no one could stop it.

Still, I had this feeling that if I got good enough, if I could roll a perfect game, maybe I could stop it. Correct action could perhaps prevail after all. I started looking for any advantage. So I asked him if I could get one of those just-out urethane AMFs that was designed for the new regulation lane conditioners, unlike the old models that were made to go on oil. He always said soon, soon—when he had time to research it, when he could talk to my mother, when we had the money.

And then, seven years to the day after I first walked into the Galaxy Lanes, on the afternoon of my sixteenth birthday in 1980, my father and I stood inside the doorway, unzipping our jackets to let some heat in. Chelsea, who already had her driver's license and a new car to go with it, was going to take me out later for dinner and a movie, and possibly some beer pinched from her father's garage cooler. But the most important thing was cradled in my arms like a baby: my own AMF Angle, still in its box, glittering gold-green through the cut-out window.

Donny was working the call boxes; he waved to me from the counter. I waved back. I could smell a tickle of chalk in the air, and I breathed it in, the way you do when you're home. Because I was, standing there with my father, checking out who was rolling that Saturday morning as the fall chill seeped from our clothing. I loved the place. I loved how it all fit together, each area with its purpose: the lines of shoes behind the counter, the rows of balls like huge Christmas ornaments, the dark-paneled lounge, where the low red velvet couches looked slouchily dangerous, even though they were faded by then from sunlight that came through the glass emergency exit Leo had installed to meet fire codes. The pro shop and arcade. And then the lanes: twenty-four of them, each crowned with rounded, chrome-trimmed ball returns like little spaceships, the red triangular hubs in the middle with the shiny hand driers and the call box if you needed a manager to set splits for practice or fix a sticking sweep. Fanned around the returns were the booths and chairs for the different teams, and behind them, the consoles where you kept score, with their fold-out drink holders and ashtrays I had to clean out each night if I closed.

My father looked at me and smiled, tapped the box in my arms. He was feeling good that day. This was the ball I'd go pro with, he had already explained. I hugged it to my chest and smiled back.

"Now, we know the local color and you've got the city tourney in the bag, right?" My father paused, and I finally looked up from my gleaming new ball. He was waiting, eyebrows raised, a crackle of electricity in his gaze. "Right?" he said again. I nodded.

"Then there's district. We could even skip city if we want to. And then you'll qualify for state." He scanned the lanes, rubbing his chin. Leo was behind the counter as usual that day, handing out a pair of rentals, phone pinched to his ear—this was before Donny put in the second line. My father chewed his bottom lip and then nodded— he'd decided on something. "Now Leo's going to want you to do the scratch division this year, and we know why, because you'll make him look good. But you might not have time for that. Then again, it's pinfall only."

"And the JTBA, that's scratch, too," I said.

But my father wasn't that excited about the Junior Bowlers Tournament Association. A kid my age from Mount Vernon had just started it that fall, and there'd only been a couple of events, and there was no route to go national. But I liked that there wasn't a girls' division, though that was only because the participant numbers were still so small.

I shifted from one foot to the other. I squinted down at my ball, and the glitter seemed to float just above its blue-green surface. I wanted to roll it right then, though I knew that even if Leo could drill it that day, I'd have to wait a couple of days for the grips to set.

My father, meanwhile, had moved on to how we should convince the PBA to agree to full membership instead of just the junior even though I was only sixteen, or maybe we should just get through the current season, and after that my birthday wouldn't be that far off, and we'd have a better case if I was closer to seventeen. Which was the age he'd been when he went to Vegas. He had that look on his face—wide-eyed now, jaw set—that I imagined he'd had when he stood at the top of the lane at the Showboat, just before something in him gave.

And that was what made me ask if he was sure.

"Sure about what?" he asked, that flash again in his eyes.

"Just because I'm so young," I said, meaning because *you* were so young.

"We're doing this right," my father said then. "Textbook."

I nodded. I was on board, as long as I could roll that ball. My mother would be none too happy about how much it had cost, but I knew that what mattered more was that my father and I had our plan, and that we were prepared.

My father headed for the lockers, and I followed. Only the slightest hitch in his stride suggested he might be feeling less well than he acted. We passed Leo at the counter. He still had the phone pinched to his ear, but he nodded to us as we passed and jerked his head toward the pro shop to say he'd be right there.

"The Tour," Leo had always said when people asked him what it was like being a pro, "is a great place to starve." He was quoting someone on this, I'm sure. But in his case, timing had worked in his favor, and when he'd come back to town after his ten-year absence,

Bern Schnipke, his old boss and the former owner of the Galaxy, had been ready to retire. And then it turned out when Bern died, he'd left everything to Leo, even his house and the furniture inside it. Another item in the timeline, if Leo were to tell it, was when Eddie Elias from over in Akron started the PBA to increase the purses and standardize the sport, which might've seemed to be a good idea, but which Leo said took the soul out of bowling. He said things were better when Walter "the Cigar" Ward had made his name in the Cleveland All-Stars, always rolling with an unlit stogie in his mouth and racking up more 700 series than anyone else in history. Or Tony Sparando, who was nearly blind, out of New York, or Joe "Bick" Wilman out of Chicago—you could know Leo ten years and he'd come up with some name you'd never heard of who'd broken all the records back in the day—and not only that, he'd fixed them drinks and fixed them up on dates with barmaids when they'd come through town. And there were his days setting up match plays down at the State, where the bookies took bets from traveling salesmen, small-time players, call girls, and fixers. He made them feel at home, since they couldn't get into the country clubs, where their bosses, sponsors, and johns worked other deals.

But the present, I always got the feeling, was a bit faded for Leo. He had bills to pay, leagues to coach. That's the way I saw him then—worn out, irritated, but a fixture. He was my friend Donny's uncle, and I still didn't know then why he'd come back to town in the first place after leaving my father in Vegas and then disappearing. My father had never discussed it and Leo hadn't either until the day I came in with that ball.

My father and I stopped by our locker to get our bags and shoes. Beyond the pro shop, the arcade sounded like a giant ringing jar of change.

"Damn racket," he said, as if the place hadn't been loud before. He reached for my bag, but I grabbed it before he could try to lift it. I had the AMF under my other arm. "Look at those skinny necks," he said, jerking a thumb at the arcade, where, in front of each machine, a boy flailed and swerved with the screen action as if plugged into a socket.

Donny had talked Leo into putting in Pong, Galaga, Space Invaders, and Asteroids, and the newest, Pac-Man—and now the place was packed every day after school. Before the arcade, it was dead on the weekdays except for the retiree leagues and team practice.

"They ought to try a game with real skill," my father said, winking at me. We stopped at the Lustre King ball polisher, and he dug in his pocket for two dimes, handed one to me. You could choose Gloss, High Gloss, or Super High Gloss. My father put his dime in the slot and chose Super High Gloss, as always. I chose High Gloss. It was a personality test, I think. My father wanted things perfect, and I did, too, but some part of me could live with good enough. If he thought his pain was a punishment for not living up to his own standards, he never said so.

Leo was grinning when my father and I came back to the counter. He reached across and clapped my father on the shoulder, and my father did a good job of not wincing. He hadn't told Leo anything; I knew that.

"Hey, hey Joe-Joe!" Leo said. He loved his bowling stars, even his former ones. They were good for the game and good for business. Then, to me, "You ready to drill that ball?"

I looked at my father and he smiled back at me. He was as excited as I was. "Yeah, let's go in there," he said. "I'm thinking top weight positive, and maybe she's ready for the fingertip grip, what do you think?"

Leo put up his bowling hand like a traffic cop, the fingers twice as thick as his left-hand set. "Whoa there, Joe," he said. "Only room for two in the drill room. I'll give her some options."

My father pursed his lips, looked away. "See you over there, then," was all he said to me. I could've maybe protested, but I didn't want my father to feel I was defending him, to give the impression he needed defending. I watched my father walk away—he'd adopted a slow stroll intended to look casual rather than careful. If Leo noticed, he hadn't mentioned it. He stepped through the swinging door, and I followed him into the pro shop, a tiny square room with new balls on curved, Astroturf-lined shelves. Behind that room was a closet with a counter on one side and a modified mill press on the other. I carried my sliding shoe so I wouldn't scuff it on the linoleum.

Leo opened the box and held up the ball. "So these things are going to be the next big wave," he said, as if he doubted it. But he knew better. He may not have liked it, but he knew. "So Wyecheski Junior is sweet sixteen. How's the old bleeder anyway? You still like it?"

He meant my White Dot. The covers were so soft they'd soak up conditioner from the lanes and you had to keep wiping it off. Overall, I liked it because it was easier to hook than a Black Beauty. "I don't know," I said. I felt loyal to it in a way. I had an uneasy feeling that I might be betraying it. Leo looked at me, bushy eyebrows raised. He was starting to go gray by then, specks in the hair around his temples. I straightened up, and it seemed to me that he wasn't as tall as I'd always thought. "My mom'll be mad," I said. "It cost a lot."

"Your dad's the one bringing home the paycheck," he said, shrugging.

"Leo," I said. "You know my mom." She didn't come to the lanes except for tourneys, but even when I won, she congratulated me as if she were really trying to comfort me instead. She called Leo "the Blob."

"A lovely woman," Leo said, smiling. He set my new AMF in the machine. He leaned against the cinder-block wall, one foot crossed over the other, one hand resting on the ball. He patted it like the top of a child's head. "I'll bevel it so you come out clean," he said. "And listen, if I could have all the time back in my life I spent worrying about what someone else thought, I'd be ten years younger."

I considered saying that was fine for him; he wasn't living with my mother. He wasn't watching her go through the bills, her eyebrows hitched up with worry. My father was working reduced hours by then, a deal the union had worked out. But it was temporary, we all knew, a step that would lead us to even more uncertain territory. Leo didn't have to watch my parents tiptoe around that fact, my mother folding the paper to the classifieds, hiding the circled ads under the phone book. In fact, Leo had never married, which didn't surprise me, and not just because I couldn't imagine it with him being fifty by then, his belly pooched out under his favorite Beers of the World shirt with all the labels in different languages. It was just that I couldn't imagine him ever loving anyone that much. And I had this feeling, even after seeing him almost every day all those years, that he could disappear again the way he had after my father had frozen up at the Showboat. I'd come by some morning to practice and the doors would be locked and no one would know what had happened. Maybe Donny would take over.

"Maybe I'll wait," I said. "It's like you said, a good bowler can roll with a rock, right?" I didn't want to wait, of course. But I wanted him to tell me not to.

"It's all the same to me, Wycheski." He bent to lift my White Dot out of my bag and turned it around. He put his fingertips on the holes, but he couldn't even get the first digit in. "You can do fine with this," he said.

"What's that supposed to mean?" I said.

Leo spun the ball on his finger and caught it in his palm like a Globetrotter, all while looking straight at me. "You think anyone's pining over what happened to your father out there in Vegas?"

Obviously, the answer was no. I shook my head. I was shocked he'd brought it up. Since I'd never heard Leo talk about Vegas in connection to my father, I could believe it wasn't quite true, like those stories your parents tell you when you're little—about how babies are born or why a fair number of men in our town were missing limbs or seemed a little nervous—because they figure you're not ready to know the truth.

"No, no one's sorry about it anymore, probably not even him," Leo was saying as he stuffed my White Dot back into my bag. "He's got this idea that you'll go pro someday, right?"

"You think I can't?" I said.

Leo nodded. "That's right. I think you can't."

I stared at him. "Thanks, coach."

"Look here, Wycheski. When I was a kid working in the basement down at the State, no one wanted to be the last one out of those lanes. You know why?"

"Why," I mumbled, not really asking. I felt dizzy with his dismissal; I reached carefully behind me for the counter so I wouldn't knock too hard against it if my knees gave.

"The place was haunted. That's why." Leo gave me a look. "You believe in ghosts?"

"Sure," I said. If an adult asked whether you believed in something, you believed. It was good policy.

"No you don't," he said. I shrugged.

"When I started down there as a pin boy, it was like as if you fell into a movie. You'd have all kinds of stars come through there after a show upstairs—Shirley Temple, Marilyn Monroe, even. And the bowlers," he shook his head and looked at the floor as if words had escaped him. "The Budweiser team came there once, back when they had Weber, Carter, Bluth, all of them. Bluth shot 834 once, unheard of in those days. But that's not my point. My point is that a kid I worked with down there had a seizure one night and choked on his tongue, and after that you could hear a ball rolling down the lane after everybody cleared out. You were the last one out, you got to hear him rolling a few lines after work."

Leo squinted at me as if he wasn't sure I deserved to hear the rest.

"Okay," I prompted.

"Okay, here's the thing. I was a cheat. Not for myself, but I'd bunch the pins for guys I liked so they'd get more strikes, and they tipped me in. I didn't believe in all that. So I never heard the ghost ball."

He stopped and looked at me again, as if trying to decide whether I'd gotten his almighty point. "Look out there," he said. I looked over my shoulder; through the door I could see the usual run for a Saturday: parents with their kids doing grandma rolls, retired leaguers getting their practice rolls in, guys from school cranking the ball as hard as they could down the lane, their girlfriends rolling limp-wristed, the best way to get tendon strain. And my father, already at Lane 3, leaning slowly forward on the bench and putting on his shoes. I looked back at Leo, biting my lip to steady myself—all those little tricks my father had taught me: a quick bite on the inside of the cheek can distract you from your fear and help you get back your focus; blow on your wrists if you start to feel dizzy, deep breaths. All those tricks, and none of them had worked for him after all.

"If you believe you're like them, you're like them, just having fun," Leo continued. "You can't just be good. You have to want to win."

"I win a lot!" I said. My voice quivered, which infuriated me. I thought about what my father had said, about how you could be talented, but without a plan you'd get nowhere. But we had a plan, and it was a good plan. The whole situation had gotten confused. "I've been Junior Bowler of the Year for three years!"

Leo waved at the air. "Your father thinks you're God's gift. So what are you going to do? You want to go pro, fine. Your dad may have bad nerves, but he can help. But if you really want to win, you come see me again. I'll get you ready. Just no talking about it. I don't want everyone bugging me."

I swallowed. I knew he was saying my father wasn't good enough to make me a pro. I knew he would think that even if he'd been aware that my father was sick. I hated him for saying it. But I hated even more that I believed him. "Drill the ball, Leo," I said, bearing down on my voice so it wouldn't shake.

"Here," he said, handing me the finger-sizer. "You've got some skinny digits, lady, but let's see if you've changed any." He winked at me, and then he was back to the behind-the-counter Leo, the good-time guy. But there was still that layer beneath, like the weight in a ball. Or like the deeper you go in water, the colder it gets. I was pretty sure that if I'd brought up the ghosts again, he'd ask me what the hell I was talking about.

Turned out, my fingers had gotten a half-size thicker since he'd drilled the White Dot for me. Leo said it was good we were sizing in the afternoon, when your hands swelled; that way he wouldn't drill too tight and risk making the ball hang. You could dislocate a finger that way, he told me, filing each slug to soften the edge. "The professional treatment, that's what you're getting," Leo said, blowing away the dust. It hung in the air for a moment, a glittery cloud. I couldn't wait to roll that ball, and at the same time, my throat ached. It was maybe the first time I remember being heartbroken. It was the first time I understood the word.

Leo ended up drilling my ball the way my father suggested. He just didn't want to take orders from a guy he used to coach, was what I thought. I hated him for that, too. And yet what he'd said about winning seemed to be about more than just being good. Or even perfect.

He finished drilling the fingertip holes and said he'd slug it deeper if I didn't like it. He put it in my hands, and I slid my first knuckles in, the holes still friction-warm. "You're going to have to give it some time," he said then, watching me try it. "It's gonna be like as if you're starting over."

"I know, I know," I said. I thought he meant about going pro. I was thinking about the next tournament, and how it would be to sail that ball. I was thinking about my father, and how I wanted to do everything we planned. Everything. I wanted to stand at the head of that lane at the Showboat, go all the way. Settle an old score. If Leo could help me do that, I'd take him up on it. But the credit would go to my father, every bit. "I'll put my time in," I said.

"No," he said. "You're gonna have to get used to it is what I mean. Try it out and I'll adjust it, and then we'll put in the grips."

So, for a short time, I had two coaches—an official one and a secret one—Leo behind me and my father on the other side of the glass, who I could see at the top of our lane then, pulling his arm straight across his chest to stretch the muscles. Everybody had been waiting for me to beat him, my father included. I hadn't yet, though plenty of times I'd rolled well enough to do it. "The key is," my father would say after each game, "You have to try for the perfect strike whether you're competing or not."

But I knew Leo saw it differently. He'd say you only have to win when you're in the game.

In fact, the first time I met him for a practice, which I scheduled right after school when my father would still be at work, Leo put it like this: "The world cares about the what, not the how. The sooner you understand what I mean here, the better off you'll be." Turns out he knew that better than anyone.

Leo Florida

3

SO FOR SIX days in 1961, my older brother Walt was dead. And truth be told, everything comes down to that. I'm telling this, so I get to call it.

Now this was before I met Joe Wycheski—hell, he was still popping zits between rolls back then. One day we heard Walt had gotten blown up by a rocket-propelled grenade near a Michelin rubber plantation somewhere in Vietnam, next thing he's coming home alive. It was like as if we had a regular Lazarus in the family.

Our father worked at Engineered Fittings out on Milan Road, just like Joe Wycheski did later on, dropping nut blanks on the screw machines, moving up from the facers and the hand tappers. Our mother kept the house and kept Walt and me straight as she was able. We were seven years apart, one lost in the middle. The idea was Walt would take our father's spot—that's what people did, pass their job down. And I'd have to bid or figure out something else.

Not too many choices either. The quarry, fishing boats, factories. None of it was for me. I'd grown up at the lanes in the cellar down below the State Theatre on Columbus and Water, first crouched behind my father when he rolled in matches, then as a pin boy, then going head-to-head myself with some of the best of the day. Bowling was the only thing I ever cared about.

When I wasn't setting pins, I'd bowl a string with the other pin boys. Down there it got thick with smoke and men working bets. It was a big place for back then, thirteen lanes. The odd number was unusual because lanes were always in pairs for match play—you'd have four or six lanes, a big place would be eight lanes. People said that was bad luck, but only if they were losing.

This is in the late thirties, what I'm talking about, when I was just a little shit sneaking Drums I rolled myself with one hand because you had to know how to do that if you wanted any respect. And yeah, none of us wanted to be out of there last. We were all scared of the ghost of that choked kid.

Back then it was all local matches. People didn't travel. They went for the town action. I'm talking mostly clubs—German Social, Polish, American Legion, VFW clubs, etc. And all kinds of leagues, singles, doubles, mixed doubles, or teams. My father was in the industrial leagues, because of his job. They weren't pro, but they'd get cash prizes put up by local merchants. Quarries had their own leagues, for an example.

My father was a town hero back then. His team, the Sandusky Icebreakers, farmed for a professional team and traveled the Midwest for tourneys. The *Register* posted all their scores and standings—high single, high triple—from each night, and the team high singles and triples. He bowled in a few nationals, and one year he ranked tenth in the country. Not that he made any money for it, but that's something to say, isn't it? That's something to say.

Most of the money was made in backroom betting. The manager'd put together a team or have a head-to-head and people would bet. My father got his cut. He let me carry his equipment, keep his ball polished, and I was proud to help him. I'd watch him and I'd think, *That's my dad.* I learned my arithmetic chalking the scores next to his name. I made sure no one stiffed him and also tracked what he needed to win. He said not to worry about the scores, don't get thrown off by anybody else's game. Consistency was the key. He had it until the drinking caught up with him. There came a time anyway when I wasn't so sure he was right. Winning was key. That was where the money was.

We pin boys got paid by the string—the manager would pay six cents a string, and the bowlers would tip. My father knew all the good tippers, and so he'd send them to me. On double league nights—like, say, the St. Mary's teams would come in and bowl at six and another league started at eight or eight-thirty, scheduled back-to-back—you'd set up six hundred frames in a night, could hardly stand up after that.

Sometimes we'd bunch the pins for the customers we liked to see win. It was harmless. There weren't all the standards back then, everything all precise. My dad could read where the ball broke into the pocket after three frames, tops.

Everybody talked about going on tour back then, but it wasn't any great life. Living out of motels, driving all night, and sure, someone was sponsoring you, but if you didn't do well you didn't make any money. Meanwhile you're paying your entrance fees and expenses. Some guys slept in their cars right there in the bowling center parking lot, ate beans and tuna out of a can, just squeaking by. When you're cranking strikes all day long on your hometown lanes, everybody loves you, they're all rooting for you. Then you get out on the road and you can't read the lanes, and you're not sleeping well and probably drinking too much. Nobody knows you, and they don't care whether you win or lose like back home. Actually, they're hoping you'll lose because they're rooting for their hometown hero. Guys get so nervous they throw the ball away. I remember it happened to my father once. It happened to Barry Asher. And I saw it happen to Joe Wycheski, like everyone else around here. But that came a lot later, and I made my peace with it.

And the point. The point is how I got back here. All this leads to it. My old man had gotten to like betting too much, not just on alley matches but anything. Track, cards, baseball. He'd get nervous when he lost bets and start drinking. The drinking ruined his game and then he'd drink more, depressed for losing.

After a while, he had people after him for money. Two big slabs came to our door one night. He was on the road, and I wasn't with him that time because I had the pin-setting job at the State. Walt hadn't enlisted yet so this would have been about '43. I was eleven. The knock woke me up, but not Walt, who could sleep through anything. I followed my mother into the living room and watched her open the door. They didn't wear those undertaker suits like in the movies; they looked like they were ready to go hunting, trousers tucked into mud boots and caps pulled down over their sausage faces.

My mother stared at them for about two seconds; they didn't even have a chance to say anything. She'd grown up on a farm outside Castalia, but she wasn't a fool. She said, "Wait a minute, I think I got some grocery money." They just shuffled their feet and shook their heads; she'd embarrassed them. She pulled her purse off the table by the door, and we all watched her digging through it. One of the bricks said, "We'll come back, Mrs. Florida." But she had some bills in hand now.

"No, take it; it's fine."

The other brick said, "Mr. Florida is man enough to pay us outright, we have faith in that. We don't need to take no food from your children." And then he smiled at me like as if we were all friends now. Or like as if he was going eat me. I wanted to slit his pudgy throat. I wished he'd just taken the money instead of pretending he was doing us a favor.

They stepped back from the door, tipping their caps and such, and then they were gone. My mother shut the door, and when she turned around, she had this flat look in her eyes like as if she didn't even recognize me. I'd never seen that look before. She told me to go to bed, but I just stood there. She said, "Go on!" I shuffled down the hall and sat on my cot, and I thought I'd be sick, I was so mad. I decided then that I wouldn't have any weaknesses. I wouldn't be blowing my cash or drinking it. But I was just a kid. It seemed simple to live straight.

When I came in Walt was sleeping facedown on his pillow, arms hanging on either side of his bed like fat ropes. He'd just graduated and was working at Engineered Fittings under our father, and he smelled like hot metal and grease all the time. He didn't have anything to say to me anymore. So I made another decision right then. I was getting out of there. I didn't want any factory job. I didn't want to dole out an allowance to any woman, and I sure as hell didn't want kids who sat in their dark bedrooms and hated me.

A few months after that, Walt enlisted and got sent straight to Normandy. He lived through that somehow and then did officer training and went to Korea. Sometime after that he got married, and then he was one of the advisors sent over to Vietnam in 1961, four years before they got official with the combat troops. I was thirty by then so he would've been thirty-seven. We hadn't talked in years. I wouldn't have known he was over there if our mother hadn't let it drop and said it was a secret.

Then, just before Christmas that year, he died for six days.

By that time, I'd been out on my own more than ten years. I'd left when I was eighteen, figured I'd bowl my way around the country. I hadn't been home except for a holiday here and there, and if it hadn't been for Walt's wife getting the visit from the base officer and the chaplain, hats in hand, I might never have come back.

Because at that point, I was doing pretty good. On the road, life was tournaments and match play and betting. I didn't drink much, and I stayed smooth. I took on big-hooking crankers like Carmen Salvino, who was younger than me, and stylists like Earl Anthony, and everything in between. Saw Junie McMahon, who had to have the smoothest delivery in bowling—Salvino said you could balance a glass of water on the man's head. Might as well have been scotch because the guy drank himself to death. Back then, the game was simpler but tougher. You won on skill, not your gear.

How my mother tracked me down with the news about Walt, I don't know. I was in Minneapolis for a pro-am, sleeping on someone's couch. But a mother has a way of finding you. I took the train home the next day.

The story was, Walt's wife had planned to stay with my parents over Christmas anyway because she didn't have any family. But then the news came, and so she came earlier than planned.

Louise was sitting at the kitchen table with my mother when I walked in. I went to kiss my mother, and I thought she'd be crying. But her eyes were dull. She looked like as if she hadn't slept for weeks.

Louise had on a blue dress, and her hair hung down her back like a girl's. She wore a thin gold chain with a locket that sat in the dip between her collarbones. She didn't even look sixteen. She had freckled skin, the kind that sunburns easy. Her eyes were almost the same deep blue as her dress. She stood, and she was about as tall as me, and she faced me chin up like as if she was waiting for some kind of inspection.

We shook hands and she said pleased to meet you. Close up, I could see she wasn't a child. Lines around her eyes and mouth—smile lines. That was a good sign.

"Pleasure's mine," I said. What I always said when I met a woman. But I knew that was wrong. There wasn't any pleasure in that room.

She sat back down, and I worked my way around the table to get a glass of water. Mostly to have something to do. I didn't want to look at my poor mother's face. It was so tight in there Louise had to wedge her chair in to let me by. Her hair smelled like some kind of flower, I wanted to know what.

My mother told me my father was in back, which meant I was supposed to go see him. I made some small talk with Louise first, asked her how her trip went, because I didn't want to be dismissed like a boy in front of her. I was thirty years old, for chrissakes, and my mother was telling me where to go the minute I walked in the door.

Louise said that Walt and me had a nice room growing up. *You-all.* *You-all* had a nice room. Some southern accent.

"She's staying in your old room," my mother said, in case I couldn't follow the conversation on my own. Then she stood up and turned her back to us and held onto the edge of the counter. I remember hoping she wouldn't start crying, not because I was sorry for her, but because I didn't want to have to comfort her. That's the truth. So I just nodded to Louise and walked out the back door.

The old man had put down some limestone scrap in a path alongside my mother's flowerbeds. It crunched under my feet like bones. It hadn't been good between me and him for a long time. I'd idolized him as a kid, but the night those two jokers came to our door while he was out of town, that was when I stopped thinking his ass was gold. Pretty soon he figured that out and he stopped caring what I thought.

Walt was just like him, a worker and a drinker. He didn't bowl, but he played all the other sports—football, basketball, baseball— so he didn't compete with the old man. After high school, he'd left every morning with my father for work, both of them in their blue shirts, while I was still sitting there eating my toast before school.

Walt would sneer at me as he walked out the back door to the car. He thought I was a waste of time. He and Dad went drinking after hours, buddies all around. When he enlisted, my father went around hangdog for months. Sure, he was worried for his son. But he also missed his buddy at work and at the bar.

Sometimes I thought my father only wanted one son. Walt and me shoved together. One son who played tough on the field and worked and drank, like Walt. One son who loved bowling, but who never wanted to be any other place in the world than this town, and never got better than his father.

In the shed, he was hunched on a low metal stool, toolbox between his knees, wiping down drill bits with a rag. He still had on his coveralls. He picked up another bit, worked it over, dropped it back in the bin. His face was spongy. His hair was thinner, and his hands shook, rubbing that rag.

He dropped the last bit in the case, clanged it shut. Took his time speaking to me. "You even give a shit?" he finally said. He looked up at me then, hands on his knees.

I turned and ducked my head under the door frame, looked back at the way I came. I could see my mother and Louise through the kitchen window. My mother was working at something at the sink now, and Louise was looking out, not at me, but at something, like as if she might try to bust through that glass. I couldn't blame her.

I heard the scrape of the stool behind me. My father stood up slowly, wiping the rag on his hands. Wringing it. He took a stiff-kneed step. "I'm sick," he said.

Times like that, I think women do better. A daughter might have gone over there, patted him while he cried. No shame in that. All I did was stand there. "Let's go in," I said finally.

He turned and put the palms of his hands on his work table. Like my mother hanging onto the kitchen counter. He shook his head slowly, his neck sunk down between the swag in his shoulders. He lifted one hand and waved me off. And I was happy to go.

After the news that night, Louise got up and said she was too tired to hold her head up anymore (*mah head*, she said), and she went straight into that room with Walt's old model planes still hanging from the ceiling and my comic books slumped on the shelves, and she didn't come out again until morning.

When she did get up, I was dead asleep on the couch. I opened my eyes, not sure where I was, just as she rounded the corner from the hallway into the kitchen. She was wearing that blue dress again, hair pulled back. It was like as if she was floating past my feet where they were propped on the couch arm. I sat up and rubbed my face. I had to piss but I didn't want to wake up my parents. I hadn't had to sneak to talk to a woman in a long time.

I found her opening cabinets quietly, one after the other.

"Help you find something?"

Her shoulders jerked up; I'd spooked her. She turned around and looked at me for a second, the way women do, sizing you up for whether you'll be trouble for them or not. Maybe she could read it in me, the want rolled up like too much cash in my pocket.

"Looking for a coffee cup," she said. Not smiling, but not nervous. Careful.

I got around the table, reached past her, and pulled down two.

"Thanks." She turned on the faucet and filled up the teapot that had been sitting on the stove.

"What're you doing?" I asked.

She looked up at me, and I could see the fine hairs around her forehead and cheeks were damp; she'd washed her face and her cheeks were pink from it. And those eyes, bluer still because of her scrubbed skin. She said, "Boiling water for instant."

"I don't know if there is any." I pulled the percolator and a can of coffee from the cabinet next to the sink, where my mother had always kept it. Amazing how things come back to you. I couldn't remember what city I'd been in a week ago, but I knew where the damn coffee-pot was in my parents' house. I scooped the coffee into the metal cup, poured the water, and plugged it in.

She watched the coffee burble in the glass nub on top. "We drink instant on the base."

"Where's that?" I asked, and she glanced at me, like as if she didn't quite believe that I didn't know where she and my brother had lived, but that was the case.

"Fort Carson," she said. "Near Colorado Springs. And how about you?"

"Pretty much all around." I ignored the look she gave me, damn near rolling her eyes, like as if she was tired of hearing answers that didn't tell you anything at all. I had to piss so bad I wanted to cross my legs. "So what's it like out there?"

"Cold. It's right at the base of the Rockies. The air is real fine and the snow is great for skiing, and it's clear all the time," she said. "Not like here." She looked out the window—another gray day with the clouds hanging on the branches. No snow at least.

I heard that accent again. "Where are you from?"

"Arkansas. Pine Bluff. My daddy worked at the arsenal there." She'd folded her arms like she expected me to question her on it.

Arkansas was one of those places with no shape for me. She could see it on my face.

"It's near Little Rock. You sure don't know your geography for a guy who's been all around." She raised an eyebrow at me, gave a hint of a smile. So she was in there somewhere, sense of humor and all.

"I don't get south much."

"They have bowling down there, you know." She smiled again and bit her lip and looked down at her feet. She was wearing navy blue pumps and hose. I felt sorry for her, all dressed up in her schoolgirl clothes, waiting for her husband's casket to arrive so she could have a funeral for him in a town she didn't know, staying with near-strangers, even if it was his family.

The coffee was almost finished. I excused myself and snuck down the hall. I still remembered where every board creaked in that hallway. I shut the bathroom door quiet as a burglar and let loose, trying to aim just above the waterline. In the next room my father snored like an engine revving and dying over and over. I don't know how my mother stood it. I put the lid down to muffle the flush and turned on a trickle of water to wash my hands and face.

I glanced into my old room on my way back down the hall. My mother had gotten rid of the cots and put in a double bed, probably for Walt and Louise's visits. It took up most of the room and was already made up. I wonder if Walt had specifications on how she did that, too—quarter bounce and all that. On the floor next to the bed stood a brown hard-sided suitcase. A gray wool coat draped over it, a navy beret on top of that. Ready to be picked up and carried out the door at any moment.

In the kitchen Louise stood with her back to me, looking out at the backyard. She cut a narrow line in the room, and I came in quiet so I could look at her longer before she turned around. I'd been with women a lot more beautiful than her. Big-busted, full mouths, thick red hair—I had a thing for redheads, that's true. I'd been with women who knew how to do anything you wanted, and they weren't whores;

they just wanted to have a good time. That's all I thought I wanted. I figured people just married when they decided it was time. And I didn't want that, no way and never.

Standing in the doorway, I wasn't sure I wanted to give up finding myself in a raggy motel with a woman named Babette who had a mole on one breast like an extra nipple. I'd met her at the Arcade Lanes in St. Louis. Babette, with her big tits and the third nipple and her wide hips bearing down on me before I even got my pants off—goddamn. I tried to remember what Louise and I had even been talking about before. She turned around, and I remembered—the base in Arkansas, where her father worked.

"So what'd he do?" I asked her, reaching for the coffeepot.

"What?"

"Your father."

She looked at me like as if she was trying to figure out what I was asking—strange, because it was a straightforward question.

"He worked in the biological munitions plant there. Only one in the country," she said, and then she was the proud daughter, arms folded over her girl breasts.

"That must've been something," I said. I poured the coffee. "How do you like it?"

"Just black."

"No sugar, even? Never met a woman who didn't take at least a little." I smiled at her and handed her the cup, and she just looked back at me, all serious.

"Walt got me to learn to do it," she said, blowing over the rim. "He said we had to be able to do without."

Everything about him came back to me then. The way he used to look at me like I was a stray he wanted to kick when he walked out in the morning with Dad. The way he used to grunt at our mother when he wanted something. She'd never complained, or at least not in front of us. She just did what was expected. Women pour themselves out for you, but I didn't know that yet, standing in the kitchen that morning with Louise. What I did know was that I wasn't sorry my brother was dead, because he'd made his wife do without sugar. Just because he could, and she'd obey him, because that was what she'd promised to do. It was a small thing. Maybe it even made her feel better, thinking of that instead of the idea of him gone and her alone. Where was she going to go? She must have been scared, standing there in her pumps with it barely even light out yet, like she had some kind of plan. More likely she didn't have slippers and didn't want to go out of her room barefoot to hunt up coffee and drink it bitter like Walt wanted her to.

It was a small thing. But that's what life narrows down to. One time I decided to catch a train rather than ride with two guys to the next tourney, because even though I was almost out of cash, I was too tired to leave at four in the morning. And it turned out they died an hour out of Buffalo. Hit a patch of ice and then a truck. Most things we do don't seem to count for much, but sometimes they do. My mind snagged on that sugar.

"There's plenty," I said, scooping a spoonful.

"No, thank you," she said. "I like it this way now."

I dumped it in my cup, even though I could take it or leave it, and right then the phone started ringing and it didn't stop for the rest of the day.

By midmorning, the house was filled with women, and in spite of the cold, they spilled out into the yard, the street, even. This wasn't visiting hours or anything official. This is what people did in our town back then. After the first shifts let out, the men showed up and sat out back and drank and smoked. By then, the women were hip to hip in the kitchen. The windows were steamed from food cooking on and in the stove, the table crowded with casseroles and sliced meats and pastries. There were children all over the place. I'd walk through the living room and one would slam face-first into my thigh, bounce on his bottom and get up tearing off somewhere else. The older folks, people from mass whose faces I recognized but whose names I'd forgotten, sat in the living room on the couch and on the kitchen chairs someone had thought to drag out there, to make more room. There were people on the swing and in lawn chairs on the stoop, standing in clumps on the lawn—mothers letting their kids run wild. I recognized a few of them, too, from high school. Girls I'd tried to get somewhere with had three kids now, and their husbands looked my father's age.

My brother's body was supposed to get there in two days. I guess all those people were good for my mother, to give her something to do. From the backyard I saw her through the kitchen window, moving back and forth from the oven to the table, wearing a dark gray dress and a green apron, gray being as close as she could maybe let herself get to black at that point. Walt's was the first war casualty in our town since Korea, and we weren't even supposed to be at war. It had everyone whipped up, though. You didn't have a town more ready to get into that jungle right then than Sandusky.

As the day went by, I stayed most of the time with the men out in the back, watching my father drink himself bloodshot. I took a couple of sips from the flasks that were going around, just to be social.

"We ought to fix them up but good over there," said Horace Schlemmer, one of the guys my dad worked with. He was drunk, his talk thick.

My father nodded and stared at the ground. He drew the tip of his boot across the dead grass, back and forth, back and forth, all the men watching him, his grief on display.

"What do you say, Leo?" said Rich Neidermeyer, another Engineered Fittings guy, retired by then.

I looked at him. "About what?"

"Those Viet Cong, they call themselves. Gooks." He was redfaced, bottle choked in his fist.

"They're all gooks, aren't they?" I meant nobody here would know the difference between Viet Cong and a rice farmer, and apparently that was a problem over there. If officers on the ground couldn't figure it out, we sure as hell weren't going to.

But Neidermeyer read me wrong. "Yeah, you're right," and he grinned mean. "We oughta kill them all."

I'd dated his daughter in high school. Kept her legs tighter than a lockbox.

Then Horace asked about my game, and I said it was as good as it could be, which was the truth. I was doing the circuit, winning here and there. But I could feel my old man watching me. He'd said before that I'd be back when I'd starved long enough. I knew what I'd see if I looked at him. Too bad I didn't get it yet, that's what he was thinking. I ought to put in for a spot on the facers at the plant, get in at the bottom and work up like any other man with sense. Start a family. Give in and give up like he did.

"Must be nice out there, a different town every day," Horace said.

"Has its merits." But I knew as soon as I'd said it that I'd had enough. I wasn't ready to quit just yet, but I wasn't getting any better, neither. There was a new crop of guys coming in, eighteen- and twenty-year-olds, as hot and driven as I'd been. They'd only ever rolled on oil, never had to get over shellac they used to use on the lanes. Almost everyone my age had either gone full pro or left to get some real wages.

People started clearing out at about ten. Around here, that was practically an all-night vigil. A few of my dad's cronies stuck around in the backyard. When they moved to the shed, I hung back. Some-one pulled the string on the bulb, and it glowed like a hot piece of metal. I headed for the house. I figured they were going to pass some whiskey and my father's tools around and mutter back and forth, like a bunch of nuns working their rosaries.

Inside, my mother, Louise, and the wives of the men out in the shed were cleaning up. One wife was at the sink, washing dishes, one was loading the refrigerator, and one was picking up everywhere else. My mother and Louise were drying dishes. It was hot as hell in there, and they all looked exhausted. I stood against the wall to keep out of the way.

My mother asked me what I needed.

"Here, take a beer, make some room in here," Mrs. Loden said, pulling one out of the fridge. She church-keyed it before I had a chance to answer and passed it to me across the kitchen table. She was short and curly-haired like her husband. I thought that was pretty funny, how married couples got to looking so much alike. I wondered what Louise would look like years from now. I watched her reaching up to put away some heavy bowls, the lift in her ribs, the way her dress hung on her hips. Sweat dark under her arms. She and Walt certainly didn't look anything alike, with his bulk and the red hair he'd gotten from our mother. I was short and dark like my father. *And Walt's the one who got her*, I thought. I shouldered the wall. I didn't need any more beer but I drank it. I figured I'd turn out like my father after all, an old drunk.

"Sit down, honey," my mother said. I looked at her and she pointed to a chair. Mrs. Schlemmer had put the chairs back at the table right under my nose and I hadn't noticed. Louise smiled at me, but the smile was one she might give to clerks and delivery boys. I nodded to her and sat down at the table, jamming myself in close. I could see myself in that same spot as a kid eating cereal, metal edge at my chest. I could see Walt letting me help build a plane with him. He might have been twelve or thirteen then, and still willing to tolerate me. I could see my father heaving buckets of cement we hand-mixed for the foundation of the shed out back, how good it felt to come in and be fed and watered, as my mother had put it, farm girl that she was.

I said, to no one in particular, "I'm not the one ought to be sitting."

"Well, you're no use in here," Mrs. Schlemmer said. She didn't mean anything by it except to say I wouldn't be allowed to help, which was fine by me.

"That's about all of it, then," Mrs. Neidermeyer said, shaking water off her hands at the sink. She picked up a towel to finish the silverware.

"You all go," my mother said. "You've done enough."

Louise looked at the ceiling. I thought she was rolling her eyes. I thought there might be some snap in her yet. She reached for the wall behind her, like she meant to lean against it, but then her knees buckled and she sat down hard on the floor. My mother went to her but Mrs. Schlemmer and Mrs. Neidermeyer were faster. Mrs. Schlemmer wedged herself between Louise and the counter, each of them taking her under the arm.

"You sit down before it happens to you, too," Mrs. Loden said to my mother. "Both of you," she said to me. I was on my feet again and hadn't realized it.

I kept standing and my mother did, too, but with her back to me so she could face Louise. She said her name with a question in her voice.

Louise turned her head from side to side a couple of times as the women hoisted her to a chair. Her face was white, greenish at the tops of her cheeks.

"Now, put your head between your knees and I'll put on some water," Mrs. Schlemmer said. She slammed the teapot on the burner. "It'll settle you."

Louise leaned forward. She was at the other end of the table from me. Mrs. Neidermeyer stayed behind her, spotting her so she wouldn't fall to one side or another. All I could see was the narrow hump of her back. Mrs. Loden pulled tea cups from the cabinet but didn't offer me one. I got a couple of looks from the women. It was clear they wanted me out. Even my mother wanted rid of me. "Your father all right?"

"He's fine." I took another sip of my beer. I'd been trying all night to get away from him. "Can I help with anything?" I asked.

This was ignored. Mother asked, "Louise, do you feel sick?"

"No," the answer came, muffled, from her knees. "Just tired, really."

I caught the women trading looks. Then I got it. They thought she was pregnant, and they wanted me gone so they could ask her about it. I watched the ridge of her spine rise and fall.

"Would you like some help into bed?" Mrs. Neidermeyer asked Louise loudly.

I stood up. I could see her nodding into her lap. I looked down at her back and damp hair, and she seemed too small to be a mother, folded over like that.

"I hope you feel better," I said.

She lifted her head. Her face had started to get back its color. "Thank you," she said, and the women hauled her out of the room.

After that, the women left one by one, bustling out the back door to collect their drunk husbands. My parents went to bed and the house finally went silent, but I couldn't sleep, even after all the beer. It was all I could do to keep from sneaking the few steps from where I was camped on the couch down the hall to peek in the door of my old room, like as if maybe I could tell what was in her just by watching her sleep. I could feel the idea of taking care of her settling in my bones and joints. It made sense to me, down to the root of myself, and I knew I would try to do it.

Tess Wycheski

4

I ROLLED EVERY day after my father gave me the AMF—I called it "the Angle"—for my sixteenth birthday. The only time my father wasn't with me at the lanes that fall was when I had varsity after school and he was at work. Leo coached me one-on-one after varsity. I kept my word to Leo and kept those sessions to myself, and though my father may have suspected, he never asked. Maybe we both wanted to believe that my rapid improvement that spring had to do with his coaching and encouragement and love, as well as my commitment to the Wycheski Plan. But I knew Leo was the one who'd made it possible for me to see inside the pins—there's no better way I can say it—to know how to hit them. My father thought about the beautiful moment, the pleasure of a perfect movement. Leo thought about the next strike. I wasn't sure yet how to think, or if there was any middle ground I could find.

Leo said I had inherited plenty of natural ability from my father, but skill had to do with what went on in your head as much as your hands. "I'm going to have to teach you how to think, Wycheski," he said to me once, and then he laughed, but he was only half joking. We worked on one thing at a time—ways not to let my elbow fly, how to get the ball to curve earlier for some splits—and we drilled it until I dreamed it at night, told the ball exactly what to do. The Galaxy Lanes was a universe with its own laws, and one by one I was learning how to work within them.

At every practice, Leo reminded me to be careful to not let my style fit too close to my home lanes. "You've got to be able to work with the lay of other lanes," he told me. "You've got to read each one." So there we were, on our hands and knees, our cheeks just above the foul line, like we were listening for a train. Sure enough, there were dips and twists in every one.

"If you can memorize cards, you can get rich playing poker," Leo said as we got to our feet. I noticed he took his time straightening up. "If you can read lanes and adjust your style on the fly, you can make a living in bowling."

After about a month, Leo drilled the grips deeper on my Angle because he thought I was working too hard to hold onto it on the backswing. He made me practice splits, his nephew Donny setting them for me from the box—clotheslines, baby splits, baby splits with company. Snake eyes, barmaids, dime stores, and—one of the hardest for me—Christmas trees, a three-seven-ten for a right-hander like me, which Leo made me practice for an hour because I'd missed it in a tournament. Also, he said, to honor the season, since by then it was December—Leo's special brand of humor.

After practice, I asked Donny why Leo wasn't coaching him, and Donny shrugged. He was carrying out a crate of string lights and a plastic Santa from the back. He'd been assembling the Santa in between setting splits for me. It was nearly as tall as he was. The year before, someone had hung a sign that said "YO, HO!" around Santa's neck. Leo had taken it down but it kept reappearing.

"I'm not pro material," Donny said. He was growing his hair, and it hung in his eyes. A bit of tinsel stuck to his cheek.

"Leo said that?"

"Yeah, but I know anyway. I mean, check the averages."

"Well, I think he's way off," I said. I reached up and brushed the tinsel off of his cheek. He blinked, stared at me. The silvery strip twirled to the floor between us. He hoisted the Santa and the crate higher in his arms, and I stepped back to let him pass. If Donny was fine with what Leo thought, why couldn't I be? I wanted to stick up for him—the way I'd always felt I had to do for my father, at least where Leo was concerned.

A couple of weeks later, right before Christmas break, Leo was drilling my timing and footwork. He wanted me to start my forward swing a half-step later so I'd get more power on the release. This was a hard rhythm to change—it felt like starting all over.

"Keep your balance, Wycheski," he said. He was standing in the gutter so he could see my approach from the front. "If Count Gengler could roll a three hundred in the dark, you can at least hit your average in the light of day." Gengler had been a hustler, one of Leo's idols—"Count" because he went around dressed in French cuffs and an ascot, pretended he was a loser with big money and picked the locals clean. I could see the attraction.

We'd been working this new timing on a different lane each practice, and my score was all over the map. Lane 14 was the worst. Lane 22 was fine if you could avoid the dip at the eighteenth board, which could grab your ball right when it was supposed to hook into the pocket. ("It's like golf," I said, when I figured that one out, and Leo said, "Golf. Why don't they get some bigger balls?")

We always skipped Lane 3. I didn't need Leo to tell me the reason for that—I'd rolled it for half of my life by then, and so I always did well on it. On the day Leo was going on about Gengler, we were rolling Lane 7, and I was rolling so bad I said that maybe I actually should hit Lane 3 for a few frames. "Just to get my magic back," I said. I laughed, but I actually believed it might work.

"That's why your father likes it, too," Leo said.

I stopped and stared at him. He was expecting me to back up and roll just then, and he was looking in the other direction to see how the ball would hook. But by the time he turned around, impatient, I was headed for my bag. He got the message.

"Okay, Tess, I'm sorry," he said. He only used my first name when he was serious.

"You're a jerk, Leo," I said, pulling off my shoes. I had varsity in fifteen minutes and I was supposed to score a league match after that, but I didn't care.

He shrugged. "You're right," he said, though he didn't sound too concerned about it.

I thought about what I wanted to say, dared myself as I got on my street shoes. "You ditched my father—a kid!—and then you tell me he can't coach me to win, and now you want to knock him behind his back." *And he's in so much pain he can hardly get the pill bottles open, you mean old bastard*, I wanted to say. My hands shook tying my sneakers. But I had done this much—I'd said everything my father hadn't said to Leo; probably things no one had ever said to him.

"Come on, now, wait a minute."

I stood up anyway to zip my bag. He was walking toward me.

"Hold on!"

I straightened instead of reaching for my jacket, folded my arms to wait. Leo scooped up his ball from the return—he still rolled a bleeder that soaked up all the lane conditioner, said he didn't trust the polyeurethane balls like my Angle—and went to wiping it down.

I watched this bit of theater with a stance I hoped would convey my lack of interest in anything he might have to say. But I was interested. My skin was tingling, in fact, with interest. What did he know about my father? What had he seen in him—or not seen in him, even then? I thought about my father in Las Vegas, seventeen years old—a year older than I was then—humiliated and abandoned, turning Leo's car toward home.

"Why did you leave him?"

Leo slowed down the polishing, set his ball in his bag, straightened up. "Did you know the first time I was in here—no," he said, correcting himself. "No, it was the second time." He looked toward the windows as if trying to predict the weather. I expected him to launch into the small talk he ran with the old men at the bar. *Just wait five minutes, it'll change. I wouldn't go out on that ice this time of year for all the money there is. Green as bottle glass out there.*

"The second time," he said again, and now he was watching Donny going from return to return, emptying ashtrays into a plastic bag. "It was right after Walt came home from the war. And I was short on cash, see? And I hustled these four guys. I needed money, and there they were."

"Isn't that illegal?" I said, not that I cared. I just wanted to keep him talking in hopes he would come back to my father.

Leo waved my question away. "It's frowned upon. Betting, on the other hand, is illegal." He watched Donny for a moment more and then turned back to me. "But my point. My point is that things happen that show you who you are. Those four guys, they were just looking for a little fun after work. But then I came along and cleaned them out."

"I guess you're proud of that," I said. I was so disgusted I didn't want to look at him. My chest felt bruised.

"No, I'm not. It's just that they had their plans and I had mine. I would've traded places with them any day, believe me."

"Because your life was so much worse?" I wanted to laugh, but when he looked at me, I believed it was true. And was that why he had left my father, too? Because leaving him was better for him than staying?

He crossed his arms with his hands in his armpits—what I'd come to recognize in him as squaring off. But something seemed to have faded out of him. "Look, Wycheski. Very few rules in life outside of bowling matter, but here's one to remember," he said. "Everything that happens between people is a deal struck. Maybe for money, maybe for something else. Myself, I always watch the money. Better odds."

I folded my arms, too, but I was cradling my right, which felt heavy from the practice. My stomach felt heavy, too. "You're not going to answer me."

"Okay. I gave your father my car to get home and most of the money I had on me." He zipped the bag, straightened up, swung the rag lightly against his thigh. The kids from school were filing in, and if I was staying, I had to hit the counter. I looked in that direction and then back at Leo, who was watching me, waiting. "So how would you follow the money?"

My legs felt unsteady and I bent my knees a bit, trying to keep my balance. "You felt guilty because of what happened to him. You let him down."

Leo shrugged. "He let himself down. Guilt is not my specialty."

I couldn't have said it better. "You owed him something."

"Exactly. The universe is finite, Tess. Don't let anyone tell you different. When the numbers don't matter anymore, it's all over."

He cleared his throat, picked up his bag, headed for his closet office. "Be glad you're getting your diploma, Wycheski. You'll need it if you keep practicing like this."

"So what numbers should I be watching, Leo?" I called after him, and I thought I saw him flinch at the sound of my voice. But he kept going. And that was the first time the thought occurred to me: he was scared of me. I was scared—not just because I didn't want to lose my father, but because I didn't want to lose my certainty that everything he said was true about what was ahead of us, that the virtue of a perfect strike was its own reward no matter when or where it happened. But what did Leo think I could do to him? For all of his talk about money, he had never seemed that concerned about it, had never charged me for our coaching sessions. So maybe he felt he owed me in some way, even if he professed to feel no guilt.

I tried to make this case, or a version of it, to my mother a few days before Christmas, after she found out how much my new AMF had cost, but she was unimpressed. Arguing Leo's merits didn't get very far since she saw him as the source of the problem—the specific one of the ball purchase and the general one of bowling being, in her view, a dead-end exercise, especially after how things had gone for my father.

She'd picked up the receipt for the Angle from the garage floor, thinking it had fallen out of her purse. In the kitchen, she flashed the footprinted piece of paper at me, then slammed it back into the junk drawer, as if she meant to keep it for evidence.

"Where do you think this going to go for you?" she asked me then. I noticed she was dressed up—her hair wound into a bun, a touch of mascara, a gray skirt—and I wanted to ask why, but I knew this wasn't the time.

"It was my birthday present. It can be my Christmas present, too," I said, thinking we were talking about the money. I knew that my AMF had cost more than a week's worth of groceries. But in reality we were having two different conversations.

My mother pressed her lips together, glanced away. Maybe she thought I didn't want anything from her at all. "And then what?" she said.

I looked at her, trying to figure out what she was asking. She put her hand on her hip, leaned against the counter as if she was prepared to wait as long as it took for whatever I would finally say. All I could think of was the Wycheski Plan. It was the only plan I had, no matter how hard I worked for Leo.

"And then maybe I'll—" I started, but she cut me off.

"You'll go pro?"

"Or maybe get a scholarship. Or both, maybe, someday."

My mother nodded, looked at the floor, as if this was the answer she'd been expecting. "Your father told you this?"

"Leo, too," I said, mainly so that she wouldn't think he was the only one who believed it could happen. But as soon as I said it, I realized I'd had the wrong idea to bring up Leo again.

"So if this doesn't work out, is he going to give you a job?" she asked me. The light from the front windows fell across her face. She looked as young as any girl at my high school. I wanted to be able to talk to her as a friend, to tell her the truth. But when I didn't answer, she suggested I think about it, and then she headed down the hall.

In fact, Leo would give me a job less than a year after that conversation. But it wouldn't be because of the Wycheski Plan. It would be because my father was gone, and so the plan had forever changed.

All of this was ahead of us. We couldn't have known it was coming—that's what people said in an attempt to comfort my mother and me. But sometimes I wondered if my mother had some sort of sense of it—perhaps a dream she'd chosen not to share. The day we'd argued over my AMF and my future, my mother had been dressed up for an interview with a new storefront church in town called the Emmanuel. It was for a part-time clerical job, and she had applied for it because my father had run out of disability and had received a warning letter from the union. They had done all they could for him; time was no longer on their side or ours.

By the spring semester of my junior year, my father had to take un-paid leave because some days the farthest he could make it from bed was to the couch, where he watched Elva Matterson on *Paint!* PBS render nature scenes unrecognizable. On his good days we would roll together, and it was hard to imagine that he would feel bad again. On his bad days I came home to the blue glow of the television, and I came to associate it with sickness and fear.

The Emmanuel took my mother in during that time; there's no better way to say it. Maybe she'd always been looking for exactly what it had to offer—a place to belong which also held the keys to the universe. In the years since she'd given up on the concentrated soap sales and Dream Interpretation Global, my mother had taken a va-riety of classes at the community college, gotten certified to teach Japanese flower arranging, tried vegetarianism and transcendental meditation, and had signed up for but not completed an animal psy-chology course at the local shelter, though she would not allow me to adopt a dog. She had joined and drifted out of book clubs, garden clubs, women's awareness groups, and neighborhood watch commit-tees. She had never once gone bowling. That was my father's and my religion, not hers.

After my father was gone she tried to get me to join the Emmanuel, too. She'd known better than to ask my father while he was still with us. If she happened to catch him on a day when he could think straight, he probably would've suggested that she sell insurance as a kind of faith test—because if you have God, who needs a policy?

But sometimes she tried anyway. As we sat down to dinner one night only about a month before my father died, she prayed silently over her plate. My father went ahead with his first bite. On the one hand, I was happy to see him eating; he'd lost weight, said the drugs ruined his appetite. I sat watching, not wanting to pray and not wanting to eat. My mother prayed with determination, hands clasped, thumb knuckles pressed to her forehead. When she raised her head, she ignored the fact that my father was already chewing. Then she said there was going to be a potluck supper at the Emmanuel, and a talent show, and would we like to come with her.

My father had been on unpaid leave for about a month by then, but that night he had made dinner and vacuumed. He raised his eyebrows and swallowed his bite and I braced myself. "Will anyone be walking on water?"

My mother's face went red. She stared at him in disbelief. Her expression sent a crimp of worry from my chest to my stomach. I looked at my plate, picked up my fork, put it down.

"How dare you," she whispered, and the amusement drained from my father's face. He knew he'd gone too far. "You know, we could use a miracle around here, Joe," she said. "How else will the bills get paid? And how else will you get better?" She turned to me; her anger was too big for just him right then. "Any ideas? Any big money coming from the bowling yet?"

There was nothing my father or I could say to that. I knew that after we ate he'd take his next set of pills, and soon he'd have a sleepy, half-dreaming smile on his face. We'd do the dishes—actually, I would do them, and he'd sit and keep me company, which was a victory in itself by then—and then he would try to kiss my mother before slipping off quietly to bed. That night she wouldn't let him get near her; she was a master at closing herself off. She didn't say another word to us that night. After I got in bed, I heard my mother climb the stairs and close the guest room door down the hall from me.

I waited for sleep to come, and just as I had done every night since Leo had started the drills, I saw myself at the top of the lane, moving forward, releasing. I thought about what Leo had said, how the world came down to numbers, finally—pinfall, hours, heartbeats. The universe was finite. When the numbers no longer mattered, it was all over. But no, I was sure my father had said something different, something better—that in fact you only needed the numbers at first. And then you had to get past them so that you could actually bowl.

5

DONNY STARTED MIDNIGHT Bowling at the Galaxy once we got to high school, mainly because he wanted to have a weekend place where kids like us could go, kids who wouldn't likely be sitting on the Homecoming Court. But also because he hoped it would bring in more people in general. My father had been right—bowling wasn't exactly holding its own in the disco era—and Donny and I hadn't missed the look on Leo's face when we helped him count the till at closing.

Naturally, Leo wasn't thrilled about paying for the mirrored ball and the colored lights, not to mention staying open until one in the morning on Friday and Saturday nights rather than eleven. But Donny had made a good bet, it turned out—the teenagers came in with their minimum-wage spending money, and they bought a lot of snacks along with their games and closed the place every weekend. The money was good, so Leo quit calling Donny Saturday Night Fever, and Donny quit making cracks behind Leo's back about Leo never throwing away rubber bands or soap slivers, scared to spend a dime, etcetera. By the time our junior year rolled around, we had the arcade.

You had to trust yourself more on your roll in the near-dark with the disco ball swinging a sparkle of lights around the room. You had to let go of trying to read the lane. My father, like most players from his generation, thought the whole thing was ridiculous, shameful, really. "If you don't already love bowling, a light show isn't going to bring you around," he said. But the idea that it might work was equally disturbing—what sort of people needed cheap shiny lures to get them to play a beautiful sport? If it wasn't in your soul to roll the same lane over and over, until you knew it as well as your own skin, what would convince you? "It's no wonder Reagan got elected," my father muttered, after it was clear Midnight Bowling wasn't just a passing phase. "All fluff and no substance."

I knew for a fact that Chelsea's parents had voted for Reagan—at least Chelsea had reported as such. Of course she was in favor of the disco ball, though she still tried to look as if she was surprised to find herself in such a setting any time I got her to stop by for a while. But I was also proud of Donny for what he'd accomplished. He was watching out for Leo, whether Leo liked it or even realized it or not. And he was watching out for me, which I came to understand soon after the final time my father and I rolled together.

I'd just nailed the Youth American Bowling Association championships, which were held at State that year. I had practiced so hard with my team, with my father when he could, and with Leo the rest of the time, that I felt like I couldn't miss. I could hardly feel the weight of the ball. But that night, even though my father was near bent over with pain that seemed to circulate from his knees to his hips to his back, he insisted that we roll a few that Saturday night to celebrate.

I had just gotten my license, so he let me drive. When I coasted into the crowded Galaxy lot, overcautious because it was getting dark, I thought of my father driving so slowly the first time he'd taken me there, how it felt as if we were riding a boat to dock. I stopped as gently as I could so as not to make him wince.

On our way to our lane, he stopped once and leaned against a table to rub the place in his back that had put a hitch in his step. He was thirty-five years old, and though at sixteen that sounded old enough to me, I could see he'd aged just in the past few months. His hair was going gray at his temples; his eyes seemed faded, deeper in their sockets. There was a fragility in his movement that I felt I had no choice but to ignore, because to acknowledge it was to let everything else take its place in the room, too. I would have to ask, "What are we going to do?" I would have to hear his answer and decide whether I believed it. Instead I heard pills rattling in a plastic bottle in his pocket with his every step, and I didn't ask what they were, or which pain they dulled.

He went first. Even though I knew better, I was still expecting his long, fluid glide, how he looked as if he might be rushing to grasp someone's hand, like in those slow-motion movie shots of lovers running to each other across fields. But that night, as much as I'd wanted to expect otherwise, his timing was way off, and I was reminded instead of him standing at the top of the line at the Showboat, frozen— a vision so real to me it could have been a memory. Somehow it seemed to me that if we could get past that, we'd get past everything. We'd get a free pass, in fact.

"You're pulling the ball," I said to him, as if fixing that one problem would make all the difference. Three pins wobbled and stayed up on his second frame.

He looked away as if he hadn't heard me, but I could tell he was frustrated. "Go," he said, and he pressed his hand to his hip, his face grim.

I tried not to appear to notice as I stepped back, rolled, and got a strike. I didn't have any intention of holding back. My father had said this was the biggest problem girls had, and I wanted to make sure he saw it wasn't mine. And I wanted to goad him into stepping back into form, back into who he was supposed to be, if that was still possible.

My father powdered his hand. "What's a perfect strike?"

I rolled my eyes so I wouldn't have to see the tremble in his fingertips. "Coming into the pocket, the ball should be on the seventeenth board," I said. I paused, wondering if he was going to make me recite the whole thing. He was waiting. "The ball only touches the one, three, and nine pins. The head pin knocks down the two, which knocks down the four, and the four knocks down the seven—that's the accuracy line," I said. "The five pin takes out the nine pin, the three pin takes out the six, and the six takes out the ten pin. That's the carrying line."

"No. The five hits the eight pin and the ball hits the nine. You know that," my father said, surveying the lane. He seemed to be having trouble holding his head up.

"I switched the numbers." I was embarrassed, and irritated that I was embarrassed. "Besides," I said before I could stop myself, "there is no perfect strike."

My father stared at me for a moment. He shook his head a little as if he thought I'd lost my mind. "There's always a perfect strike, Tess. Where'd you get that idea?"

I could feel my face getting hot. I knew where I'd gotten it, and he did, too. On the topic of perfect strikes, Leo's commentary went about like this: A strike was a strike. A strike on Monday was as good as any other day of the week. The strikes that counted were the ones that were scored. When you stopped counting, it was all over.

"Well?" he said then. He was watching me, waiting. I thought of the first time we'd stood at the top of that very lane, Lane 3, *our* lane, and the way he'd looked at me, trying to see something in me that I couldn't name.

He shook his head again and set his ball. He rolled, shuffling forward slowly, and left three pins up again. Miserable. He was no longer a dancer, a man gliding through water. The gravity he'd eluded all those years had come back with interest, and my rage at this realization surprised me. That was the moment I decided I would beat him. I decided it would be a wake-up call, a warning that it was time to move on, time to quit suffering, as if his pain was something he could put away as neatly as he had done with his bowling career the year before I was born. We went back and forth, and I kept the score close, because it happened to be one of those nights when I could do anything with the Angle. It felt weightless, an extension of my arm. It sparkled all the way down the lane. I tried not to think about how my father had maybe kept the score close for me years ago, so that I would feel we were really competing.

I won 168 to 152. Gutter scores for us, but still, I'd beaten him. My father watched my last spare—it was a split the baby and I'd gotten it—and then he turned to me.

"You did it!" he said. He seemed to be gathering all the enthusiasm he had left, with great effort. His voice was thin.

"Congratulations," I said, trying to smile, because that was what any good coach wanted—for their protégé to surpass them. And yet I wanted to apologize, too. Because somehow I felt I'd knocked us out of the orbit we'd maintained for so long. I wanted to grab his too-thin arms, claw my way back through time and take him with me.

My father nodded and made his way to the booth behind us. He sat down and leaned back, catching his breath. I sat down across from him. I could hear him reaching in his pocket, the rattle of pills.

"You want me to get you some water?" I said.

"How about a beer? You can have one, too. To celebrate."

"I thought you shouldn't drink with those."

My father managed a smile, looked down at his hands as he opened the pill bottle, as if he didn't trust them to do their work. "It doesn't matter, Tess."

I stood up so fast my thighs slammed against the table edge, and he looked up at me, blinking in surprise. "Why?" I said. I had the feeling that in beating him, I was maybe killing him.

"You could've done better," he said finally.

"So could you," I shot back, but he ignored this. He dropped the last two pills from the bottle into his palm, pinched them into his mouth, swallowed them dry. He leaned forward and pulled his wallet from his back pocket and handed it to me.

"Go pay," he said softly. His fingers were cold.

"Dad?" I said.

He waved me away. I turned around and walked to the counter, forcing myself not to look back at him. I didn't want Leo to see and ask me what was wrong. But it was a busy night, and Leo had the phone to his ear as usual. He waved off the money I dug out of my pocket.

I walked back to the booth. I felt as if my ears had closed up, the sounds of toppling pins muffled and distant. My father's head was cocked to one side as if he was trying to hear something whispered to him. If you'd asked me even then, I would've told you there was no reason to consider all the days and hours he and I had spent at the Galaxy, and how at some point they came to a finite number, that there was an end somewhere. It wouldn't have seemed possible that we'd almost run out of time. My father had gone back for another round with the doctors, had been X-rayed from head to toe—he joked that he could have stopped in at Zleigman's to get his feet done if they still had that machine where you could see if your shoes fit properly by zapping your own feet. He'd said half of Sandusky probably had cancer of the sole, he joked, spelling it out each time just to make sure I got it. His doctors could find no way to hold off or relieve the progress of the pain that had wedged into his joints. All of this was what we had to live with, I told myself. He was my father; he had this pain. The days would keep passing with all of us together. It would get better. When I got back to the booth, all I wanted was to crawl into his lap, to be small enough to do that.

My father sat with his forearms on the table. His head was tilted because he had started to doze. I touched his shoulder and he jerked up straighter in his seat. He took a deep breath to steady himself.

"Help me up, okay?" he said. I leaned down to him and he held onto my neck as I pulled him to his feet. I looked past him toward Leo, and then Donny in the light box, but neither of them had seen. When I held his arms, my thumbs pressed through his muscles to the bone.

"Those were my last pills," he said, once he caught his breath. "Can't get any more until tomorrow." He gritted his teeth, held onto the table, sweating. I pulled a napkin from the dispenser and handed it to him, and he wiped the sweat off his forehead. I wondered, thinking about this night afterward, at how calm I'd been in the moment. Or maybe not calm. Flattened.

My father straightened, patted my arm, smiling tightly at me in a way that I knew was meant to be encouraging. He pointed to my jacket and I grabbed it. We made our way to the door, walking close to each other like we were having some heated talk about strategy—at least that was what I hoped it looked like, as I waved good-bye to Leo and Donny—but really I was trying my best to make sure he didn't fall.

In the car on the way home, my father said, "Did you know the Showboat has a hundred and six lanes now?" His voice sounded slurred, sleepy. He shook his head. "When I was there they only had twenty-four. Same as the Galaxy. But it seemed bigger. Everything out there was bigger. I think that's what scared me most. Not the winning or losing. Just all of that space. I don't know why, but I think that's what it was."

I glanced at him, and he managed a slow wink at me, an apology of sorts. My father had never spoken to me about the Showboat. Everything I knew I'd heard in bits and pieces, here and there. And from Leo, of course, who'd never explained why he'd left my father there. But now my question had changed.

"Why'd Leo take you there in the first place?" I looked at my father again, but I wasn't sure if he'd heard me. The drugs were smoothing his breathing, softening the lines of pain on his forehead. I turned my eyes back to the dark road. All my life, when I thought about going to the Showboat someday, I'd imagined I'd find another Joe Wycheski—still my father but also just a boy—the one who got left and never made his way home. I wanted to put my arm around that boy, tell him there would be other chances.

My father shook his head. "I wanted to go. I was so cocky."

"But that's my point! Leo was your coach. He should've told you no." In that moment, it was perfectly clear to me that all of this was Leo's fault. Not just the moment my father froze at the foul line, but the slow freezing in his joints as well.

I pulled into the driveway and put the car in park but left the engine on. My father was fighting to stay awake by then, otherwise he would've told me to quit wasting gas. He cleared his throat, propped his forehead in his palm.

"It was Donny," he said. "Leo loved him. I couldn't believe he left him."

"What?" How did Donny figure in as to why Leo took my father to Vegas? They'd gone in January of 1963, the year before I was born. Donny had been born the year before. He'd started school a year later than I had, and he'd been held back a year in elementary school, so we were now in the same grade. I didn't know anything beyond that.

"Donny was just a baby then," my father said. "Leo wanted to go out there to make money. To help out Donny's folks, with his dad so bad off."

I'd heard that Walt Florida had come home from Vietnam so damaged he couldn't go outside—his scars scared people. And Donny's mother stayed home to care for him. She never came to the lanes. I'd never met either one of them. But if Leo had wanted to help Donny and his parents so much, why had he stayed away all those years?

"So he used you to make money for Donny?"

My father snorted a muffled laugh. "Well, he didn't exactly make any money, sweetie."

I wanted to kill Leo in that moment. I turned in the seat, grabbed my father's hand. "What should I do, Dad?" I said. I couldn't seem to get a full breath. "Please tell me. Because I'm afraid—I'm afraid—"

"Of what?" He squeezed my hand, turned his head slowly, gazed at me with heavy eyes.

I couldn't say that I was afraid of losing him. Would not. Tears were running down my face.

"Hey," he said. "Hey now."

I wiped at my face, rubbed my hands on my jeans. "I'm afraid I won't ever know what to do," I said. My shoulders were shaking, and I tried to squeeze them toward my ears to stop it, but there was no point. I felt like something was flying loose inside me.

My father held my hand and clicked his tongue against the roof of his mouth. "Tess, you've known forever." I could barely understand him, the medicine thick on his tongue. "Play all you can. Do it because you love it. That's all the plan ever was."

"But didn't you love it? Don't you?"

"Always. It was just—I played with too much fear." The words came out in a sigh. His head was tipping back as if he could barely hold it up.

"Because of Leo," I said. My throat was tight, but the anger centered me, helped me stop crying. "Because he cared about himself and not you."

"Listen, Tess." My father twisted in his seat to face me, squeezed my hand. He seemed to be working as hard as he could to look at me steadily. "That may be true. But I owe him anyway."

He stopped then, either to let that sink in or to catch his breath. "If it weren't for him, I never would've met your mother. Or had you," he said, and his words rolled into my chest and caved me in. I pressed my palms to my face, hunched forward in my seat. I wanted to howl into my own bones.

But my father was still talking, almost whispering by then; I could hear him as if from underwater. "I would lose on the line every day for the rest of my life," he said, "In trade for that."

I gulped air, trying to calm myself, and he patted my back. I wanted to tell him to stop, that I couldn't take anymore, but instead I straightened up, wrenched the keys from the ignition. My father eased the car door open, standing carefully. I came around to meet him in case he needed help, but he'd started toward the door on his own.

My mother wasn't waiting at the door as I'd expected. In fact, she was nowhere to be found when my father gave a little wave before he headed down the hall to bed. Upstairs, I was almost asleep when I heard my mother turn over and sigh in the bed across the hall, and I realized she had been in the guest room all that time, sleeping alone again.

The next day, my father picked me up from league practice, and he was fine. He'd been to the doctor—the white paper bag shredded on his front seat—and he even dragged the grill onto the icy patio and cooked burgers that the three of us ate at the kitchen table. But that night in bed, I woke up, and I knew there had just been this big sound downstairs—there was still a vibration in the air. I sat up, heart pounding, listening.

I heard my mother saying something that I couldn't understand, but I recognized the tone in her voice, both angry and pleading. Then my father said, "Don't."

"What?" my mother said. "What?"

"Pray," he said. And from that one strained word, I could tell he was trying to get to his feet. And my mother, somewhere near him, crying.

February passed, then March, and we got a letter from the union about his membership expiring. Then my father called Leo one afternoon to say good-bye, though Leo didn't know that at the time, and then he took all the pills he had left and fell asleep on the couch, and my mother was the one who found him after she got off work at the Emmanuel, while I was still at school.

The cemetery was across the street from the high school, and I passed my father's marker every day once I started back to school. It was at the end of the newest section, and still bright white, like a bone stuck in the ground. It said his name and the dates and some verse my mother chose. He didn't seem to be anywhere near that rectangle of ground. The only place I thought I might find him was at the lanes, though I knew for sure I wasn't ever going to go back there. The Wycheski Plan had been only that—a plan, a dream—and it was finished.

Part Two

Leo Florida

6

WISH I COULD say that after the neighborhood showed up for Walt, I'd gotten myself clear of Louise. Not too much to ask for being brought up decent and fed well. I could have helped as long as I was needed and then gone on. But there was no way I was going to do that.

My father went in to work that morning. His boss said stay home, but he wanted to toil on in view of his working buddies, suffer heroically in the rattle of the machinery and so forth. Meanwhile, my mother and I took Louise to the Pfieffle funeral home on Columbus. My mother and Louise wore black. Louise's dress had a small white collar. It looked homemade. I only had one suit, and I was damned if I'd wear that to a meeting where, as far as I could tell, the point was to see how much money was behind our grief.

My mother and Louise sat in the deep chairs across from Mr. Pfieffle's big desk and I stood. Mr. Pfeiffle himself was a round-faced man with a sunburn on his nose. I wondered where he got that sunburn in the winter. He looked like he should've been guessing your weight and age at Cedar Point, not selling coffins.

"We might consider opening an additional room," Mr. Pfieffle said. "For a young man like this, lost in service to his country. The receiving line will be long."

"Is that all right with you, Louise?" my mother asked.

Louise fidgeted with her pocketbook, eyes on her lap. "That's fine."

My mother cleared her throat.

Pfeiffle started in on the flowers then. What kinds did we want to order? How many around the coffin? Did we want to consider the foyer? He and my mother went back and forth—extra chairs in the side room? Guest book? On and on. But Louise kept it zipped.

"Do you have any requests at all, Louise?" my mother asked finally.

Mr. Pfeiffle leaned across his desk. He smiled like a doctor who'd seen our ailment before. "It's all right. Maybe you can discuss it this afternoon and give me a call." He stood up.

"When my parents died, they had chocolates at the funeral place," Louise said. "I remember that."

Pfeiffle didn't blink an eye. A pro. "Certainly, Mrs. Florida."

When we got home, my mother told me she needed help with something in the shed. She waited until Louise went in the house and then she told me about Louise's old man killing her mother.

"She found them," my mother said.

I thought about how Louise had looked at me when I'd asked her what her old man did. So that was why she was so locked down. She wasn't timid. She was just prepared for the worst.

"And so, now what?" I asked. "Is she going to live with you?"

My mother shook her head. "I don't know. She doesn't have anywhere else to go."

"What about last night?" I asked. "What was wrong with her?"

"Nothing." My mother sighed. "She was just tired." Then I knew. She'd hoped it was a baby. Then there'd be something of Walt left. I wondered why, after all those years, they didn't already have any. I figured she'd probably given up on me.

Inside, we found the door to Walt's and my old bedroom shut.

Louise had gone in for a nap, looked like. My mother turned to me, an idea lighting her eyes. "You ought to take her out when she wakes up. Get her out of the house a little."

Just what I wanted to hear. The hair on my arms stood up. "Well, if she's up to it, sure."

Downtown was lit up for Christmas. Storefront windows lined with cotton to look like snow in the corners. No snow on the ground, though, and dark patches on the lake where the ice was thin. I showed Louise the working clock built into the hill in Washington Park. I'd thought it was one of the world's wonders when I was a kid. "In the spring and summer, this is all covered in flowers," I said. "And they change the date at the bottom there every day."

"I remember this," she said. "We had our picture taken here." She had on that coat I'd seen over her suitcase. It came to her knees and looked thick as a couch. I just had my jacket over a sweater.

"I didn't know you'd been here before," I said.

"On our way to Niagara Falls. Honeymoon."

The wind picked up off the lake, wrapped around buildings. People hurried in and out of the post office carrying packages. The dome was dark under the low clouds, and the flag could hardly flap from the wind pasting it to the pole. Louise shivered.

"How about we just drive around," I said. I felt pretty stupid, a tour guide for a widow. I guess I'd wanted to see the town more than she did. It had been a good place for a kid, swimming and fishing in the summer, skating and hockey in the winter. And bowling anytime. I'd been in a hurry to get out, but now I realized I had a soft spot for it. It was a nice town, and I got the first idea that maybe I could come back someday and stay.

We were only a couple of blocks away from the State, so I thought to take her downstairs to the lanes. I could see my father as a young tough again, ball set firm right at his chest. I was heading down the hill on Columbus toward the water, and I thought maybe I'd just stick my head in, take a quick look. But the place was dark.

"Wait a minute," I said, pulling to the curb across the street. I looked back over my shoulder. The windows under the Spanish arches were black, nothing on the marquee. Coffman Optical next door was apparently doing just fine though—he had tinsel draped along his windows, and the place was packed.

"You okay here?" She shrugged and nodded. I jogged across the street, tried the Water Street entrance. Locked, and it would've been open by then. Should have been. I rattled that metal door and thought I could smell the smoke and lane oil coming up from those metal stairs. I walked around to the Columbus Avenue side, where the theatre entrance was. Locked there, too.

The wind was strong now. I shoved my hands in my pockets and walked back across the street. I felt like as if I'd been punched in the chest. Like I should've been notified. The truth was I was sorrier about that place being closed than my brother being dead. I could go to hell for it, but that was the truth.

Louise watched me start up the car. She didn't ask, and I didn't try to explain. "I hear they built a new road up here," I said. We drove by the Feddersen Building and Jackson's Pier, where I'd hopped ferries to Kelleys Island in the summer to swim off the beach or fish. I turned down a side street off of First Street and pointed down a row of boat-houses. "There's the park, over there. Place is closed this time of year, though. Me and Walt used to fish right here," I said.

She blinked but didn't say a word. The town was pulling me back in again. It wasn't even five o'clock but the streetlights were on. The warehouse windows behind us were dark.

"This is it, the new road," I said as we turned from Cleveland Road onto the Causeway. "This takes you right into Cedar Point, so now you don't have to drive as far out of town or take the ferry, but I like the ferry, myself," I said. I was just running my mouth, because she was so pretty, and I didn't know what else to do. I tried to keep from looking at her. I got to the gates and turned the car around. The water was gray and choppy; it was like as if we were driving right through it. I asked her if she wanted to eat and she said sure, and I told her I'd heard there was a new bowling center in town—state of the art and all that, and right then I realized that was probably why the State had closed.

She said she could go for a burger. "Walt told me you bowled. He said you hustled."

"Is that so," I said. But I wasn't really asking and I wasn't going to try to defend myself against whatever my brother had to say about me. *I can go straight, but you're dead, big man. No changes left for you.*

The Galaxy Lanes was a box of a building with three metal arches over the doors and huge bowling pins with metal sparkles meant to look like stars, I guess, mounted to aqua blue panels under the arches. Underneath that, glass doors and bright lights inside. I sat in the car looking at it for a moment. I'd been in all kinds of bowling centers of course, and they were building them like crazy all over the country by then. In fact there was another place called Bonnie Lanes in Sandusky, but I'd almost never gone there except for an occasional match. It was a fine place, but it wasn't the State. None of these places were.

We went in and ordered beers. There was black carpet run halfway up the walls with little metal stars and planets and rockets stuck to it. You could still smell the dye and the paint, the place was so new. Above the sweepers, the name of the place was spelled out with those sharp curved letters like they used on Martian movies.

Oversized silver bowling pins at various stages of falling were hanging below that.

"Well, this is quite a place," I said. "Sandusky enters the space age."

"We had lanes on the base," she said. "Seems like an awful lot of fuss for a game where you do the same thing over and over."

That irritated me. At the State I could have shown her the difference, lane to lane. So when I asked her how old she'd been when her parents died, it was to get her where she lived. It was a mean thing to do, but I never claimed to be better.

Louise looked up at me, dabbed beer foam from her lip. She put her napkin on her lap and smoothed it. Several times. Like you'd pat a kid's hair down. "Did you know I met Walt when I was only nineteen?" Her smile looked pasted on her face, her voice thin over the noise. "I thought he was my age when we met. He still looked like a boy, even after everything he'd been through. But he was thirty-two! He was visiting the arsenal. I was a secretary there, after."

The waitress came with our food, ripped off a ticket, smacked it down next to my drink. I didn't even look at her, and neither did Louise.

She started in on her burger, took her time chewing. "We got married a year later," she said. "He got me out of there. Pine Bluff wasn't somewhere I wanted to stay." She picked her napkin up and spread it out on her lap again. She took another bite, turned to watch the lanes. She was done talking to me about it.

League play that night. On Number 3, there was one guy who kept rolling strikes. Young, skinny kid with red hair and ears like knobs on his head. Muscles like string up the back of his arm when he swung his release. I'd seen him come up on several rounds by then. You can tell the ones who have talent. They're smooth, no rush in their approach. Even the crankers seem to be moving too slow for all their force. And he was definitely a cranker, a lot of power whether he needed it or not. But that's the way kids are, boys especially. I had to squint to read the name on his team shirt: Wycheski. That night I saw him leave a spare maybe once. The next year, I'd be his coach, and he'd be on national television and of course, everyone around here knows that story. Only a couple of months after that night eating burgers with Louise, Walt would come home, alive again, and I'd be working the counter not ten feet from where Louise and I were sitting, trying to get over her.

We finished our beers and I helped her with her heavy coat and wished for one too when we got outside again. The wind aimed at our faces, and the snow hit like needles. I caught the gleam of it melting on her hair when I opened the car door for her. We passed the empty marina, and beyond the lights along the docks, the sky and water were black. For some reason I thought right then of going hunting with Walt and our father. I wasn't much for it, mostly because I didn't like getting up that early, freezing your ass off in the woods, burying your shit so the deer wouldn't smell it. I hated the waiting. Once on my watch a buck slipped out of a stand of pine. Everything around him was still. You think an animal doesn't know. But they know. I had a clear shot and didn't take it. Not because I felt sorry for it. But there was something I didn't want to lose, the animal listening, a branch against his chest.

"Nothing's sticking yet," I said. "Ground's too warm."

I put on the wipers because our breath was steaming the glass. She drew the pad of her finger across her window. "How about you? You sticking around?"

I'd just turned onto our street and was regretting it, thinking maybe we should've stayed out a little longer, maybe the beer had loosened her up a bit. I don't remember if I said anything. Then I saw a woman standing in our yard. She flashed through that watery line Louise had made on the window. I slowed for the driveway. The woman was my mother. She didn't have on a coat, and her hair was slicked against her forehead. She had on her green apron, I could see it in the porch light, and she was shouting something. Louise sat up, wrenched the door handle. She was out of the car before I'd cut the engine, about tripped on her coat.

My mother's voice sounded like something torn. I couldn't understand her. My father shambled down the porch steps, already drunk, likely. He wrapped his arms around her, pinned her arms to her sides. Louise said something and my mother turned to her.

It took a moment, but then her words came together for me: *They found him and he's alive.* My mother fell on her knees then and my father lurched, stumbled backward. Louise got down with her, the two of them hugging and sobbing under that dark, snow-shot sky. And my father and I—what could we do? The women were handling all the wailing. We just stood there, stunned.

Too hasty on the reporting, that was the explanation for the mix-up. We never questioned it. It would be nearly two months until Walt came home. The headless man whose body had arrived in Sandusky that afternoon, maybe just as Louise and I were sipping beers at the new lanes, would be sent to blow up another family.

The telegram read: WE ARE PLEASED TO INFORM YOU THAT SERGEANT MAJOR WALTER B. FLORIDA IS SAFE AND WELL.

I took off the next morning. I figured there was no point in staying since he wouldn't be home for a while. I figured I could make that tourney in Harrisburg if they'd still let me do the qualifier. My mother put out a feast for breakfast, all the food people had brought. I ate as much as I could handle, then took my dishes to the sink, grabbed my bag and jacket, and kissed my mother good-bye. She'd put on lipstick for the first time since I'd been home; she rubbed it off my jaw when she let me go.

She and Louise followed me and my father outside. "Good to finally meet you," Louise said. The snow had come the night before. It lit up her hair.

"You, too," I said. We'd all been up late, my mother trying to call a number she had over and over, not getting through. Then, when we'd finally all gone to bed, I still couldn't sleep, thinking of Louise asking me if I meant to stay. I leaned down and kissed her where her cheek had gone pink from cold, and I didn't try to rush it. If she thought anything of it she didn't show it, only smiled and patted my shoulder and told me to have a good trip.

My father drove me to the depot. "You taking any side action out there?"

"Occasionally," I said.

"I'm putting a bid in for the tool room," he said. "I can put in a word for you anytime." He was solemn as a judge. Ready to save me from my imminent failure.

"I'm not done yet," I said.

My father pulled to a stop but kept the motor running. He had that dead-sour alcohol smell on him. His hands were red and chapped on the wheel. I'd never seen them completely clean. Grease had seeped into the calluses on his thumb and forefinger from years of dropping nut blanks off the screw machines. A fine snow dusted the windshield.

"Tell Louie Bertrell I've seen his hook and he ought to save it for the church leagues," he said. He sat there and watched me walk away, I knew.

I came home again two weeks later for Christmas. Louise was still there, waiting with my folks for Walt to get home. My mother had gone over the top; the Christmas tree took up half the living room. On that visit Louise showed me a letter on Army stationery written with a fat-tipped pencil with letters that sprawled across the page:

I am not here the same way. Feel fine   See you.
Walt

If Louise was scared, she didn't show it. She smiled like as if this was her kid writing his first letter. Every time my mother looked at it she cried, but kept saying she was happy.

As for me, the last two weeks had been a wash. I carried around a little extra cash, and I was eating into that. Maybe my body had already given in to what I wanted, but it was a hell of a way to end a career. Of course, at the time I told myself I just needed a break from the road for a while, and that I'd get back to it in January.

While I'd been gone, Louise had bought the house on Pipe Street. Apparently, Walt was headed for retirement, and they'd all decided it'd be best to keep him where everyone could pitch in. The house was a one-story bungalow; big front room, two bedrooms and a bath in back. Nice backyard and front porch. Needed a little repair here and there, some painting. I didn't like how close it was to the train tracks, but the price was right. My folks had helped her out.

So I offered to help Louise get the house in shape. I thought I'd talked myself out of her, one woman at a time, in Harrisburg, Philly, and Baltimore over the past few weeks. I told myself I was only in town until the next qualifiers. I told myself I felt sorry for her.

One afternoon she was sanding a spot on the floor behind me and I was on a ladder scraping trim. "You have furniture to ship?" I asked. The house was empty except for the bed my folks had given her out of me and Walt's room. I was sleeping on a cot.

She stood up and stretched her back. "The place we had on the base was furnished. There's his trunk and a rocking chair, that's about it."

She wore a baggy pair of trousers cinched at the waist and cut off at the ankles. I wondered if they'd belonged to Walt. "I guess I'll get us a couch and a TV for in here, and a table and chairs for in there, and a bed and dresser. Walt's stuff will fill the spare room, easy."

I didn't have kids on the brain for myself, but I was kind of surprised she didn't say that second bedroom might be a nursery someday. I scraped at some loose paint.

"Probably going to cost a lot shipping a rocking chair."

"Yeah, but I want to keep hold of that." *Aholt.*

I looked at her, and I knew the chair had come from her parents' house.

"Why you looking at me like that?"

"I guess I could ask you the same thing." A paint flake got in my mouth, and I tasted metal. I fished it out with a finger. "Matter of fact, I am asking you the same thing."

Louise got on her knees again, grabbed the sander and leaned into it, back and forth, like that was all she wanted to do in the world.

"Here I am working on your house," I continued. "I don't even have my own bed."

She didn't look up. But her face had gone red. She shook her head, and I wondered if she was going to say anything at all. If she hadn't, I would have walked out of there, left her to do her home improvements solo. But then she nodded, like as if to say fine, you asked for it. "My daddy shot my mother one day after coming home from the arsenal," she said. "Then he shot himself. I guess he thought she was cheating."

Her arm worked fast, the muscles ridging up in her neck. "I'd decided to go home with my friend Mary Fran." She stopped then, eyes steady on me, chin tilted up like the first time I saw her. "So I wasn't home."

I hung onto the ladder. "I'm glad you weren't there."

She shook her head, almost smiled, looking at the new wood she'd sanded down to. Obviously, I'd missed something. "Either he was going to shoot me, too, or maybe, if I'd been there, he wouldn't have shot either of us."

I got down off the ladder.

"Don't." She waved her hands in front of her, like trying to slap down cobwebs. I kept coming anyway and then I kneeled in front of her. She moved fast as a cat, grabbed my collar, fingernails scraping my neck.

"Don't." Eyes narrowed, lips tight against her teeth. "You can go and never come back if you want."

She let go of me and I pushed myself up. She got up and went to the bathroom, and a few minutes later she came back out and started working that floor again, like nothing had happened.

Just after New Year's, there was another note from Walt:

Feeling fine. There's no winter here. Home soon, miss you.
Walt

This time, not in the shaky child's hand but a neat script. Louise unfolded it in the living room of my parents' house and read it out. My mother had hung a banner with 1962 in big numbers over the front door. We passed the note around.

Leave it to my father to say something. "Who the hell wrote this?"

Louise folded the note and put it back in the envelope, like as if she hadn't heard a thing.

Walt was due back in a month. She found ways to perk the house up. She borrowed my mother's sewing machine to make a slipcover for the scratchy old couch she got from the Salvation Army. She made curtains—those were from new navy blue cloth, same color as the dress I first saw her in. My mother's friends brought her things, too—dishes, linens, pots and pans—everything worn or chipped or mismatched, but clean.

We finished painting and cleaning, and I helped her haul things in the house and moved them around until she felt they were right. I helped her hang the curtains, too. "You're going to have to have the in-laws over for a housewarming party, you know," I said.

"I know." She held several hooks between her teeth and worked them into the pleats at the top of the cloth. Her hair was bright over her shoulders. She looked happy. She looked like any woman waiting to see her husband after being apart for months. So I tried to be happy for her, even though I didn't like thinking of Walt sitting in that living room instead of me.

Helping Louise had gotten me in good not just with my parents but also my mother's friends. Several had offered up their still unmarried daughters. I went on dates just to have something to do, but I knew I wasn't going to get anything out of them, and if I did I might as well just sign the mortgage papers. I didn't remember a lot from school but I did recall from French class that *mort* meant dead. I said that anytime someone asked why didn't I settle down.

"I'll bring the bubbly," I said. "Make it black tie." I guess right then I missed life on the road, the win or the lose, how the women took me out of myself, the yellow lights sliding over my face on night trains.

She smiled. "You got some money you're not telling about?" She sat across the room from where I stood screwing in the hardware for curtains only a bit darker blue than her eyes. A detail her husband would appreciate, if he had any wits left.

I shrugged. "I've got what I need." Though the truth was, I was low on money. My mother had offered to make me a loan, indefinitely, if I'd settle down, buy some woman a ring.

I thought of Walt on the couch beside her, sewn up from whatever damage had been done to him. What would they talk about? Would I have wanted Louise at all if she hadn't been his wife? Plenty of other women out there. You could find something to like in any of them—one might be plump but pretty. Or skinny but busty. Or weak-chinned but leggy. A lot of the things that bother a man when a woman is painted up and trussed into girdles and stockings sort of ease off when she's stretched beside you, all bare skin and loose hair. Low light doesn't hurt the situation either. So why Louise? You could say it was just as simple as one brother wanting what the other had, the second oldest story in the world. Maybe that was reason enough.

She slid in the last hook, held the curtain panel up to me. I worked the hooks into the hardware and she held the other end, feeding it to me. When we finished, she stood back to look. She smiled, gazing up at them like as if God had damn hung them.

I'd left some beers on the porch and asked her did she want one. She said sure, so I brought in two. Still fingering those curtains, she said she wanted to make a loop for each side, so she could draw them back to frame the window nice. She'd put in hooks to catch the loops. She pulled the fabric back to show me what she meant.

"You could put it right here," I said. I put my finger to a spot on the wall next to the window frame where the hook could go, and I pressed hard until my skin went white around the nail, right where I thought I'd drive in the screw.

* 7 *

A COUPLE OF weeks later, there was one more letter from Walt, with a picture.

To prepare you. It's still me.

Louise had been drinking a while by the time I came by with a pair of rusted iron gates from Sandusky Scrap that afternoon. There I was dragging bits of metal to her like a sad old jay. I didn't care. I figured I'd end up on the road again eventually, play out a couple more years. Set myself up booking or start coaching somewhere, whatever. It was so cold the metal hurt my hands. The sky was flat and low, gray as pavement at four o'clock. I knocked on the door. She didn't have a car, but I figured she wouldn't be out with the wind slicing off the lake and the air ready to burst with snow. No answer, so I knocked again, then tried the door. It was unlocked, and I opened it a little ways.

She was sitting cross-legged on the couch facing the window. There was a box of my beer cleaned out beside her, the empties neatly lined at her feet. She had on a sweater and those old trousers, no socks. Her hair was down.

"Mail came," she said, swaying with just the effort of talking.

I saw the Polaroid on the couch next to her. I rubbed my hands together, flaking off the rusty dirt. I picked it up, brought it close to my face. There he was, one big smashed thing slumped in a wheelchair. There was either a glare in the shot or his hair was white. And a gash on his head, scarred flesh and a dark red valley. Then the sag on his left side, the cheek and bottom lip slack. The bandaged left arm resting on his right. He was trying to smile, but the smile was only on half his face. I looked closer. That blur above his head was his hair, all white. I hoped she didn't hear me swallow.

"So, he's beat up. You knew that."

She tucked her feet under her, looked out the window.

I laid the Polaroid back on the couch beside her. "Want me to put this on the fridge?" I said. I can't figure what I was thinking, trying to joke with her right then.

She dragged her hair back behind one ear and took another long drink of beer, eyes darting from crack to crack on the ceiling. I could see them glassing over with tears. She lurched forward again and reared that arm back and threw the bottle as hard as she could at the wall. Actually, I think she was aiming at the window, framed with those blue curtains we'd just hung a couple days before, but she missed. The bottle didn't even break, just bounced and spun a couple of times, leaking foam onto the floor.

"Whoa now," I said. "Wait." I reached for her and she shook her head and tried to stand up but caught her foot in the cushion and fell on her knees. I tried to help her up, but she swung at me. I grabbed her hands so she couldn't hit me. They were thin as bird bones. I kneeled in front of her and pulled her into me, folded her arms against my chest.

She curled, chin down, and sobbed, sucking air in, forcing it out. Her hair stuck to her face. I rocked her, and I thought of my father pinning my mother's arms to her sides in the snow the night we'd found out Walt was alive.

She raised her head, lips curled back from her teeth, caught her breath. She squeezed her eyes shut and then opened them. She looked at me for about five beats, her face still wet and flat, like as if she'd just woken up.

"At Fort Carson he used to ski like a bullet," she said.

Then she kissed me. Salt and beer on her tongue, a rattle in her breath. She edged into me, until my head was back far enough so I couldn't swallow. She lost her balance and grabbed my shoulder, and I threw an arm back to keep us from falling. I saw the edge of the Polaroid on the couch like a slice in the cloth.

I turned my face away from her. "You need to sleep it off, maybe." Not what I wanted, obviously, but I was trying to be honorable, or at least put up a convincing front.

"You think I don't know myself?"

I kept quiet, kept my head down. It was the only way I felt I could keep from screwing the situation up, whatever that would have meant.

"I know myself." She sat back down on her knees. "Ever since—all this time I've known exactly who I was." She cupped my jaw in her palms, eased them down to my neck. "A lot of people might be grateful for that kind of clarity, early in life." She leaned into me again, and I tried to stay upright.

I wanted her; sure I did. Some might say wanting's the same as doing, but I say it's different.

"Are you?" I asked.

She straightened. "What?"

"Grateful?"

"I've never been grateful enough," she said. "It's one of my failings." She kissed me again, and I kissed her back. I couldn't get my breath, holding her, my mouth dry and heart whacking at my ribs; I hadn't felt like that since the first time I'd found my way inside a woman's dress. And with that Polaroid there, too, inches from my face.

She got to her feet and I followed her into the bedroom and sat down next to her on the bed, on my mother's rosebud sheets that smelled of whitener and the inside of our closets. She turned on the lamp and started pulling off her clothes. I'd only just kicked off my shoes. Most of the women I'd been with liked to slip out of their dresses in the dark, and a lot of them dressed again in the dark and took off after, like as if they couldn't see, it might not have happened. And, sure, some of them were bold, they had something to prove, going to bed easy as a man. But those women were the ones most likely to stay the night, look at you with big girl-eyes in the morning and ask you when you'd be through that way again.

Louise took her time. She folded her sweater before setting it on that rocking chair of hers with a back like wheel spokes, which had arrived a few days before. She folded her trousers and panties too. She was a narrow girl, hard to believe she was a grown woman, pale flat belly and small breasts high on her rib cage. Lamplight orange in her hair, shadowing her face. I sat up and unbuttoned my shirt. She took it before I could throw it on the floor, hung it over the back of the chair. Hung my trousers over that and stuffed my socks in my shoes.

"You shy?" She asked me, climbing onto the bed as I stood up, thumbs hooked in my shorts.

Why bother to say I thought to stop, if only to point out I knew better? I kicked my shorts off my ankles and let her guide me onto my back, and she kept her eyes open the whole time she rode me. I reached for her shoulders to pull her down to kiss me, and even then, she watched me. I slid an arm tight around her shoulder and rolled onto her, because I wanted to go as deep as I could into her, make those dark blue eyes close under my weight. But instead I felt her eyelashes against my cheek as she blinked. Then she was done with that and pushed me back to straddle me again.

When I finished she rested on top of me, face against my neck. Then she rolled off of me and laid on her hip, facing me, a hand on my belly.

"Don't fall asleep."

I was trying not to shiver now, the heat sliding out of me. I looked at her. Her eyelids were so heavy, she looked like as if she might fall asleep herself any minute. But I understood then why she'd hung my clothes so neat, because she knew where I'd be going after that, and she didn't want me looking rumpled in front of my mother, who already knew how much time I'd been spending there.

"I'm not worried about being late for dinner, if that's what you're saying." There I was, a grown man. I didn't have it in me to say I loved her. I didn't believe it then anyway.

She smiled. "But you still have to go." She closed her eyes, nudged my hip.

"What about you? You ought to put something in that stomach, keep the beer company."

She brushed her hair back from her neck, and I thought of the first time I'd seen her in my mother's kitchen, the cloudy light, the gold thread at her throat, and it hadn't been too much more than a month, but it was like as if someone else had seen it and had told me about it. You think you walk around free and then you remember yourself from back when maybe you really were free, meaning you didn't have anything to think about except what you were doing right then. You know the difference.

She slid her hand up my chest, cupped my cheek. "There's nothing you have to do about me."

I turned to face her. Her palm slipped from my face onto the sheets. "What do you mean?" I asked.

She sat up, reached for the bedspread, pulled it to her waist. "When I was alone, I wanted to run, but I had nowhere to go. So I just went on for a while until I figured out something else. That's all I'm saying."

She swung her legs off the edge of the bed and reached for my trousers, but I was already on my feet. "Got it," I said. I grabbed my shirt, too, and she watched me dress.

"So when I see you again, we'll just shake hands," I said, sitting with my back to her, shoving my feet into my shoes. I stuffed my socks into my pockets. I felt like I was the one who'd been drinking, fumbling with my laces.

"Leo."

I turned and she sat up and reached for me. I ran my hands down her naked back and kissed her neck and asked her what she wanted me to do, and the only thing she told me was not to ask anymore.

There were only a few other times in the next few weeks. It ran the same: I came by with some excuse, and it was easy to do. I'd found something she could use at the house, I could plug the chinks in the window frames, I could see if she needed to get groceries. She didn't have a phone, so I had to stop by. One night I came and she was setting the table for two in the dining room, and when I said I didn't think she'd be expecting me, she laughed like as if I should have known better. She'd fixed pot roast and potatoes and gravy. She'd bought an electric heater because the radiator didn't do much in there. She lit candles and put out blue napkins creased from the store and smelling of dye. We drank beer from the bottles and water from jars.

After we ate, I stood up to clear the table. She followed me into the kitchen.

"Did you always help your momma so nice?" She stood behind me with her arms at my waist while I rinsed. She'd trimmed her bangs crooked and all night she'd been tilting her head the other way and asking me if that made them look straighter. That was the thing about Louise. She could make me laugh.

"Sure I did," I said. And I had, after Walt left, to make up for him being gone. But I kept that part to myself. Before we'd gone to bed, I could've talked about Walt all day if I'd wanted to. Now I could kiss her in that kitchen, undress her, but I couldn't so much as say my brother's name.

And that was a bargain I could keep. We carried the candles into the bedroom.

"I always thought you'd be rougher," she said after. I'd hung my own clothes over the rocking chair, not wanting her to do it for me. The candle flames were nearly flat in the draft; I hadn't plugged that room yet.

"In bed?" I laughed, pulled her into me, her back against my chest.

"Not like that."

"How'd you think I'd be then?"

"I didn't think of that at all."

"Don't lie," I said, but she didn't argue.

"I thought you'd have a beard or a moustache, and I thought you'd be beefier."

"You thought I'd be fat and hairy? I'm flattered, truly." I asked her why.

"I don't know. Maybe your name. Like a lion. The only picture I ever saw of you was from when you were kids."

There was Walt again, not mentioned but in the room with us, just the same. He'd said my name, and maybe he'd said other things. And she'd seen a picture and then decided what kind of man I was.

"Well, I can see how you might think it," I said. "I was a fat kid and bowling makes you hairy, starting with your knuckles."

She laughed. "You were skinny in that picture." She turned over to face me, her breasts cool against my chest. "You were a little guy. You had a cowboy hat and a toy gun in each hand. Walt had his face painted like an Indian. He had a tomahawk."

I stared at the shadows on the ceiling. I remembered that Halloween. Walt and his friends wanted an excuse to run around half-naked in the cold. I dressed like a cowboy so I could hunt him. He'd said to me, *You may be the cowboy, but this time the Indian wins.* Tomahawk in his fist, a lethal smile. It was a real pointed rock he'd tied to a stick. I ran like hell. I really believed he'd kill me.

"Made me want to have a boy," she said. " 'Til then I'd always wanted a girl."

And there he was again, Walt in the rocking chair across from us now, reminding me just who was going to be there with Louise for that next chapter, and who wasn't.

Louise nudged my hip again, my signal to get dressed, but then we fell asleep, and by the time I got back I found my mother sitting in her robe on the couch, watching Jack Paar. Seeing the blue flicker from the living room, I figured on finding my father asleep in the recliner. But she was alone. I stopped in the doorway from the kitchen.

"You're up late," I said.

She looked at me like as if she wasn't sure it was really me. At first I thought she had bad news. I thought of the night those goons came pounding on the door for some bet my father hadn't made good on—probably small change now, something you could win in a frame—and there it was twenty years later nearly, but I still remembered that blank way she'd looked at me then. Then I thought maybe she'd heard something about Walt. I even hoped it was bad news.

"Mom?"

She stood up and came over to me. Her hair hung in a braid over her shoulder. She studied me for a moment and then slapped me hard in the face.

I rocked back on my feet. "What the hell?"

"You think I didn't hear you whistling all the way up the walk?" She turned away from me then, leaving me with the TV chatter.

I had time, as she walked down the hall, to deny it. But I didn't try to. Anyway I knew she wouldn't believe me, because I hadn't even heard myself whistling. When you hustle, you control every muscle, every sound. When you can't do that, it means your life has spilled over you like ink. Far as I could tell, she'd seen the stain on me for weeks.

Tess Wycheski

* 8 *

AFTER MY FATHER died, I felt the weight of my body in everything I did—reaching for a glass, pulling on clothes, walking anywhere, only to forget the point of my errand. My father had left his body, I was told in the funeral service he hadn't wanted, but I was trapped in mine. In one way I was like those ghosts on Johnson Island, drifting through the rooms of our house, the doorway my lake's edge. In another way I was the lake itself, heavy and cold. Bowling was out of the question. I couldn't handle my father's picture on Leo's Hall of Fame wall with his hair slicked back and the smile he gave to people he didn't know. No physics could explain what I couldn't let go.

The Overdose was how my mother later referred to my father's death, if she referred to it at all, as if it had been an event all its own, not happening to anyone in particular. The coroner called it narcotic-induced cardiac arrest. At the funeral, the preacher from the Emmanuel, Pastor Jake, told me that because my father had become a drug addict, I would have to be more careful, I could get addicted to anything. He told me he was speaking from experience. He smiled and patted me on the shoulder. Me, standing by the hole with the velvet skirt around it and the coffin looking like it was hovering, about to blast off.

Chelsea was there with her mother and father, all of them looking scrubbed and sleek in their dark clothes. She squeezed my hand as if she was trying to pour her fierceness into me. The only moment

I almost lost it was when Leo tried to speak to my mother and she turned away from him. He looked so pained that I knew I couldn't risk trying to talk to him if I wanted to keep my own composure, which had seemed so important at the time. And there was Donny, who came alone, his mother at home with his father. When he said my name in the receiving line I heard it as if from far away.

After the funeral, my mother and I went through most of our pots and pans—their bottoms blackened from being left on a live burner, my mother having decided to make some attempt at dinner and then forgetting. We never replaced them; we got thinner, sat for hours without moving. People visited, some wives of the men who'd worked with my father, but mostly members of the Emmanuel congregation, bringing food, saying prayers with my mother in the kitchen. I stayed in my room for those visits.

Mr. Todd, my journalism and history teacher, stopped by every few days with homework and lecture notes. After a couple of weeks, he was the one to tell me, gently, that I had to come back to school or repeat the year. That was enough to propel me into my jeans and backpack the following Monday. Walking to school, I felt weak and unbalanced, like after I'd broken my ankle in second grade and the cast had just come off, my foot limp and pale. I came home exhausted each day but could not fall asleep at night. Or I jerked awake with my heart pounding, like I'd just remembered something important, but it faded as soon as I opened my eyes.

And there was the problem of the crying. I'd be walking to my next class and tears would start streaming down my face with no warning, like an allergic reaction. I started keeping extra cafeteria napkins in my back pocket. I asked for bathroom passes so often that one of my teachers pulled me aside and asked if I had any female issues I wanted to discuss. As if my father dying in our house had not been issue enough. I felt cold all the time. Sometimes my eyes wouldn't focus. I was clumsy, dizzy; I wondered if I'd absorbed the poison that had twisted my father's joints. In a way, I wanted that to be the case. I wanted a reason for feeling as if I would never be right again.

Mr. Todd either didn't seem to notice my red eyes and shaky handwriting, or he chose to ignore these things. Instead, he caught me at the doorway of his room after journalism class the week I came back and handed me a certificate.

I'd won third place in a state contest for an article I'd written about Joe Schnipke—no relation to Bern, the former Galaxy Lanes owner—who'd lost his arm in a tractor accident but still went on to nail one of the first 800 series in Sandusky. Mr. Todd had entered everyone in the class. Now I barely remembered writing the piece, but somehow it made sense that I'd profile someone who'd had his arm torn off. The certificate was stiff in my hands. I gave Mr. Todd the best smile I could manage.

"Thanks," I said. Mr. Todd smiled back, handed me another paper.

"Here's something else I think you should take," he said. It was an application for State. "Your time out won't hurt you, Tess," he said, as if I'd just taken a long vacation. I stared back at him. I was still stunned by the amount of noise there was in a high school; I hadn't noticed it before. Kids yelling to each other down the hall, lockers clanging, the long electric whine of the second bell signaling the buses would leave soon.

"They have a good journalism program there," he continued. "Of course, you could figure out what you want to major in after you get there. Anyway, I'll write you a letter." Then he said that while State was only a couple of hours drive, it was far enough away to, "You know, have your own life."

He stopped then, blinking, and I realized he was talking about my situation, since, having come to my house with the assignments, he knew it better than anyone else at school other than Chelsea. I think on one of his drop-bys while I was napping, my mother had even tried to convert him, or whatever it was they called it when they snowed you.

He pushed his glasses up on the bridge of his nose. He wore his sandy brown hair kind of longish, just to the collar, and feathered on the sides in a sort of disco time warp, and if it hadn't been for the glasses and the beard shadow, I could've confused him with the blond, blue-eyed Jesus gazing from the covers of those slippery little Emmanuel pamphlets my mother brought home and stacked on her bedside table. But Mr. Todd was forty, older than my father had been before he died, and he had a son in eighth grade special ed and a stern-faced wife who wore the same cobalt blue satin sheath dress with a black rose on one shoulder to every prom and homecoming she chaperoned. This was what I'd heard, anyway, since I hadn't gone to any of the dances. Mr. Todd was just a man, but I wondered if he also might be trying to be my savior, now that my father was gone.

The hallway was jammed, and I concentrated on not getting knocked into Mr. Todd's chest. He tapped the form, which I held between us like a flimsy shield. "The application is pretty straightforward, okay? My sister-in-law is there; she'll be on the lookout for it."

I thanked him, and he said, "Hey, fill it out," and I said I would.

He caught my wrist as I turned away, and I remember the shock of being touched that way by him, by any teacher—it wasn't sexual, but intimate, or maybe it was sexual, but at the time I couldn't be sure. His fingers circled my wrist easily, and he held on. "Promise me, Tess."

I promised, and he let me go, and then I leaned into the kids pushing their way past me, the books slammed into lockers and girls spraying perfume in their teased hair, guys pretending to choke on the sweetened alcohol clouds. I slipped the form into my backpack before I rode my bike home. I didn't want my mother to see it. She wouldn't have understood, given the fact that, even though she'd gone full-time at the Emmanuel, we still barely had enough money to make the bills. Every day she brought home food for us. The Tupperware and CorningWare dishes were labeled on the bottom with not only the owner's name but also the name of the meal: Christ Casserole, Savior Three-Bean, Miracle Bread. Chelsea thought they were hilarious. For my part, I lost even more weight trying to avoid that stuff, but hunger would always eventually win.

My mother had started back to work at the Emmanuel when I started back to school. Having daily schedules again forced a kind of normalcy on us, though to me the routines still felt like a script I couldn't memorize. One morning maybe a month after my father died, as we sat at the kitchen table eating cereal, my mother told me she had good news.

"I've been promoted," she said. She was dressed up more than usual, in a silky lavender blouse, navy skirt, and heels. She gave me a shaky smile. Her skin looked thin and pale; I could see a blue vein along the edge of her jaw.

She was the church secretary, charged with typing and mimeographing the bulletin and whatnot. I must've looked confused about what a promotion could entail, because then she explained that it was more of a promotion in title than in pay. "I'll be Pastor Jake's assistant starting today," she said, beaming a professional smile. "We've had to hire another secretary—we're growing so fast!" Then she said maybe I should visit, that "it might help."

What she'd said before rang in my head: *we're*. I needed a moment to think about it. In the past, *we* had always meant our family. I didn't believe the promotion had suddenly changed her allegiances. Maybe she'd thought of the Emmanuel as her family for a while, even before my father had died. And maybe becoming Pastor Jake's assistant was her reward. It wouldn't be so far-fetched to think of it that way if you believed in a universe where there were rewards for good behavior—correct action, even—which in my case I'd begun to doubt.

"Congratulations," I said to her. She smiled distractedly and gathered up her jacket and purse. She seemed so eager to get going, and I couldn't blame her.

MY MOTHER'S FULL-TIME work schedule meant most of the housework and yard care fell to me. Mowing had been my father's department, and I was more than willing to take over the responsibility for the same reasons I pressed my face into his shirts as often as I felt I needed to. He'd maintained our mower with the same care as his bowling gear—I found it oiled, gassed up, shiny new spark plugs in place. He might have been getting it ready in the days before he died, a thought that got me mad enough to throw all my effort into starting it. But the thing wouldn't kick. We didn't have the money for repairs, and anyway my mother and I couldn't even lift it into the trunk of the Buick. She refused to let me borrow one from any of the neighbors. She wasn't concerned that our square of grass was knee-high in places, and I didn't want to press her about it in case she decided to bring in some team of evangelist yard-care people. Once or twice someone anonymously mowed, probably a neighbor. I'd come home from school to find our yard naked and startling in its neatness, and I'd think for a moment that my father had come home and finished the mowing early so we could head out to the lanes. It was as if whole stretches of time could disappear for me.

Then, early that summer on a Saturday morning, Donny Florida came to our house. My mother was getting ready to make a rare trip to the grocery store; we were out of basics—toilet paper, dry cereal, toothpaste—the kinds of things my mother never would've allowed us to run out of before.

And there was Donny, already blurting out before I'd managed a hello that he would be happy to help us out with the yard. It had rained the night before, and the Wycheski lawn had soaked his jeans to the shins. "No charge; I have a job," he explained, as if I wouldn't remember he was working at the lanes.

I hadn't seen him since the funeral. We'd never had any classes together—he was Vo-Ed, though I'd always believed he could've been fine in my classes. In two months he'd gotten taller, and his voice had gone deeper in his chest. He'd let his hair grow, and it curled around his ears, blond at the tips from the sun. We stood there at the door while I tried to take in what he'd just said to me. He waited patiently, even though I could tell he was nervous—and I couldn't blame him, given the way we were living, with our sealed house and overgrown grass and prayer pamphlets stacked by the door.

Finally I thought to invite him in, and my mother came in from the kitchen. Donny did all the right things. He said, "Nice to see you, Mrs. Wycheski," and smiled and nodded to her.

"He works at the lanes," I said, though I knew she knew this, too. But she managed to say, "Good to see you, too," and he said thank you, and she went back to her list of things she would forget to buy at the store.

I offered Donny a seat on the couch and he busied himself looking around the room. He showed no reaction to the airbrushed pictures my mother had hung in the living room, of Jesus walking in a crowd of children, preaching on the mount, crying on the cross. I asked him if he wanted something to drink, and he said thank you and asked if he could help. He looked so sane, smiling his careful smile, and he didn't look worried about breathing the air or sitting on our furniture like other people had, even the evangelists who were supposedly immunized by God's love—as if you could catch an overdose, accidental or otherwise. I shook my head because it felt too dangerous to speak. It wasn't as if I'd been missing him, or maybe I had been without realizing it, but that wasn't the point. He represented a world I had cut myself off from. I hadn't even taken my AMF Angle out of the bag, afraid I wouldn't be able to handle its weight, much less the sight of it.

I brought him a glass of Vernors and sat down on the other end of the couch from him. "Our mower is broken," I said. It seemed to sum up the overall situation.

"I can probably fix it," he said. "I fix all the mowers on my street. Anyway, Leo'll let me borrow his riding mower from the lanes."

My mother headed down the hall to find her purse, saying in a kind of warning, it seemed, that she would be right back.

Donny set his glass on the coffee table, on top of a prayer pamphlet, which he also appeared not to notice. He sat with his elbows on his knees and looked at me. "And how about you?" he asked. "How are you?"

There wasn't time to answer—or to answer truthfully—with my mother coming back down the hall already. I said I was fine, smiling like I meant it, and he nodded like he believed me. He stood up and said he would take our mower with him if I didn't mind, and we both looked at my mother and she said that would be okay.

He came back the next afternoon with the riding mower on a flatbed trailer towed by Leo's winter-beater pickup truck, and once again our yard was shorn and perfect, a model citizen in the neighborhood. When he came back a few days later, he had our mower with him, and he proudly started it up for me in the front yard. Then he decided he would go ahead and mow again, since he was there, even though the grass didn't really need it yet. So I made lemonade and sat out on the stoop, pretending to read while he leaned into the mower, back and forth, muscles moving under his skin. Afterward, we drank lemonade together and I tried not to let him notice me looking at his brown arms, sweat-slick and flecked with grass.

When my mother commented on how promptly he arrived each Saturday morning to mow, I suggested that she mention his good work at the Emmanuel in case any older folks could use his help. That caught her by surprise. As far as I knew, no one took him up on it.

Then school started again, and Donny offered to take me to school and back each day, though I wasn't on his way. He drove a mostly brown, pieced-together Trans Am that he called the Turd, but he loved the thing. His legs were so long he had to drive with the wheel between his knees. He cranked the wheel lower to emphasize this, though.

On one of those trips to school, early in the fall of our senior year, he asked me to come back to the lanes. He still had a T-shirt tan from mowing lawns all summer; white skin showed under the edges of his sleeves.

"Leo misses you," he said.

"Leo hasn't shown his face since the funeral," I said. And I thought of him watching my mother turning away, a weight in my chest.

"Well," he looked away, toward the sky over the lake, which was violet at the edges. "He told me he could use your help. Scoring and working the snack bar and stuff."

"And what will you do?" I asked.

Donny shrugged. "More of the same." He turned into the student parking lot, and when he parked, as far from the building as possible, he turned to me. He was shaking a little when he kissed me, but he was gentle and steady, and he smelled like fresh-cut grass. He kept his eyes open, as if to tell me he knew what he was doing, even though later he told me I was the first girl he'd ever kissed. It was my first kiss, too.

"Come back," he said, and I decided I would.

I didn't bring my AMF because I hadn't planned to bowl—I'd told Donny the best I could do was stop by. When we went to the counter, Leo had a pair of shoes waiting for me, just like the first time I'd come there, holding my father's hand. Only these weren't rentals. They were custom Linds, just like my father's, red kidskin like they made back in the day for the Hamm's and Stroh's bowling teams.

"Don't say I didn't want you back," Leo said, pushing them toward me. He was smiling, proud of himself. I reached to pick them up, but they blurred in front of me, tears rolling down my face. I couldn't touch them, couldn't seem to get any air.

"Hey," Donny said, pulling me to him. "Hey, you're okay."

I shook my head, closed my eyes, drank in the smell of the place, the oil and smoke and buttered popcorn. There were the clattering pins and the squeak of the swinging door—Leo never oiled it because he wanted to hear if someone was trying to sneak back there when he was in the shoe room—and then Leo was next to me, too, clicking his tongue against the roof of his mouth and patting my shoulder.

"I think you need to break these in, kid," he said, but that only made my muscles clench tighter. My hands and feet prickled as if they were getting no blood.

"But first," I managed to get out, "I need you to take that picture down."

"What?"

Donny and Leo looked where I was pointing, at the Hall of Fame wall. It was bad enough that I had gone back to the lanes without my father, and that in doing so I'd let whatever was left of him slip out of the place. I couldn't face his polite, unaware smile.

"That's a fine thank you," Leo said.

"I mean it," I said.

Leo shook his head. "Not an option, sweetie."

"Then I'm going." I got my balance again, turned to look at him. My face was wet, my cheeks twitching with the effort of fighting down another sob. "I'm sorry I came."

"You'll be sorrier if you don't stay."

"I'll get it myself. It's mine anyway," I said, but Leo snagged me by the arm.

"Can I talk to you a minute?" he said. He tugged me toward the pro shop. Donny took a step back from us to let us pass. It was clear he didn't know what to do.

The pro shop had the burned plastic smell of a ball recently drilled. I thought of the day we'd drilled my Angle, the glittery cloud of dust in the air, Leo's story about ghosts. That's what we were—clouds and dust—how had I not known? And then Leo saying my father couldn't coach me to win. Why had I believed him even for a moment? And why had winning ever mattered to me anyway? I had the idea that if I could fling everything off the walls, I might feel better. Leo maybe saw it in my face. He pointed toward the Hall of Fame wall.

"That over there belongs to your father," he said. "It's his, no matter where he is. He earned it—you get me on this?"

I stared at him. I wasn't sure I'd be able to speak without screaming, but I decided to risk it. "You have a lot of nerve talking about my father."

Leo sighed. "You want me to say he was the better man? Then fine, you got it."

I hoped my expression conveyed how little I cared for this obvious fact. "You left him," I said. "You broke his heart. And you never even said you were sorry."

Leo leaned against the counter and looked at the floor, blinking as if trying to remember something. "Tess, my whole life has been an apology."

"What? What do you mean?" This was just my point; he'd never apologized for anything.

He looked through the window at Donny, who was set at the top of the lane, getting ready to roll. I thought of what my father had said on that last night we rolled, how Leo had loved Donny—but left him, too.

Leo turned and walked out then, flipped off the lights, didn't check to see if I was following. I rubbed my arm where he'd grabbed me, even though he hadn't hurt me. I gazed at the rows of balls mounted on their Astroturf shelves.

I had, as I saw it in that moment, a choice. I could walk out of that room, and then out the front doors of the Galaxy, and find another way to live. I was almost done with school. I could fill out Mr. Todd's application, major in journalism like he'd suggested. Leo could feel sorry all day, he wouldn't chase me down. And Donny—I watched him through the window as Leo passed him—he was facing my direction now, his chin tilted up just so. He was looking for me but he couldn't see me through the glass in the darkened room. But he was waiting just the same. Maybe that was the key, I thought; maybe he could show me how to hold out for something I couldn't quite see.

I took my time pulling the door closed behind me and walking over to him. Leo was at the counter. He pushed the Linds toward me, reached across to pat my rolling arm.

"You're weak as a baby, Wycheski," he said, and there was nothing in his face then that showed his regret, such as it was, from a moment before. "You might need to start back with a lighter weight," he said. He gestured toward the racks, where the nicked and dulled house balls sat in rows, and then he stepped back and folded his arms. He'd made his best play and now he just wanted to see how it would roll out.

Donny picked up the Linds off the counter, reached for my hand. I looked back and forth between Donny and Leo—Donny lanky and already taller than Leo with his coarse brown hair, and Leo with his thick arms and chest, his dark hair tipped in gray now—I'd just noticed—but the same dark brown eyes, the corners tilted down just enough to carry some kind of sorrow, even when they were smiling. I looked at my father's picture. I couldn't think of any other place where I was wanted—or even seen. *I'm coming back because of you,* I thought—wondering if it was the same reason my father had, that first time he'd walked in with me.

Donny took my hand. "Let's go pick one out," he said. He led me to the racks, and I picked a ball. He steered me to a lane on the opposite end of the house from Lane 3. I rolled and let the rolling lull me, like watching water rolling into shore.

We kept going until closing time. Leo shut down the bar instead of having Donny do it. He cut the house lights, pulled out the cash drawer. "Looks like it's all coming back to you, Wycheski," he said, while Donny rolled.

"Thanks," I said. The muscles in my arm were quivering, but I didn't want to stop. With the lights down, I remembered those nights not so long ago, when my father couldn't sleep and Leo had let us in, and it had seemed we were on a ship, skimming over a starlit lake.

"So maybe when you come in tomorrow to help Donny score, you can give those pretty shoes a whirl," Leo said then. I had to hand it to him, not giving me a chance to say no.

I didn't want to, anyway. This was where I belonged. "Okay," I said, and Leo gave me a thumbs up and headed for his office.

Behind me, a whisper of a sound, and I turned. It was Donny, holding my house ball, letting out a sigh of relief.

* 9 *

THOUGH DONNY AND I had grown up in the same town, he knew places I'd never noticed—pockets near the quarry, or the golf course, or the woods between Remington Avenue and Pipe Street, where his parents' house was. He showed me paths in those woods. We found scattered tins and bottles, campfire ash. Once, a muddy blanket that we thought at first was a dead person.

We told each other stories. He told me about the year he'd found packs of gum in the back of the freezer that his mother put in his stocking every year. They were frozen, she'd explained, from flying across the sky in Santa's sleigh. How one year they'd had so little money, she'd wrapped up the phone book just so he'd have something to open. But that had made him fall in love with big books, even dictionaries, and later she'd given him one of those, too, and when he'd looked at those words he didn't feel so bad about the grades he got on spelling tests—how could anyone memorize all those words? He loved dictionaries, encyclopedias, and yes, even phone books—he admitted that he looked his family up every year, something I did too.

We brought blankets on our expeditions into the woods as the nights got cooler, and six-packs Donny lifted from the Galaxy. We explored each other carefully with an odd combination of urgency and slow motion, our hearts thudding in our throats; sometimes I thought I could hear his pulse, a vibration in his breath. Afterward, all I wanted to do was look at him. It wasn't as if I'd slept through sex ed; he just fascinated me. The hollow between his collar bones and the ridge of muscle fanning from his neck to his shoulders, the skin taut across his belly, the line down the middle of him, between the muscles of his chest, which became a line of fine, curled hairs, then spreading, the slight curve of his cock—I had to admit that I'd spent a good deal of class time thinking about it, how no matter where he was, that part of him had been inside me, and his fingers, and his mouth on my breasts. We didn't have anything to say about the sex. We just needed it. At first I suspected that the ache I felt for him was a distraction from my own loss. But then, by the time winter settled in, it became real.

One night I told him I was moving into my parents' bedroom. My mother had moved into the guest room upstairs next door to me on the very first night after my father died. Since then, she'd been keeping me awake at night playing audio tapes with titles like "Finding Comfort in God" and "Self-Denial for Self-Fulfillment." I'd finally talked her into letting me move downstairs to the master bedroom so I could get some sleep.

Donny and I were in the woods again near his house. It was dark, but in memory I can see everything—the gloss of his eyelashes, our clothes scattered on the ground at our feet, the bare branches above us lining a moonless sky. Whatever chill there was, we didn't feel it. I could tell he hadn't put together what I meant by mentioning my move.

"It's downstairs," I explained. "I can leave the window cracked."

Donny shook his head slowly. "Your mom."

"She won't have any idea," I said. "Not with those tapes she plays."

"It's not that," he said. He didn't need to say anything more; he was really talking about my father. I understood his fear. I had felt it just sitting down on the living room couch in the same spot where my father had died, and in lifting the glass of water he'd left by the sink. I knew the glass was his because my mother only drank Vernors 1-Calorie or Tab since she didn't like the taste of tap water. His body was gone by the time I'd gotten home, but his glass of water was still there. And I drank it, every drop.

"Please," I said. I rested my head on his chest and slid my hand down to his belly, and I felt him pull in a breath, his mouth against my hair. He sat up to put on a condom, and I stroked his hip, waiting. He pushed into me, and I pressed my face into his neck and pulled my knees up to squeeze his ribs. He breathed my name into my hair, and I'll admit that I felt what we were doing was our own kind of worship, finding our own comfort in this world.

After that I started waiting for him in the master bedroom, a window cracked, a seam of cool air off the lake seeping in. One Wednesday night he came over when we were both off from the lanes and my mother was at church, at something she called a miracle meeting. We walked into the living room to get glasses of water. I knew which glass was my father's; I used it every time, washed it and put it in the back of the cabinet so I could use it again. It felt more risky to me to walk naked through the house with Donny than anything else we'd done.

When Donny snuck in the window when my mother was home but still awake, he said nothing about my mother's droning prayer tapes, which we could hear through the vent, a warning to keep silent ourselves. When she got rid of my father's clothes and shoes and then our kitchen table and chairs, talking about "making a move," and how we wouldn't need any of it where we were going, he understood why I had to stuff my father's league shirts between the mattress and box spring in the master bedroom. The shirts were Buckeye beige with "Wycheski" sewn in maroon cursive on the sleeve and shirt pocket. Aside from a few photographs and my father's gear, which I'd also managed to save, those shirts were all I had left, but I didn't have to explain any of that to Donny. He had a talent, as it turned out, for coexisting calmly with the bizarre and unfixable, which made him perfect for me.

This talent, I knew, came from his own family situation, though I had never met his parents; didn't even know what they looked like—a strange thing in such a small town—and I told him I thought it was odd that I didn't know his family.

"You know Leo," he said, his voice muffled because he was resting his head on my belly, facing me. I was on my back and he was on his stomach, legs hanging off one side of the bed in the master bedroom; we were catching our breath.

"I don't know Leo at all," I said, and Donny frowned, maybe because he felt the same way and didn't want to admit it. I thought about what my father had said to me about Leo that night in the car after our last night at the Galaxy. What I did know, because it was common knowledge at the Galaxy, was that as far as anyone could remember, Walt Florida and Leo Florida hadn't spoken, hadn't been in the same room, for years. People had various theories as to why, and my father had told me the ones he knew. Walt the war hero hated Leo for not enlisting; Leo had shamed the family by going to prison somewhere, which would explain his long absence; Leo's father, who'd been a big bowler in his day, cut Leo off for hustling, and that had split the family. No matter what the truth was, the general idea seemed to be something between disgrace and desertion.

But now Donny was talking about his father. "I've never been close to him," he said. "Whoever he was isn't who he is now."

"But he's there, in the house with you," I said, almost whispering. "You can be with him whenever you want."

He dragged himself by his elbows so that he could lie on his side facing me. "So he's started in on these confessions lately. That's what he calls them." He shrugged. "We were shaving this morning—I help him shave—and he told me he'd stolen a coat off a private who'd frozen to death, in Korea. Said he had to break the guy's arm to get it off."

Some confessions were small—once he'd told Donny he'd once eaten heaping spoonfuls of sugar out of the bowl even when it was war-rationed and he was old enough to know better. Some confessions involved people begging for their lives; some nights he woke up screaming.

Donny let me take that in, then told me about the seizures. They started like a switch flipped. His father would be spreading butter on bread and then fall to the floor, knife bouncing off his chest. He was on medication, but it didn't always work, and that's why he stayed home.

The cold air slid through the window over our bare feet, and I thought of the ice-sealed eyelids of the sleeping dead men in Korea, their breath frozen in their lungs. I understood that Donny was the most alone person I'd ever known other than my own father. But Donny—and it pained me to realize this difference—he wanted to survive. He was willing to drag through school days which didn't matter to him, to stash work gloves in every room of his house in case he needed to fish his father's tongue from the back of his throat during a seizure. He was willing to work for Leo for an hourly wage, and to accept that he might not work or live anywhere else. And he had risked asking me to come back—to the lanes, and to him.

Our birthdays were a week apart. When my seventeenth came, my first birthday without my father, I insisted on no cake, no dinner out, and my mother didn't argue. Ahead of us was Thanksgiving, Christmas—days to get through rather than to celebrate; we were already worn out at the prospect. Instead, I left the window cracked and Donny came over after my mother finally shut off her tape recorder and went to sleep. He gave me a silver necklace that sat like a line of water on my skin. We made love, and I paid attention—to how his eyes moved under his lids, how his hands tightened on my thighs, how his breath sounded in his throat, how we were in the room, the streetlight slipping under the blind, the glow of my AMF in the corner next to my father's gear, all blue-green swirls and gold, like a little planet. I leaned over Donny, my cheek to his chest, and told him that I loved him. He held me, whispered that he loved me, too. We said we'd wait until graduation; we said maybe we'd head out west so we could see the Grand Canyon and the Showboat, maybe roll a line or few. All we knew at that point was that we'd soon be able to do what we wanted, whenever we figured out what exactly that was.

10

THAT WINTER THERE was an early warm spell, meaning the temperature got into the high forties for a few days, but that was enough to make people roll the windows down in their salt-streaked cars, radios blaring. Kids at school wore wrinkled shorts dragged from the backs of drawers. The week before, they'd been skating on the lake in their tennis shoes. The first hint of wet earth in the air made everyone crave spring. But then the cold came again the next day, and anything that had melted froze again. By the time Donny and I left school that afternoon, the parking lot looked like the solid surface of the lake, and the light was already dropping from the sky.

We were headed to the woods anyway. We were both supposed to be working at the lanes that afternoon right after school because it was a league night, but really, we couldn't hold off until later; we didn't even consider it.

We hiked into the woods. The ice-crusted trees were shot through with the low light, just the dark veins of wood showing beneath their glassy skins. Donny laid back on the crackling leaves and I straddled him, leaned over to ease the backpack under his head for a pillow. I kissed him, slipped a hand inside his flannel shirt to feel the line of his collarbone, the rise of muscle at his chest. He slid his hands under my thighs to his jeans, working at the buttons, and I eased back so that I could get mine undone and slip one leg off, then my underwear. I helped him push his jeans past his hips, stroked him as he tied the arms of his dark blue ski jacket around my waist to cover me. His hands shook as he rolled on the condom. He was pulling me forward then, pushing in, and for a moment neither of us could breathe. We were still, nothing but the ice ticking in the branches above us, the low whine of a passing truck, and then our own breath again, steaming out of our mouths, kissing then as if we could only get air from each other. We were both trembling from the cold and from our own need, and it wouldn't be until later that I realized I had jammed my knee hard enough into a rock to break the skin.

We rested, holding each other against the cold—my knees clasped against his flannel-covered ribs, my forehead pressed against his neck where I could feel his pulse against my temple. We eased ourselves apart and dragged our clothes back on, the denim ice-cold on my skin. Then Donny touched my shoulder and whispered to wait.

We were immediately still. I could hear my blood moving, my breath in my ears.

"Listen," he breathed, and then I heard it. Footsteps, slow and searching. Not someone trying to get from here to there—careful, hunting steps. But I couldn't see anything, and I knew Donny couldn't either, because I was close enough to sense the movement of his eyes, scanning the woods. The sound was off to the left of us, which was good, because it wasn't between us and the car. But that was also where the woods were thickest, and we couldn't tell who or what it was—though it sounded like a man, those crunching, deliberate steps—and then we were running, shoulder to shoulder for a few strides, and then Donny just in front because he knew the way to the car. I could feel whatever it was crawling all over my back; it was like all those horror movies except worse, because I couldn't hear anything except the noise I was making, crashing back through those woods to Donny's car. He threw open my side first, then ran to his side and started the car before I'd even hit the seat. I pulled the door shut and we looked back into the woods as we got going. We saw nothing different. But I could still feel the fear, a pressure in my chest.

"Jesus," Donny said. He had both hands on the wheel. His voice shook. I tossed his jacket and my backpack, which I'd somehow been clutching the whole time, into the back.

"Are we crazy?" I asked.

Donny shook his head. "We're safe. Whatever that was—it doesn't matter."

But we agreed we'd stay away from there for a while anyway. My legs were still weak when we got to the lanes.

Leo had been watching for us. Now that I'd been working for him for a few months, it was business as usual. I was an employee, and there was no more talk of ghosts or regrets. He'd offered to start coaching me again, and I'd said I wasn't ready, so he left it at that. It seemed to me that we could just keep going as we were, even with school out in a few months and nothing official to hold me here. But when we got to the lanes that day, ice melting on our jackets, it felt like we had a lot longer than that.

"Florida! Wycheski!" Leo boomed, turning his palms out toward the line at the counter that was ten deep. "What the hell?" he asked.

Neither of us said anything, but Leo looked at me like he knew the answer. He waved me behind the counter. The phone rang and he made a dramatic grab for it. Then he handed it to Donny. "Your mother."

Donny got very still. Of course, his mother never called, just as she never came. I felt a wave of resentment that she'd always stayed away, never even coming to tournaments Donny had competed in. Even if his father was sick, couldn't she manage an hour away to support him? And then the look on Donny's face when Leo handed him the phone. And what's more, the look on Leo's face, the same dread. Was that what it was?

The other phone line started ringing, and I pushed through the swinging door to get behind the counter. "Answer that," Leo barked at me, just as I picked up—some lady asking about late league, if it was still going to move to Tuesday nights. The second phone line had been another one of Donny's improvement ideas so people didn't get a busy signal all the time, but it just irritated Leo, having the other line ring when he was already talking to someone. If he was there by himself, he'd jerk the second phone off the hook and leave the receiver dangling until he was done with the other call. People got used to it.

I tried to listen to what Leo was saying to Donny while I told the woman the schedule. "No one knows where he got off to," Leo said to Donny just as I hung up.

"Who?" I said.

"His father." Leo jerked a thumb in Donny's direction. "He got out. Wandered off."

To hear Leo refer to his own brother that way—*his father*—as if there were no other connection really threw me, and I could tell Donny was as thrown by it as I was. The muscles of his face were tight, the way he'd looked in the woods. He turned toward the door, and I started to follow.

"Wycheski," Leo said. "I need you. I'm on my last tub of conditioner."

"Leo—"

"You're staying."

I turned—I was going to go anyway—but Donny put his hands on my shoulders. "I'll be back in a little bit, okay?" he said, tilting his forehead close to mine. I nodded and then he went out the glass doors. I watched him go. The fact that he didn't want me with him sent a dull ache into my chest, and when I went back to the register I was careful not to look in Leo's direction, because I was worried that if he made a crack of any kind, I would lose it in front of everyone in the place.

I went to look for the conditioner, and I thought about what Leo had said. *His father.* He'd never said, "When my brother and I were kids," or "Walt and I used to." Nothing. Like there was an invisible wall, and Donny was the only one who could go through it.

There wasn't any conditioner in the back, so Leo made the run to get some. He grabbed his keys and jacket off the hook behind the counter, muttering to himself, but clearly for my benefit, about Donny needing to keep his shit straight on the inventory and he had a pretty good idea why he wasn't. He didn't look my way, didn't need to.

"Aren't you worried?" I said to him.

Leo looked at me like I'd lost my mind.

I thought of saying *about your brother.* "About Mr. Florida?"

"I tell you what. I'll decide what I should worry about. Okay?" And he was out the door, and by then it was dark and the air coming in behind him smelled of muddy ice.

It was a fifteen-minute run to the supply store for the conditioner. Leo came back over an hour later. Under his jacket, his shirt looked wet. He put the conditioner tub on the counter and walked right past me to the storage closet that he called his office, and he didn't come out for a good half an hour. When he finally did, he was wearing a different shirt, the one he kept on a hanger on the back of his door. I asked if he'd heard anything, and if we should call.

Leo looked out at the lanes. "Even if they've found him by now, she doesn't pick up. You know that, don't you?" He knew that I did. He popped open the cash drawer and counted out some bills and handed them to me for my week's pay. I put it in my lockbox in the bottom drawer of the desk wedged in Leo's closet office, because, as he'd explained when Donny had convinced me to come back to the lanes, I should have a safe place for my own money, too. The idea of a bank account never came up. And while he understood my mother needed all the help she could get, money wasn't the answer to all of her problems. "Our problems," he corrected himself. But I'd gotten the point.

Donny hadn't called by the time we closed at eleven, so Leo took me home. He pulled up to the curb rather than into the driveway, even though our street dead-ended at the lake and he was going to have to turn around anyway. "Listen," he said, "you might have a lot of questions."

"About what?"

"About tonight. For Donny. But I'd let it rest."

What do you care? I wanted to ask him. "Donny and I tell each other everything anyway," I said.

"No you don't," Leo said. He kept his eyes straight ahead. "No one tells everything, trust me on that one."

I wanted to remind him that we weren't children. Ever since my father had died, I'd had the sense that some wall between me and the rest of the world had fallen away. My mother and Donny and Leo were what I had left. And bowling.

"Not if you love someone," I said.

Leo threw his head back, barked a laugh. "Especially then."

I wondered who Leo could have possibly ever loved. None of the rumors about him included a marriage, and I'd never seen him with a woman in the eight years I'd known him. To me he was an old man, any love already behind him.

"You and Donny have a good thing going," Leo said then. "So be careful, that's all."

"Fine. Maybe you should write a column," I said, and I realized that this was exactly the kind of thing he would've said.

He laughed at that, too. "That's the spirit." I got out of the car, and I didn't miss the fact that he waited until I got inside before he drove away.

I hoped Donny would come over that night, let me know everything was okay. I kept the window cracked as long as I could stand it, and I heard Mr. Ontero's roof tarps flapping in the wind off the lake. A low whistle wrapped around the house when the gusts turned a certain way, a sound that had once comforted me but now seemed to be a moaning in my own skull. My father had said once that if the house had been a ship it would sink, *not enough caulk in the world for it*. What would keep us afloat now? When I finally shut the window and huddled in my cold-stiffened sheets, the wind sounded like a voice calling.

The next morning my mother left early for the Emmanuel and I wondered if I should wait to see if Donny would be there to pick me up for school or if I should just start walking. He pulled in the drive just as I was getting my coat on.

He looked like he'd just rolled out of bed, his thick brown hair dull and sticking up in places. As we drove to school, he told me that he'd found his father in the woods, sitting on the train bridge, shivering but uninjured, not far from where we'd stopped earlier that day on our way to the lanes. I asked him if he thought it was his father we'd heard crashing around in there, the sound we'd run from. He said he didn't know.

Then I asked him about Leo. Nothing specific—I just said his name because I was thinking of how long Leo had been gone on that errand the night before, coming back only to hide in his office and then telling me not to ask any questions. I said, "Leo," the way my father had said it on that first day we went to the lanes, the beginning of a thought he wouldn't voice.

Donny looked at me and looked away. He was quiet for a while, driving on the frost-laced streets like he really needed to pay attention. Then he said, "Leo doesn't know shit."

And I knew then that Leo had been there with him. I knew it. And for some reason Donny wasn't going to tell me about it, at least not right away—just as he hadn't told me about his father's confessions at first. The only thing I could do was wait.

Donny let me smooth his bed-head hair down in places before we got out of the car and crossed the potholed student parking lot to go inside. I couldn't blame him for what he kept to himself. I'd never told him how, lying in bed after he'd gone home, I sometimes talked to my father's Amflite. I would ask my father how he could leave me and whether he was somewhere now where he could decide whether it had been worth it. I would catch myself doing this and think about my mother praying fervently over her plate and at the Emmanuel. Maybe she was crazy, but if she was, I was, too. I was seventeen and talking to bowling balls, and as far as I could tell, there wasn't much of a difference.

Leo Florida

✳ 11 ✳

MY MOTHER HAD her suspicions about me and Louise. She didn't put me out, but she stopped asking where I'd been when I came home at night. Then, one morning in February 1962 I'm standing with her and Louise waiting for Walt on the platform in Toledo. My father, too, red-eyed from a late drunk. I'd been in Louise's bed the day before, and I would've been back for more except she told me not to.

"You know we can't keep doing this." Still out of breath, saying it.

I thought to ask her what the difference was, next room or another continent. Then I thought better of it, seeing her face. I got up before she could hand me my clothes. I didn't believe she'd stick to her word. She couldn't kiss me at the door like that—made me want to take her back to the bedroom again—and really mean it was over. What I thought at the time.

At the station, men in suits and hats shot past in a way that made you feel a sorry sap for not being as grim with purpose as they were. Two privates unloaded Walt from the train in a chair, but he wanted to walk. The privates tried to help, but he ignored them. He pushed and sank, grunting. Louise went to him first. I had to look away. I could handle the caved in side of his face, but her hanging on his neck was too much. She stepped back, and the privates hauled him to his feet. He shook them off and lurched toward us. His hair was white as a spiderweb in that winter sun. He looked terrifying.

The privates turned, picked up their chair, and got back on the car.

They came out again with Walt's trunk, set it on the platform. Walt turned. The smashed arm swung and stilled at his side. The privates saluted, and he did it back. Then they hustled back on that train.

"'Lo," Walt said. He grinned. On one side, the mouth drew up, the eye crinkled. On the other side, a trance stare. My mother was at him next, hugging him and crying. He toppled back a step, but Louise held him steady.

My father and I stood wide-legged like sailors. I could hear him taking a deep, rattling breath. No question what he was thinking. This white-haired, crushed giant didn't look anything like the Walt we knew.

The women backed off and I stepped up to shake his hand. The other one hung at his side limp as lettuce. "Welcome home," I said. I felt like as if my chest was getting crushed. I guess I'd been hoping somehow he wouldn't show up. Walt looked at me with his half-smile. I wondered if he could read it in me.

And I got right out of the way so my father could try a handshake that ended with Walt reeling him in with his right arm. My father hugged him, face in Walt's shoulder. He stepped back red-faced and sniffing like a swatted dog.

"Home?" Walt said, that slack grin.

The women went to his arms, Louise to the good one, my mother to the left, swinging one. She cradled it on the inside of her forearm. There was a streak of water running back toward her ear when she tilted her head back, blinking. I couldn't see anything of Louise's face because her head didn't clear Walt's shoulder. But she held his hand like any woman on a date, her skirt swinging under her wool coat. The sight of that was enough to make me want to cry.

I went for the trunk. My father got the other end, and I heard the old man groan with the effort. We huffed along behind the women.

It occurred to me that hauling was pretty much all we were good for. Louise was telling Walt about the house, everything she'd done to it.

"Leo too," she said. "He did a lot."

That was almost more than I could take. Walt said something so quiet I couldn't get it, but I didn't care. Myself, I wanted a drink. I wanted to take some money.

That afternoon, after Walt ate applesauce and dumpling soup and Louise wiped him down and the women installed him in that rose-sheeted bed in his new house, and after Louise said we could all come for dinner when Walt woke up, even though she didn't look like she wanted us around at all, I begged off and headed to the Galaxy Lanes.

I'd bought a car off Rich Neidermeyer, and that's where I kept my ball and shoes. Sometimes I'd bowl with my gear on a hustle, sometimes not. It depended on the place. Sometimes I'd go in talking big, lose a streak and then win it back and more. Or go in all humble and make some small-time guy think he could steal your shorts. That's what I did at the Galaxy because I didn't have much cash to put up or lose after buying that car. On one side of my head I'd been telling myself I'd need it to get back on the road before long, and on the other I'd decided I'd need it to get me and Louise around town. I hated to admit it.

It was Friday, and the place was packed with guys coming off shift from the quarries or the boats, hunched over those brand-new plastic tables, probably missing their old haunts. I felt for them, sure. But hustling's a two-way street. You aren't mugging anyone. You can't play if they won't, that's how I see it.

And I needed to punch down a sickness. My brother was a gray, twitching giant and he filled the room with his cracked smile and rattling words. *Good, Happy-be-here* he'd said, about himself. And *Pretty*, about Louise. *I'm-most-metter* to Mom and Dad. And *You-*

old-mastard to me. A grin as sweet as an infant's. I could see Louise pulling his face to her breasts just like that.

I found four guys talking big on two lanes. I bought a beer and took the lane next door, struck up a conversation. A good night to work people over, cash in their pockets from the week. Those four worked the docks, loading off the quarry trucks, I could tell from their coveralls. All of them a few years older than me, and I wondered if I'd ever set pins for them at the State. They were already up to ten a game, a few beers in them. They asked me if I wanted in. I introduced myself as Roy, my middle name.

I had my last couple hundred on me. I changed my delivery to throw myself off, did a five-step instead of four. Lost a few rounds. I was real apologetic. "Sorry," I kept saying, "I'm not much of a challenge." It was true. I'd already been beaten pretty good that day, how I saw it.

They ate it up. They upped it to twenty to see if I'd give up, but I lost that one, and the next, keeping it close. Bought some beers. Lost the next round, and up it went to thirty, then fifty. I was pretty much out of money at that point. I had to win, and of course you can't go back to your normal style or people know they've been had. So I kept shuffling up with that extra step in my approach. The ball broke early on these lanes, they were short-oiled, so I had to compensate for that, too.

But that's when you know you're alive. Tight in my belly, not nerves but focus. My back and arm were loose, and this was what mattered. I wasn't doing deals in a suit in big cities. I wasn't dragging myself out of a jungle. I hadn't gotten the girl. But I could do this. I could be the asshole who'd beaten them up in sixth grade or the guy who'd stolen their girlfriend, or the sap they'd done these things to and more.

A few people were watching by then. Some standing behind us

at the tables, some checking us out from their lanes. I wondered if anyone would recognize me, almost hoped for it.

I won that round. Kept it close. The biggest one looked at me different then. "You fuckin' with us?"

"No," I said. "No way. Look, you take the money. I won it, but if you want to bust a guy for a little good luck, well, you need it more than I do."

The other guys slapped him on the back, saying, "Easy, man."

"All right then, double," the big man said. The bull. "You in?"

No question I was in. But I stepped back. I said, "A man knows when he's pushed his luck. I oughtta walk."

"I'm out," one guy said. The oldest one, probably in his fifties. Close to the end of his quarry days. He tossed his cash on the console. "The wife is waiting," he said, but he was grinning, like as if he knew what she was waiting for.

"I'm in trouble, too," I said.

But I let the other three draw me in. The nice guy, who called off the bull, I felt a little bad for him. You could tell he was a decent sort, married, thinning on top and a church boy face, probably led a Boy Scout troop. Probably didn't get out much, and he'd have some explaining to do. My heart was leaning on my ribs, pumping. Times like this, things are clear. There's a win or a lose, but there's an ending.

I started out, remembered halfway through that I'd gone back to my four-step. Had to stop and start over. It pissed me off, but they were laughing, and I realized I couldn't have played it better. They thought I was freezing up.

"Lotta money," I said, shaking my head.

"He's like that kid Joe Wycheski," the third guy said. I think that was the first thing he said all night.

Wycheski, I thought. "Who's he?" I asked.

"Oh, he's the star around here," Bull said. "Except he gets nervous and chokes."

"Gets stuck," Choir Boy said.

"Damn if it isn't happening to me, too," I said. "Must be the place." And they laughed again. But they weren't laughing when I edged them out by ten points.

You gotta be humble, times like this. When working men just got beat out of a good chunk of wages, you better look sorry. It's a fine line, see, because either way they've been had. If you beat them fair and square, then they just aren't that good. If you hustled them, they're dumb.

Bull wasn't going quietly. "This guy screwed us," he said.

I didn't defend myself, just hung my head. And let me tell you, I wasn't that concerned. People were laughing at old Bull. Apparently he never lost well. Beyond that, I wasn't hardly there. Soon as I stopped rolling I could see her again, the points of her hips, her fingers pressed into my chest. Those fingers wiping my brother's mouth.

"He won, Perry," Choir Boy said.

I thought, *Bless his decent heart.*

"We'll get him next time," the third guy said.

When they deal out the cash, you can't be eager, and you can't talk too much. "Look," I said, leaving it there on the console. "Let me buy some beers."

"No, you keep it, Roy," Bull said. "That's your travel money. Understand?"

I nodded. "Drinks?"

"Go to hell," Bull said. Grabbed his gear and got out of there. I held back my smile until I was sure he couldn't see me through those glass doors. There was always a bull.

The other two weren't far behind him. I went up to turn in my shoes. Put down my fifty cents for the rental and a five-dollar tip in front of the old man at the counter.

"Nice place," I said. "Name's Roy."

The old man left the money on the counter right between his knuckles. "You ever heard about not shitting where you eat?"

"Pardon me?" I was still in my pleasant-guy-on-the-street act.

"Bern Schnipke," he said. He checked my shoes like as if he thought I'd stolen the laces, shoved them in a slot. "I own the place, and I know who the fuck you are. I remember you from when you were a little shit setting pins for your daddy."

"All right then," I said.

"Listen, my customers don't need that crap you pulled out there." His face was gray as his hair almost, eyes hunched under his brows. "You do that again and I'll beat your ass and take your money."

"Whatever you say," I said. I turned around to leave. There were a couple of guys standing around, pretending not to listen.

"Okay, Florida." He didn't raise his voice, but I stopped anyway. He flipped the little wooden door open and came toward me, and I thought he was really going to try it. That was the last thing I needed, getting jumped by the owner, and an old man to boot. There wasn't going to be any winning that one. But instead he picked up a White Spot off the rack and walked over to the lane I'd just left.

"I'm not going to hurt you, boy," he said. "I just want to show you how to roll."

Half the place heard that. No getting out if I ever wanted to come back.

We rolled maybe ten games, and he did what he said he would—beat my ass every time. I was trying, believe me. I thought I was rolling with damn Don Carter. He didn't take a dime off me. He was just laughing at me by the end. Then he offered me a job.

12

WALT'S HEAD CLOSED up more after the first month, and more patches of hair grew back, all white. He got better at moving around and talking. He knew what you were saying to him. The words came slow, and he slept a lot, and sometimes he'd get to staring and you'd have to shake him out of it. But he seemed to be gaining some ground.

I saw him and Louise once a week, at Sunday lunch after my parents got out of mass. Louise had us over. I didn't go to mass. I'd taken a room from Bern Schnipke, an efficiency over his garage. It had a kitchenette and a bath and a fold-out couch. I didn't care. It was temporary enough that I didn't have to think too hard about it.

I stuck around for those Sunday lunches at first. I was still hopeful. Walt would go down after eating and he'd twitch and yelp in his sleep, like a dog dream running. My mother and Louise cleaned up, and my father and I sat in the living room on opposite ends of the couch, pretending we couldn't hear Walt whining in the other room.

Whenever I was there, Louise talked to me like as if she was a coat check girl. She asked me if I wanted my beer in a glass. She offered me seconds and wouldn't let me take my plate out. But sometimes I'd catch her eye. Before I could've sworn she loved me. Now it was different. More like she was sorry for me.

But I kept coming back for Sunday lunch. I offered to help out. One time in early April I asked if they needed anything done around the house. My mother looked across the table at me, then at Louise.

Louise pressed a gravy bowl in her mashed potatoes with the curve of her spoon and didn't say anything. My father wasn't there; he'd had a bad drunk the night before.

Walt cleared his throat and wiped his mouth with his right hand. He said, "Help me cut the out mrush in mack before the green comes mack." He still had trouble with those "b's."

"Sure," I said.

"Gonna get some monkey mars mack there," he said.

Took me a minute to figure out what he said. "Monkey bars?"

"Sure," he said. "Got an officer in training." Big grin on the side of his face that worked.

My mother looked at Louise. "Are you—?"

"I'm due in November," Louise said, smiling. My mother stood and hugged her across the table, rattling the glasses. Walt beamed his half-smile and snuffled a laugh. I leaned back in my chair. I'd fallen out of a tree in the backyard one summer when I was ten and landed on my back. I remembered opening my mouth to breathe or scream but couldn't do either. Couldn't even hear for a while, the blood in my ears. That's how I felt. Doing the math, it was possible Walt was the one. I didn't know which made me feel worse, thinking it was his or mine.

My mother come around the end of the table to hug Louise some more. I looked away, toward the kitchen. Through the windows I could see the brush I'd cut through. My mother was telling Louise to sit down; she'd be doing the cooking and clearing from now on, and just wait until she told Roy. She turned to Walt. "Oh, your father won't know what to do."

I pushed myself to my feet. They all looked at me, Walt with his silly grin, my mother, too happy to think of anything else but babies right then. And Louise, turning to me as my mother leaned to kiss her cheek, and I couldn't read anything in her dark blue eyes.

"Show me what you need done," I said to Walt.

Walt stood and smoked cigarettes while I hacked. He pointed to this and that and then eventually got to saying something about what he was pointing at, and I nodded and started swinging the machete he'd bought, and I just kept chopping and chopping.

AROUND THAT TIME, Joe Wycheski came to talk to me one afternoon at the lanes. He was in every day after school, hadn't said a word to me. And that was fine. I didn't have much to say to anyone by then anyway. What a twerp he was, red hair buzzed and he still tried to slick it down so it just kept popping up in needles like a shocked raccoon, all knobs at his elbows, wrists, and ears. And the way he moved, jerking his arms back and forth, walking on the balls of his feet, like he was trying to cut through something. Skin so pale you could see his veins.

He was one of those guys who'd never had anything go wrong for him. His mamma adored him, and she beat his daddy back anytime he tried to suggest that, God forbid, the boy might get a job. I knew all that from Bern, who ran a commentary on all the regulars, a little entertainment between renting shoes and pulling beers. But I could tell it had all been smooth for him because he wasn't afraid of anything. And I don't mean fearless like Walt, because broken as he was by then, he still had a way of staring out over your head like he figured something was going to explode and he just wanted to give you fair warning. No, I mean fearless like a puppy doesn't know to avoid the street. Floppy, wide-eyed, crazy, stupid. Begging for a disaster.

But Bern had a good feeling about him. "That kid could be a real kegler if he learns right," he'd say. "Skinny little bastard."

I agreed with the second part. Far as I could tell, all Wycheski ever wanted to do was bowl. So when he loped up to the counter and said Bern had told him to ask me about some coaching, I didn't tell him to go to hell like I wanted.

"How old are you anyway?" I asked him.

He leaned those pink-white elbows on my counter and looked at me earnest as an acolyte. "Sixteen," he said. "I know that might surprise you, looking at my game."

"It surprises me looking at you," I said. "I'd put you younger."

That knobby spine sank a little between those pointy shoulders. Kid was half my age and twice as good as I'd been at that age. I didn't give a shit how he felt about it.

"Bern said you were a jerk but you'd help me go pro." Rolling his eyes now, like he thought he was wasting his time.

"Bern said that, did he?" I shoved the register drawer all the way closed. Bern didn't like the ding sound it made so he left it cracked all the time. I wasn't upset to hear what he thought of me. Coming from Bern, that was a compliment.

Wycheski shrugged, like as if he thought my feelings were hurt. I said, "Why'd you suppose Bern said that?"

"Dunno," he said, sticking a dirty nail between two teeth, digging at something. "Maybe because you tried to go pro and didn't make it."

"That so." I ripped open a pack of chalk bags. White dust rose between us. I was trying to think if I'd been that much of an asshole at sixteen. Wycheski was right; I might not have been much of a pro, but I was still better than most guys walking around. At least I had that.

"Well," I said, "I can't see why you'd think an old wash-up like me could help an obvious talent such as yourself."

That stumped him. "I trust what Bern says," he mumbled, inspecting his nails again.

"Trust will take you a long way," I said. "Not in bowling, but somewhere."

Wycheski slapped a bony hand on the counter. "Think about it," he said.

"That your bowling thumb?" I asked.

He looked down at it, nodded. It was all red, the knuckle swollen.

"Your ball isn't drilled right. That's one thing. You can get Bern to take a look at that. But in the meantime, I can tell you right now you'll have to make some changes."

"Like what?" He was trying to act bored; he thought he was humoring me now. Well, maybe he was. I needed to feel smart in some way, I guess, and bowling was about the only option. I hadn't made much of a career unless you counted betting and hustling, and I certainly hadn't been a comfort to my family. Louise rose in my eyes so thick right then I could barely see Wycheski. Felt her knees pressing on my ribs, hair brushing my shoulder, back and forth. Fingers nudging my hip to tell me to go.

"Like your approach, for one," I said, dragging myself out of that bedroom, where my brother slept now. "You rush the line," I said. "And you hang onto that ball so tight it's a wonder you still have a thumb, much less hit anything."

Wycheski took a step back like as if he thought I was crazy. "The grip and the swing is where the power is," he said.

"No," I said. It was four o'clock, people pouring in off the first shifts. They were going to line up and I was going to get their shoes and beers and burgers. I could do it, I told myself. I could make this kid into something, and that might make the rest of it bearable. "No," I said again to Wycheski. "The power is in the letting go."

13

I TRIED TO let go, too. I came for those Sunday lunches—either to Louise and Walt's or to my parents' house. I ate creamed corn and three-bean salads and salted hams. I drank a beer or two with my father and helped out where I was needed. It got warm. The ice pulled back from the shore and the water turned from gray to green to blue. The ferries started running, cars lined up headed for Kelleys Island or Cedar Point. My mother brought cut flowers from her garden to Louise's house. Every week Louise's belly got bigger. She had my mother's sewing machine on permanent loan, making shifts for herself and baby clothes. She trucked out the little white or yellow things, no bigger than socks, to show my mother, and the two women cooed over them like as if they already held an infant. All I could see was the questions I couldn't ask about it.

One Sunday, early summer, my parents left early. My father was complaining of a bad stomach, no mystery where that came from. I'd noticed my mother didn't like leaving before I did. That was fine by me. Louise and I were talking easy enough, but I was being careful. I didn't want anyone catching me staring. Because by then, I'd given into it. I knew I was in love with her. I'd done that to myself, let it happen, and I could live with that. I figured I'd meet someone else in time, and then what I felt for Louise would fall away like a scab.

After my parents left, I sat on the back stoop with Walt while he smoked and Louise finished cleaning up. He sat on the rusted glider that came with the place, and I sat on the steps. He was yawning. The new grass I'd helped him seed was lime green, tufts in the dirt where we'd cut away the thorn bushes and poison ivy a month or so before. And monkey bars, made from a ladder nailed to four fence posts, right in the middle.

"Make his arms strong," Walt said.

"What makes you so sure it's a boy?"

He looked surprised, but not a lot, since only half his face worked. "Dunno." He shrugged one shoulder. "Girl's fine, too."

"What does Louise want?" I asked. Even saying her name stopped my breath for a beat. I thought of her drawing a line through the steam on the car window the night we'd found out Walt was alive. It was like as if she'd drawn that line through the middle of my chest.

Walt shrugged again. "Girl, promally. Dresses. Women, hmm?"

I only nodded, seeing as how I couldn't speak right then. Walt dragged the last off his cigarette and dropped it in the coffee can. He clapped my shoulder. "Din't think you'd come mack," he said.

"It's because of you," I said. I leaned back against the stair railing. "You got me into this," I said, trying to make a joke, but Walt didn't laugh.

"Mayme you'll settle down."

"Sure," I said. "Maybe."

"Don' wait," he said. "Someone'll come along and do it for you." He laughed, kind of gurgled, so I laughed, too. I figured he meant the explosion that had torn half his face off. Right then I was thinking how life was all position and timing. Like bowling, but worse. There wasn't more than ten feet between me and Louise where she was in the kitchen right then, but I couldn't touch her. I wished I could put Walt back on the other side of the world. In the grave, even.

"Fucked me up, they did," he was saying. "Can't even get it up."

I looked at him. "What?"

He didn't repeat it. I was sure I heard right. I pulled my knees up and propped my elbows on them. Tried to look casual.

"You'll get better." I lodged my back against the railing to keep steady.

"Won't matter, will it?" he said.

I could hear his breathing, feel him watching me. To look at him would give me away. Not looking meant the same thing.

Next door, the neighbor's back screen slammed shut, and he flinched so hard it looked like he'd been shot. He almost tipped out of his seat.

I got to my feet, put a hand on his shoulder. He was shaking. He was watching his fists clench and unclench like they were doing it all on their own. "You okay? You want a beer?"

He started to stand up. I couldn't read his face. I took a step back. But then he stopped halfway up and fell on top me.

I didn't have time to do anything but grunt. I fell down the steps on my back, his weight full on me. I tried to jack up his shoulder to get out from under him, but there was no moving him. Louise heard me yelling and came running. I twisted onto my belly and got free, and the two of us dragged him up the steps.

"Let me do it," I said. "You'll get hurt, too."

"Just help me," she said through gritted teeth.

"I got him, let go."

Back and forth we went as we hauled him into the bedroom. But the truth was I couldn't have carried him alone. She was strong. We sat him down on the edge of the bed, on those rosebud sheets, the bed already turned down for Walt's nap, I guessed. Last time I'd been in there I'd left Louise naked and sleeping, Walt's train on its way east. I leaned him back and Louise swung his legs up. His cheek and nose were bleeding. She went for a rag.

"Take off his shoes," she said. "Put his feet on a pillow."

She came back in to clean him. Her face grim and set as his, wiping at the blood.

"What's going on?" I asked, lifting one of Walt's feet and then the other, to shove the pillow under.

"He just passes out sometimes. If he's tired, or doesn't eat. I don't know, they can't tell me why."

"Do I call the doctor?"

She shook her head. "You oughtta just go. I've got it from here."

"Louise," I said. I hated hearing her tell me to go again.

"He'll be fine. He'll sleep. Go on, it's okay." She sounded professional as a nurse.

The room was different now, in small ways. On the bedside table next to the lamp, Walt's watch, some change. His trunk in the corner, though Louise had said she'd wanted to put it in the spare room. His pants hanging over the back of the rocking chair.

"He told me," I said. I said it quiet. I picked up a quarter and turned it in my fingers.

She kept her back to me, pulled the blanket over his legs. The room smelled closed up. She walked out of the room and I followed. She was wearing one of those shifts she'd made, yellow flowers and green vines, looked like another one of my mother's sheets cut up. The light from the front windows came through the cloth. I could see her thighs, the thickness at her waist.

She turned for the kitchen. "Please go," she said.

"You say it to me," I said. "That's all I want."

She stopped. We were in the dining room, all the windows open. Bees thumped the screens. She had that rag with Walt's blood on it, and she twisted it in her hands.

"He doesn't know," she said. Her mouth tight now, eyes hard on me.

"He told me," I said.

"What? What did he tell you?"

"That he—that he can't." I stopped.

Louise stepped toward me. Her belly stuck out more than her breasts now. "What did he tell you?" She asked again.

I didn't say anything. I could smell her, the warmth of her skin. I wanted her. It was that simple. I wanted to lie down on the floor and let it take me over.

"Did he tell you that one night he'd been sleeping and then crying and sleeping for hours, not really sleeping but something close, and I got on top of him and tried to put him inside me but it didn't work?"

She stopped and looked at me, lips parted just so I could think about that. All the color gone from her face.

"So I used my mouth. And he started crying again, but after that I could put him inside. But not for long. And then I realized the back of his head was wet with pus. His bandage was leaking, see? But by that time he'd fallen asleep again, so I waited until he turned on his side so I could clean it. I did it just the way the nurse told me. You know, they're nice at the Vet's Home out there. Very nice."

"Louise." I leaned against the table.

"And since then, nothing," she said.

I was trying to breathe, head down. I could see the paunch of my belly, my scuffed shoes, all there was of me.

"I begged him a couple of times. If I crawl into bed with him he tries to get on the floor. So I sleep on the couch. You know, it used to be good with us. He took it slow with me. He was the only one I'd ever been with."

I didn't want to hear anymore. "I'm sorry," I said, turning, a lurch in my stomach.

But she was right behind me as I made for the door. "This baby isn't yours, Leo, or his," she said. "It's mine."

14

DONALD WAS BORN at the beginning of November. They named him after my father. Might have been a week or so late, as far as I could figure. But early, as far as everyone else was concerned. My mother never asked any questions. Whatever she thought, she'd put it out of her head and believed other things instead, just like she believed that the bread and wine at his christening turned to flesh and blood. Well, I took my sip from the cup, too, and let the wafer melt on my tongue. I looked at Donald in his white gown when the priest raised him in front of the congregation, his skin all velvety and loose, flat-nosed, black hair slick like as if it was wet. It was the first time I'd been in a church in probably fifteen years. I hadn't missed it.

My mother wore a dress that brought out some color in her cheeks. My father was scrubbed and combed and gray as his suit, shifting from foot to foot. Louise stood with her arm on Walt's, him leaning on his cane. He looked happy as any father, and she looked tired, but still beautiful. She'd pulled her hair back in a blue headband that matched her dress. Her breasts were larger and hips wider, and I could almost look at her and not be sorry for wanting her.

It helped that I'd dated a woman or two in the last few months, and I worked all the time, all that Bern would let me. Wycheski had gotten it in his head that he wanted to try the pro circuit. His scores were high, but he wasn't consistent, and he was nervous. I tried to talk him out of it but he didn't want it any other way. So I figured it might be good for him to fall on his face. I got his mother to sign a release, and we started going to tourneys in Toledo and Detroit and Paramus and Atlantic City. The guys I knew there had a good time watching me be ball boy for the Twerp, as I called him, but they didn't laugh so much when they saw him score. So that was all right. Everyone figured I'd hung up my gear, but I was getting a cut of the take—Joe's and what I made on the side, betting. I never mixed the two. I was doing all right. We had a little ways to go to get ready for the US Open in January. It was going to be at the Showboat in Vegas. TV, big money. I wouldn't have minded it happening for me, but I was fine to watch it up close and make money on it, too. It was a far cry from shining my father's ball down at the State lanes. It was something.

I didn't see Louise and Donald until about a month later. This girl from Sandusky, Jackie Mayer, won Miss America and the whole town was in an uproar. I never knew her; she was younger than me. Her mother had a clothing store downtown where my mother liked to shop.

Walt was in the Christmas parade, one of the veterans now. I'd always thought of them as the old men, the World War II and Korea guys. Walt had only been a kid then. But with his white hair and lurching walk, he fit right in. My parents had taken Louise to lunch, and she had Donny all bundled up. The four of us stood on Columbus near Washington Park. The parade came down Hayes to Columbus, all the way to the water. There was the high school marching band and the softball team, and fire trucks and Jackie sitting on the back of a red Mustang convertible next to the mayor. She had on a fur coat and her dark hair twirled up. She really was a beauty.

"Here she comes!" My mother was so excited.

Donald started crying, and Louise hunted in her bag for a bottle.

"Here," she said to me. "Hold him."

I looked at her.

"Go ahead. You can do it."

"You want me to?" My mother said, reaching, like as if she thought he might fall to his death with me trying to hold him.

"I got it," I said. "I got him."

It was the first time I'd held a baby. He was lighter than I expected. He cried with his eyes closed, head turning side to side. He sounded like the cats at the docks begging fish. He yowled until Louise put the nipple of the bottle against his cheek and he turned to it, calming himself as he sucked.

"Here," she said, tilting the bottle's end toward me. "You can hold that, too."

"You think that milk's warm enough?" my mother said.

"I just warmed it a few minutes ago and wrapped it," Louise said.

"Well, if it's too cold it gives them nightmares."

Louise smiled at me like as if we had a secret joke, and the joke was that my mother was all over her, fussing. We did have a secret, that was for sure. I don't know why she decided to let me hold Donald right then. Maybe because Walt wasn't there. Maybe to piss my mother off. I guess it doesn't help, at this point, to try to figure it out. But I do know this. When I held him, well, the day fell back— the marching bands, the veterans, the waving beauty queen. I'd never wanted a kid. But I wanted this one, and I knew I wouldn't leave him.

Tess Wycheski

15

THEN CAME THE first anniversary of my father's death. Some part of me wanted to refuse to grieve it, just like refusing to be happier on your birthday, or more in love on Valentine's Day. I already felt dulled by all the days he hadn't been with us—not just holidays or tournaments, but the string of school days and weekends when nothing much was going on and there was no official reason to miss someone and yet you missed them just the same.

One thing was different. By that first anniversary, I'd stopped willing my body back in time, imagining myself coming home early somehow, catching my father falling asleep on the couch before it was too late. I'd stopped asking myself why I hadn't taken him to the hospital that last night we'd bowled together. Instead, I'd started thinking about how, when my father died, Donny and I had just been two kids in the same school. If you'd asked me then, I never would have believed I'd be sneaking into Donny's house with him a year later, hoping to get some time alone.

That night was also when the Vet's Home held its annual banquet, the one night a year Donny's parents went out. And Leo had given us both the night off, a rare thing for a Saturday. If it was because he remembered the anniversary, he hadn't said so.

I told my mother that Chelsea and I were going for a burger and maybe a movie—in fact, Chelsea was going to take me to Frisch's Big Boy on Milan, where Donny would pick me up.

I came downstairs after my shower and found my mother at the kitchen table, typing the Emmanuel newsletter. When I told her Chelsea would be there soon, she took a long look at me over her half-typed sheet, her hands perched on the keys of her typewriter.

"I won't be late," I said.

My mother stood up from the table. "I'd thought that we—" and then she stopped herself, either because she'd forgotten her thought, or because she didn't want to voice it. I wanted to apologize—for leaving her, for being in love—I wanted for a moment to give in, call off my plans. But there was no way I could do it—the desire to see where Donny slept and showered and ate breakfast, to make love to him in his own bed, was too great.

"I hope you don't mind," I said.

"They prayed for us," she said. "At the miracle meeting this week. For me, and for you."

I looked at her, wondering for a moment if she somehow knew I was lying to her. But instead she just looked as if she was trying to give me some encouraging news. I hugged her, and pretended not to feel her jump, startled, when Chelsea honked from the driveway.

Chelsea turned down the stereo as I got in her red Prelude, a present for her sixteenth birthday. She'd only had it a few weeks, and she'd been stopped for speeding four times—three of which she'd gotten out of. The fourth time, the cop had been a woman, and so Chelsea's expert flirting skills hadn't worked.

"My mother dragged me to a scrapbook class at her friend's house or I would have gotten here earlier," Chelsea said. "I mean, picture this: eight middle-aged women playing with construction paper and funky scissors and shit. At least they weren't looking at their pussies."

She looked at me, expecting me to laugh. "Are you okay?" she asked, and I told her I was fine, but she said, "Yeah, right." I knew she thought it was her job to help me get over my father's death. She used terms lifted from her mother's self-help books, like *acceptance* and *healing*, and suggested that I try breathing exercises or even Jazzercise, perhaps to sweat the past out of my system. But I also knew she'd loved my father—she'd cried at the funeral, quietly, coughing sometimes to choke down her sobs, while her parents had sat stiffly beside her. And she knew what day this was; she'd called me that morning to check on me and had offered to pick me up so Donny wouldn't have to.

We pulled onto Columbus Avenue, and she gunned through the intersection as the light flashed red. She was wearing her nylon cheerleading team shorts and matching zippered jacket. It was still too cold for shorts, but she was already making regular visits to the tanning bed to prepare for prom, and she wanted to show off her orange skin. She had the heat in the car cranking. At a stoplight that she actually stopped for, she reached toward the tiny back seat and pulled a can of Schlitz from her backpack, handed it to me, asked me to open it for her.

"Cherokee's stash," she said when I handed the beer back to her. "He thinks he's so slick. He moved his pot, though."

Cherokee, named during her parents' brief stint at the Willow Commune somewhere in California before they'd moved to Ohio, was two years older than Chelsea and still living at home. He was studying kung fu and trying to find himself—which apparently entailed dealing dime bags out of the garage. He looked like a male version of Chelsea, except with acne and a lot of tie-dye. Chelsea's other older brothers were twins with black hair, big noses, and thick arms like Mr. Vickham. Chelsea and Cherokee had taken after their mother and didn't even look related to the twins, who were both in college by then with golf scholarships at Miami.

Having three brothers seemed to have given Chelsea a special ability to see into and through males of any age. Guys at school were no match for her. She could talk them into doing whatever she wanted—you might say the breasts and the blond hair helped, but it was something more, the way she seemed to feel a certain sympathy for them; she could see the worry behind their hard stares, the sorrowful way they threw themselves into their desk chairs, slammed their car doors, fought in the parking lot over what they thought someone had said about their mothers. The boys followed her in jerking, mumbling packs. They were polite to me because I was her friend, under her protection. But that was as far as it went. And that was fine with me.

"So do you want one?" Chelsea said, lifting her beer can.

"No, thanks," I said. Beer made me have to pee right away, and I didn't want to have to go to the bathroom the minute I walked into Donny's house.

"Your mother isn't getting to you with that holy roller stuff, is she?"

"Chelsea—"

"Okay, I'm sorry, I'm sorry," she said, patting my knee. "If you had Cherokee high as a kite at the dinner table every night, you probably wouldn't worry about a beer. Anyway I, for one, always like to have a beer before a date. You would, too, if you were dating Taft."

Taft Peeler, the basketball team captain, had sand-colored hair and hands the size of pancakes. Chelsea had told me that, at least in Taft's case, the rule of the direct relationship between hand and dick size had held true. She was conducting a survey of sorts. She'd been with three other boys so far, and she'd described to me in detail their bodies and the things they did to her or asked her for, the way they sounded when they came. I passed those boys in the hall, and it was a kind of power, what I knew about them. My mother had told me that men would say anything, do anything, for sex, and that girls who fell for it were stupid and pitiful and ruined. I didn't think I was any of these things because Donny and I were in love and we were each other's first, but I didn't think Chelsea was any of those things, either.

"I thought you liked him," I said. I was thinking about Donny, waiting for me in the Frisch's parking lot, of what I was willing to do to get a couple of hours alone with him.

"Oh, he's fine," Chelsea said. "Not very bright, but sweet. And anyway, there's prom coming up, and we already have the matching cummerbund, and you know, graduation parties. I don't have time to groom someone else for the role." She took another swig of her beer, lodged it between her thighs while she made a turn. "You know we should double-date sometime—but then again, it's probably not fair to let Taft bore three people."

"Yeah, I don't think Donny would be that into it anyway," I said, but really I was trying to give her the out she needed. I knew Chelsea had to consider the social calculus of who you could hang out with based on who you were dating. It was a real concern, whether you liked it or not. Taft was a jock—a nice jock, but a jock. He would never date someone like me—non-blond, non-cheerleader, etc.—but it was okay for him to be seen with someone like me in a double-date situation provided the guy I was dating was acceptable. Donny, being Vo-Ed rather than college prep and a metal head with his shaggy hair and his pieced-together muscle car, didn't qualify.

Knowing that Chelsea was weighing these factors didn't bother me. It was part of who she was, and we went too far back for it to mat-

ter much. It could have been a third arm coming out of her chest—
just something we'd have to get around.

"So, how are things going with Donny?" Chelsea said.

I hesitated before answering. I knew what she thought of him—
that he was no smarter than Taft Peeler, but at least Taft came across
as trying to be nice. At least Taft looked like the all-American, hearty
midwestern boy we were all supposed to want. And I knew that in
asking how Donny was, Chelsea was actually asking about something
else—what, I wasn't sure.

"He—he's fine," I said.

Chelsea turned into the Frisch's parking lot. I craned my neck to
look for the Turd, but I couldn't see it.

"Well, has he asked you to prom yet?"

I looked at her to see if she was joking. She was completely serious,
and I wanted to laugh out loud. Prom, at that point, after the year I'd
had, sounded like those plays we'd done in the cafeteria in elementary
school. Fun and cute and a thing of the past.

"No. But anyway, I don't want to go."

Chelsea rolled her eyes. "Of course you do! All these years when
you didn't have a date, and now it's our last year! I mean, why would
you skip your senior prom?"

I saw the Turd pulling in the other entrance, and I unclipped my
seat belt. I wanted to run out of the car without bothering to say
good-bye; I just wanted to get to him as soon as possible.

"Chelsea, listen. I don't want to go. He would go if I wanted, I'm
sure. But I don't, okay?"

She stared at me in disbelief. Then she closed her eyes for a second; she seemed to be doing a calculation of sorts. "Look, Tess. We
could get a table together. I'll talk to Taft—I mean, I'll just let him
know. And you know I have extra dresses. You wouldn't even have to

buy one. My mother will do our makeup and hair. I mean, I'm like a shoo-in for prom queen! I want you to be there. And, you know, I think it'd be good for you."

She said the last part gently, and I was sure she meant it. I was amazed, in that moment, by the number of ways one could refer to catastrophe without ever referring to specifics. As usual, she had it all figured out—the dinner, the dress—she was even going to break all those tricky social rules and sit with me at prom, until it was her time to join the prom court and accept her crown, of course. But she was missing one important detail, and I hated to have to tell her.

"I'm sorry," I said. "I just don't give a shit about any of that."

She blinked rapidly a few times, a habit she'd gotten from her mom when something just didn't make any sense to her. She pulled into a parking space. She swallowed, faced forward, put her car in reverse. "Okay," she said quietly, and I knew that I'd hurt her.

"I'm sorry," I said again.

"It's okay," she said. She gave me a bright smile then. She'd never been one to admit feeling bruised. "I get it. The minute you have a guy, you ditch your best friend. Girls do that all the time. I mean, it's common. Except I never did that to you."

Across the parking lot, Donny was getting out of his car, looking around, his face yellow lit from the diner windows. I didn't want him to think for a moment that I wasn't coming. And so it didn't matter to me that Chelsea seemed to be suggesting that she'd been doing me favors all along, never dropping me when she'd had so many opportunities. She was my friend from the days before we could speak. She was a personal witness to the way my life had once been. I couldn't let her go, if only for that. One of us would call each other, probably the next day, I knew. She'd turn it around; she'd say she was sorry she'd upset me. She knew the trick of apologizing first so she'd never be the injured party. She knew so many tricks, all slapped together like some kind of armor—who knew if they'd be enough. I hugged her, thanked her for the ride. She patted me stiffly, told me to give her a call if I changed my mind; she could still change the table reservations.

I smiled at her, squeezed her arm before I got out of her car. As I crossed the parking lot, I ignored as best I could the feeling that she was miles away. Sometimes I felt like shouting in conversations, because it seemed I was standing on one side of the Wagner Quarry just a little farther down Milan, and the rest of the world was on the other side. Or—as I looked in the windows at Frisch's, all those couples and families leaning toward each other in the warm light—that they were on one side of the glass, and I was on the other. I wanted to believe that someday this feeling would pass. The only person who never made me feel that way was Donny.

Ten minutes later, Donny and I parked down the street from his house. We avoided streetlights as we walked, glancing at the lit windows in the houses, trying to see if anyone had noticed us. I had chosen to wear a knit skirt and light sweater, no buttons—a practical outfit for what we had planned. I wouldn't even have to get all of the way undressed in case Donny's parents came home early. I shivered; it was too early for bare legs. We sped up a bit once we could see his parents' car was definitely gone. He squeezed my hand to signal a change of direction, and we turned toward a fence that bordered his neighbors' backyard. We stopped at the bushes by the small front stoop of his house.

"Wait here," he said, and he followed the line of the house around the back. I listened but couldn't hear him at all until he was back in view again.

"Storm door's locked," he said. "I should've thought of that."

So we climbed the front steps and stood at the door under the dim porch light, listening. I put my hand on the siding beside the front door and thought I could feel a ticking, a breathing inside. Donny propped the screen door against his shoulder and turned the key in the doorknob lock, pulled it out, tried the door. It didn't open, and he frowned. I touched his arm, and he shook his head and slipped the key in the deadbolt slowly, but then the door opened like something falling away from us, and Donny's father stood huge and white like a giant moth in the doorway. Donny and I stepped back and the screen slapped shut and I pinched off a yelp in my throat.

"Hi Dad," Donny said. His voice was calm and even. I'd always thought he was tall until I saw him next to his father, who towered. I could tell he was trying to figure out what to do—he reached toward the screen door handle and then stopped and tilted his head, trying to look past Mr. Florida, who was looking down at us with a not-quite smile—half of his face not moving. He nodded, or lowered his head, and he hunched forward, and I wondered if he might pass out. Then I saw he was pawing at the screen door handle. His other hand swung at his side like a scarf end, fingers limp.

"I got it," Donny said. He opened the screen a crack and turned to me. "I'll be right back—you want to go to the car?"

The suggestion felt like a punch. "No—let's— "

But Donny shook his head no, looking at me with a pleading in his eyes that I hadn't seen before. His father brushed a hand up the wall and flipped on the hall light, which gleamed on his glossy scalp, where a red scar ran from over his left eyebrow to behind his ear, twisting and branching like a riverbed. His fine white hair stood on end. He looked down at me without smiling, but not unkindly; it seemed he'd just forgotten to. He wore light gray cotton pajamas, thin from washing, the cloth pilled and gauzy, and navy slide-on slippers, which I hadn't thought men actually wore; I'd never seen my father in slippers.

"Stay," he said, and the word seemed to move through Donny's shoulders, and he looked at his feet and held the screen door open for me. We followed his father into the living room. With each step his pajama legs hitched, and his bare ankles were white and brittle looking.

He sat down in a blanket-draped recliner, his usual place, you could tell from the magazine rack next to it stacked with *Stars and Stripes* issues and the side table with a lamp, tissues, deck of cards. He pulled his limp arm into his lap and settled back in the chair, and I willed myself not to look between his spread knees, not wanting to see through the thin cloth.

I sat on the faded blue couch and Donny sat beside me. The room smelled of mothballs and newspaper ink. Donny perched forward on the couch cushion, elbows on his knees, as if he might need to spring to his feet at any moment. "Where's Mom?"

"Getting ice cream." His father's voice was husky, too much breath in the words.

"Why didn't you go to the dinner?" Donny asked.

"Had birds in my chest," he announced. He tapped his chest and then his head, near the seam of his scar, and then he looked at me as if he'd just noticed I was in the room and raised an eyebrow on the side of his face that worked. He asked me how old I was, and I told him seventeen, and he said, "Too young for birds, that's for sure." He slapped his knee, as if to make a point, and Donny straightened up at the sound.

"Well, we'll go," he said, standing. He looked down at me, waiting for me to stand, too, but I was dazed by finally being there in his house. I was trying to find the ways he might look like his father, in the shape of his face, his eyes—or the eye on the living side of his face. The lower lid of the other eye sagged, pulled down by the slack skin, and there was a rim of red under the white of his eye like a line of blood. But other than his height, and maybe the broadness of his shoulders, I couldn't see anything in Mr. Florida that had made its way onto Donny's face or in the shape of his body. I couldn't even see how Mr. Florida looked like Leo; there was so much damage to his face. It was hard to imagine that Leo could also be called Mr. Florida. Leo was Leo; this man was definitely Mr. Florida.

"I'm too dizzy to go anywhere," his father said, misunderstanding what Donny meant. Donny shook his head, about to explain, and just then the key rattled in the front door lock, and we all got very still. There was a pause, the sound of the key pulled out, and I figured Donny's mother had just realized that the door wasn't locked. The door swung open, and there were a few hesitant steps, and then Donny's mother stood in the living room doorway. She froze when she saw me, hugging the paper grocery sack against her chest. She was thin and freckled and narrow-faced, faded strawberry blond hair tucked behind her ears. The blue hem of her dress matched her pumps—the rest of her was covered in a black belted coat. She was still dressed for the dinner, I guessed; the bright line of lipstick didn't seem right on her face. Her eyes shifted back and forth between me and Donny—and I saw then that she was the one he looked like—the high cheekbones, the coloring, a slightness in her frame that in him had become lankiness.

"Mom," Donny said in that same careful, quiet tone he'd used with his father. "This is Tess."

I said pleased to meet you and she nodded once, a tuck in the chin, like she was trying to swallow something caught in her throat.

"We just stopped by," Donny said. He looked at his father, avoiding his mother's eyes, and I knew then that there had been an agreement, broken by my presence there. "We're just leaving."

"Where's everyone going?" Donny's father demanded. "I told you I'm not up to it. My chest hurts."

"We're not going anywhere, Walt," Donny's mother said, a sigh in her voice. She had some kind of accent, southern, I guessed, but not like the southern accents you heard in the movies. Kind of flattened, maybe—"where" sounded like "weer." She looked a lot younger than Donny's father, maybe because of his white hair and quavering voice, but with her small wrists and her hair tucked behind her ears she seemed more like an older sister to Donny than his mother. She shifted the bag of ice cream into the crook of one arm, touched the buttons of her coat with the other. She looked at my bare legs and then at me, and I was sure she knew everything—why we were there in her house, my skin flushed and damp in anticipation of what I would do with her son. Ever since Donny and I had first gotten together, finding time alone had meant hiding from my mother, but I hadn't thought about Donny's mother, how maybe she might worry for her son, his body, his heart.

"We'll go," Donny said.

"No, now that you're here, have some ice cream with us. It's fresh," she said, blinking at us, as if the sight of us blinded her. "Sit," she said, and then she hurried down the hall, pumps clomping on the bare floors, and I understood why there were no area rugs—one less thing to trip on. And no mirrors, no pictures on the walls, no knickknacks of any kind, nothing that could be broken during a seizure. Donny's house, as it turned out, was as bare as mine, just the reasons were different—his because of his father's presence, and mine because of my father's absence.

We sat again, knees pressed together, hands clasped on the tops of our thighs. "Are you in school?" Mr. Florida asked me, sounding perfectly reasonable.

Donny cradled his forehead in one palm, not trying to hide his dismay. I touched the side of his leg, where Donny's father couldn't see, wanting to say it was okay, no shame in a sick father and a shy mother. So he'd said something funny about birds. So what? He was alive; he was in the room, asking his son's girlfriend questions, like a father should do.

"Yes," I said. "The same year as Donny."

"Good," Mr. Florida said. "Stay in school. Better than getting your ass shot off."

Donny looked up. "You graduated."

Mr. Florida looked at the ceiling as if trying to remember if this was right. "Yes, I did. Nineteen-forty-three. Then I helped finish up the war. Lived to tell about it despite those fucking Germans." He coughed, touched his chest. "Birds are bad tonight."

Donny flinched at the curse—not that it wasn't something he said himself, but he was embarrassed. "Maybe you want to get some rest?"

Mr. Florida looked down at his chest, plucked at a pajama button, and Donny's question fell apart in the air. Then he looked up at us, good eyebrow raised, which made him seem skeptical of us, or maybe just surprised to find us still in the room. I could hear Mrs. Florida down the hall in the kitchen setting bowls out on the counter, tapping clumps of ice cream into them. My mother had taught me to offer help in situations like these, but I couldn't imagine walking down the hallway toward her. I didn't want her to look at me that way again, knowing why I was there. I didn't want to offend her any further.

"I think the Catholics have it good with getting things off their chests," Mr. Florida said. "Say a Hail Mary and your sins go away and all that."

"Dad," Donny said, but his father batted at the air with his good hand as if to knock something out of his line of sight.

"No use in a soldier confessing. But the time comes. A man has things to say."

Donny's mother clomped back down the hallway, bowls and spoons rattling on a tray. Donny was drumming his fingers on his jaw, looking at the ceiling, as if trying to remember the words of a song, but really he was lifting out of the room, bumping the ceiling like one of those birds trapped in his father's ribs. Maybe his father had done desperate things, but he had paid a price, and the least we could do was listen to him. I wanted to say this, but of course there was no way, with Donny's mother rounding the corner, heading to the recliner to serve Mr. Florida first.

"Thank you, dear," he said, and Donny sighed and he seemed to be fully back to himself again on the couch. Maybe he thought his father had been distracted, whatever secrets he'd meant to tell already forgotten.

There were two round scoops of ice cream in each bowl. Mr. Florida shoved half of one in his mouth on the first bite. Mrs. Florida sat in the arm chair across from us, on the other side of the side table next to Donny's father. She shaved off a small bite, working her way toward the center. Donny's father chewed huge bites of ice cream; it gave me an ice cream headache just to watch. He was like a big child, I thought. He caught me watching and I looked away, but when I looked up again he was still gazing at me. I was thinking right then that Donny must have gotten his darker coloring and the wave in his hair from Leo, and it was satisfying somehow to trace where each of his features had come from—his height from his father, but his bones from his mother—jawline, mouth, forehead—and then his coloring from his uncle. That's why I'd wanted to come there, I realized then, to find out the source of him.

Then Mr. Florida's eyes widened and he jabbed the air with his spoon, pointing at me. "You look like her," he said, his eyes bright with the recaptured thought.

"Yes?" I said. I thought he meant I looked like Donny's mother, and although I didn't agree, I wanted to show that I cared what he said. He might be trapped, disfigured, but he'd chosen to live, while my father hadn't. I wanted to thank him for sticking it out.

Donny's spoon clattered into his empty bowl. He stood up, wiping his mouth with the back of his hand. "Thanks, Mom," he said, and she nodded—permission for us to leave. "Let's go," he said to me. I wasn't done with my ice cream and wondered if I should try to gulp it down, if I should offer to take the bowls out, invade their house further.

"Wait," Mr. Florida said. "Wait." He let go of his ice cream bowl so that it tipped sideways in his lap, and he turned his hands palms up, as if this might help him hold onto his thought. He cleared his throat. "The girl who was raped." His eyebrows drew together, as if the words surprised even him, as if he'd meant to tell us a funny fishing story, and this time, it would be the truth—the fish wasn't that big but he'd kept his thumb on the scale. Or that's what I'd expected, a kind of fishing confession, but the actual words clanged in my head and I had this sense that I was slipping on an icy hill, and there would be no stopping.

"I could have saved her, see, but I didn't," Mr. Florida continued. Some melted ice cream dripped onto his lap and he must have felt it because he grabbed the bowl and set it on the side table, wiping his thigh with his good hand. "Don't leave yet."

Donny's mother was on her feet now, too. She set her bowl on the side table. "Walt, I think they have plans."

"Wait a minute. In the dark, with the other men, it was hard to tell. Maybe they'd paid her," he said, his eyes glassy and not quite focused on me, but he stood up then, working hard to get to his feet, and stepped toward us, hands gesturing in shaky circles, as if trying to explain. He filled the room. "I watched. I didn't do anything but I watched."

Donny took my bowl, put it on the coffee table. "We're going," he said. His mother was between his father and us now, trying to settle him down in a low warning voice. Mr. Florida told her to get out of his way, he couldn't see, and he did seem to be trying to peer through the darkness, and I wondered how hard it would be to tell what was going on, a screaming girl—or did you scream? Would you? At a certain point would you give in and busy yourself with trying to live through it? I felt like I had no blood in my legs. Donny's mother was telling his father to say good-bye, and Donny pulled me toward the door. "Now," he said through his teeth.

"I'm not sure," his father said, blinking, the fingers of his good hand fluttering in the air. He seemed about to reach for us, and then I felt Donny's hand on my arm.

"It's okay," I said, a reflex, to comfort him maybe, but Donny was pulling me and we stumbled through the front door down the steps and across the dark grass to the street. We got in Donny's car and he took off. We were airborne over the tracks by the time we got to the end of Pipe Street, something we'd done in the past for fun. I thought he might be heading to the lanes after all, and that we might not talk about what his father had said. I was willing to wait. But then Donny pulled over into the gravel lot right before the turn, where we'd parked before to go into the woods, and he leaned forward, his forehead propped on the steering wheel between his knuckles. His shoulders tightened and tightened, and then he fell back against his seat and put his hands over his face.

"It's okay," I said, the same thing I'd said to his father.

"Look at me," I said. I wiped at his wet face with the heel of my hand. "You're not your father." I said it again because the first time it seemed he hadn't heard me, even though he was looking at me. He closed his eyes, turned his face toward the bare metal roof of the car. We had the windows up, but he was shivering. He hugged himself, hands tucked under his armpits.

"He's not my father, either, Tess." He put the Turd in park, and it lurched in place, and for a moment I thought the parking break wouldn't be enough—it might take off on its own.

"You remember how I told you I used to look myself up in the phone book? My folks?"

I nodded. I did remember. I thought of his mother wrapping a phone book one Christmas so that he'd have something to open. Now that I knew her face, her strawberry-blond hair tucked behind her ears, I could picture her leaning over a length of shiny paper, could imagine her sorrow wrapping such a thing.

"One year, I was like eleven, I found Leo's name, too. There was one Florida in the phonebook, and then the next year, there were two. That's how I found out about him." He turned in his seat to face me then. "So I asked my mother one night. I asked her why she'd never told me I had an uncle. I mean, you know, we never had any pictures up in the house because of my dad knocking things around. And she tells me he left and never even told them where he went. She didn't even know if he was alive."

He paused, and I waited. I was afraid he would stop, and almost equally afraid he would keep going. I reached for his hand, squeezed it. He squeezed back.

"But the thing was, after I started coming to the lanes, Leo asked about her all the time. Never about him. One night I woke up and my mother was talking with someone in the front room. I was used to my dad waking up at all hours. So I get up out of the bed and come down the hallway, and there's Leo. My mom's in her robe, and Leo's got her by the shoulders. But he's not yelling; it's like he's asking her for something. And she was saying no. So I start backing up, because I was scared. He saw me, Tess. She didn't, because her back was to me. But he did."

Donny took his hand away from mine and pinched the bridge of his nose. I thought he might be trying to stop himself from crying again, but when he raised his head again, he looked completely calm. He reached up, flicked the keys hanging from the ignition. "After that, he never mentioned her to me again." He shrugged, and I eased over closer to him as best as I could in the seat, the gear shift poking my thigh. I could feel the shake in his breathing.

He put the Turd back in gear and backed out of the lot, and we headed out of town toward the airport. We carried a blanket and a six-pack toward the runway, not far from the glow of the red lights. We spread the blanket and the ground was damp and cool, but we wrapped the edges around us, and I didn't even let him get his jeans all the way off the first time. Then we rested on our backs, sipping beer and looking at the stars.

After a while Donny said, "There's one other thing."

I waited, threaded my bare legs between his for warmth, rested my head on his chest. I listened to his heartbeat.

"That night, when my dad wandered off," he said. "Leo found him."

I nodded; I knew this, had known it at the time, but I was glad he'd finally said it to me.

"He said something when he was leaving—" Donny stopped, took a drink of his beer. He seemed to be trying to make a decision. He balanced his beer in the grass and pulled me close again, the bones of our ribs rubbing together. "My mother was upset. So I asked her."

I propped myself on one elbow. "You asked her what?"

Donny closed his eyes. "To tell me the truth."

"And what did she say?" I took his hand, stroked his fingers one by one.

He looked at me then, and I loved him, loved the line of his cheekbone and jaw in the far-off glow of the runway lights.

"She said it didn't matter what she told me, I'd believe what I wanted to anyway."

We looked at each other a long time. I thought of what my father had said about Leo, and why he'd gone with my father to Vegas. *It was Donny. He loved him.* I could have repeated this to Donny, but I didn't. At the time, I wouldn't have been able to explain my reasons. Later I decided that maybe it was because, no matter how much Leo might have loved Donny, it wasn't enough. He'd deserved better.

"What do you believe?" I finally asked.

He looked down at our hands. "I don't know," he said.

But your father is still your father, I wanted to say, no matter what—which was what I said to myself anytime I caught myself wondering why my own father had given up, left me. A father stays. I thought of Mr. Florida filling the doorway, of the birds trapped in his chest. I thought of seeing Leo for the first time at the lanes with my father. And the first time I'd met Donny, Leo nudging him forward to say hello just like a father would, though I hadn't thought of it that way then. Donny proudly pouring me a soda at the bar, because Leo had just given him privileges. And all those years in between. Donny rolling with Leo a few lanes down from my father and me. Donny pitching Leo on the arcade, the light board, and the disco ball. The way Leo yelled for him: Florida!

My father had said that he'd played with too much fear. I decided then, as I leaned against Donny's chest so that I could kiss him, that I wouldn't make the same mistake.

* 16 *

GRADUATION CAME, AND Chelsea invited me and Donny to a party at her house. As I'd expected, she got over me not going to prom, and she won prom queen. So she'd stood on the platform as we'd filed up, blue white blue white, to get our diplomas in their vinyl cases (which, Donny said, looked like what waiters carried, and which wasn't too far off the mark for most of us). When my mother took me home to change, I told her Donny and I were just going to the lanes, knowing she still had bruised feelings about the Vickhams.

By the time Donny and I got to Chelsea's house, there were probably fifty people milling around the pool carrying blue or white plastic plates—kids, parents, a few teachers, and a lot of people I didn't recognize—neighbors, maybe, or Mr. Vickham's business associates. Card tables covered with blue paper dotted the patio around the kidney-shaped pool. Blue and white lights stretched between the house and the massive three-car garage, which Mr. Vickham had added to keep their boat in the winters.

Chelsea called out to us and waved us over. She still had on the strapless white sheath dress she'd worn under her gown. Next to her, Taft Peeler wore a blue golf shirt and white shorts. The two of them stood in full prom court stance, shoulder to shoulder. She'd just gotten accepted to Bowling Green and was leaving in a couple of weeks for cheerleading tryouts. There was a big orange and brown banner for the Falcons hanging at one end of the pool.

Chelsea said hi to Donny, and Donny and Taft grunted hellos at each other, and then she and I hugged. She smelled like coconut oil and hairspray. "I was wondering when you'd get here. Listen, after the parents pack it in, then, you know, the real party." She winked and her sparkly eye shadow flashed.

Taft had made a point of turning away from us, surveying the scene, hands in pockets. He frowned, pursed his lips, did the chin-lift hello to certain people. Whatever any of us had to say to each other was of no interest to him, and he wanted us to know that. It was an old guy's stance, and I felt sorry for him. Donny, for his part, was working toward being invisible: hands in pockets, neutral expression as if watching something of mild interest taking place far away. He seemed to be receding even as I watched.

Chelsea's father came over from his post at the grill, smelling of lighter fluid and beer.

"There's my princess!" he boomed. Chelsea shrugged and smiled up at him, and he swung a bear arm around her, scrunching her shoulders up to her neck. He swigged the last of his beer. "Lydia!" he yelled to Chelsea's mother across the pool. When she looked over at him, he held up his empty beer can and shook it. She sang back an okay and hurried toward the house. She wore shimmery pants and heels, her blond hair twirled in a high bun that bounced as she walked. She looked like a sitcom mother, so perfect, and for a moment I was jealous of Chelsea, of all this great packaging, even of her loud, meaty father. "Tell her to bring some towels, would you?" he said to Taft, and Taft marched off with a business-like scowl.

"Dad, don't order him around all the time," Chelsea said, and Mr. Vickham loosened his grip on her a little and shrugged.

"Sorry, honey." He squinted at Donny. "Do I know you, son?"

I didn't wait for Chelsea to handle introductions. "Mr. Vickham,

this is Donny Florida. His uncle owns the lanes," I said, and I felt
Donny flinch, his elbow knocking against my arm.

"Business good?" he said to Donny.

Donny nodded, looked back at the water. "We're doing fine." Mr.
Vickham scowled, waiting, his rodent eyebrows pinched together.
But Donny seemed to have nothing further to say. I thought maybe
I should put a hand on his chest and gently tip him into the pool—
something to distract everyone, so we could escape in the commo-
tion. Then Mr. Vickham noticed someone in the crowd and dropped
his slab of a hand on my shoulder. "Now there's my buddy," he said.
"Charles!" he yelled, as he strode away from us.

"I'll grab us some drinks," Donny said then, and he headed out
of view beyond the blue glow of the pool. I tried to watch where he
was going, because I was still worried about him, but Chelsea tugged
on my arm.

"So, I'm getting rid of Taft tonight," she whispered to me.

"Why?" I scanned the crowd for Donny and couldn't find him. I
wondered if he was okay and whether I should try to go find him or
leave him alone for a while.

Chelsea laughed. "Oh, we're just done. He's served his purpose, you
know? I mean, I would've dumped him earlier, but we had the matching cummerbund." She sighed. "Anyway, my dad will be bummed
about it. He was already planning the wedding."

I looked at Taft across the pool, hands in his pockets still, oblivious
as to what awaited him. I felt a rush of sympathy for him again, even
though we'd never so much as said hello in the hallways at school.

She patted my shoulder. "You feel bad for him? I bet I could blame
you for world hunger and you'd apologize. Listen," she said, shaking
her head, "we aren't kids anymore. We graduated today, remember?
We're done—real world, right? He'll be with someone else in a week."

"That's not the point," I said. But I wasn't sure what the point should be.

"So we're just supposed to hold out? Me and Taft and—" she looked down at her pink-polished fingernails and laughed. "And you and Donny—we'll get married and bowl doubles on weekends, that's what you're thinking?"

She was all prom queen right then, already in acceptance-speech mode. I couldn't admit to her that maybe I had wished things could turn out that way, Chelsea inheriting her mother's clientele, Taft selling insurance or real estate, the two of them coming over to dinner—to where?—with me and Donny. And what would he and I be doing? Working at the lanes, maybe the owners after Leo retired?

"No, you're right," I said, trying to sound convincing. "You really should cut him loose."

She nodded and patted my shoulder. "I don't know about you, but I'm going to have some fun before I settle down. You should, too!"

I smiled back at her and decided to ignore the insult of that suggestion. Clearly, she hadn't been having much fun either and maybe hadn't admitted it to herself. I watched her walk away, holding her cup of punch like a cocktail. I headed for the snack table, looking for Donny.

"Tess," I heard someone say behind me, and I turned around to find Mr. Todd looking down at me with his sad smile. When I asked him if he'd seen Donny, he seemed a little disappointed. He shook his head and said something I couldn't understand, what with my classmates milling around us, calling to each other across the pool—someone was daring someone to jump in. He set his pop can down on one of the paper-covered tables and lifted one of the light strings next to his head so he could duck under it and get close enough to talk.

"I talked to my sister-in-law about you," Mr. Todd said. "At State. She's in admissions."

"I never filled out the application." My hands felt sweaty, and I rubbed them on my upper arms to dry them, but also to steady myself—a trick I'd learned from my father.

He nodded. "I know. Listen, Tess. I'm trying to help you, but this is not the normal way." Mr. Todd looked at me for a moment. "She wants to talk to you. All you have to do is let me make you an appointment."

"Because of my dad," I said without thinking, but I knew it was true. He felt sorry for me; he had all along. He was doing his part like the people who'd made us Jesus casseroles and mowed the lawn.

"No. Okay, yes. Maybe that's part of it. But it's mainly because of you. You can always come back. But you might not get another chance like this. Do you understand?"

I looked around the crowded patio. My father had said once that people sometimes gave the things they wanted for themselves—at least that was how he explained the plaid wool scarves my grandmother had given him every year for Christmas until she died. So Mr. Todd was maybe giving me the thing he wanted, or had wanted when he was my age. But I wasn't sure if it was what I should want. I imagined myself disappearing from this, from the blue-lit party, the echoing chatter, the people I'd always known. I turned back to Mr. Todd. He'd done more for me than anyone could ask. No one could say he hadn't tried. The least I could do was be thankful.

"I'll fill out the application. Promise this time," I said, and Mr. Todd looked down at his hands and nodded. He seemed relieved. "If you want to get in touch with me," I said, and he nodded again, waiting. "Just leave a message at the lanes."

He said okay and congratulations, and I thanked him again, and then I turned and threaded my way across the crowded patio. I found Donny standing at the edge of the grass, looking for me. Everything seemed blurred under the almost-dark sky. I saw the quiet searching in his face, and as I made my way toward him, I knew I would send in the form, because I'd promised. But that was the end of it.

* 17 *

AS DONNY TOOK me home that night after graduation, I wondered if my mother would be up waiting for me when I got home. She'd known about Chelsea's party, after all; she could've found me if she'd wanted to. I debated as to whether I should ask her if Pastor Jake worried at all what people might say about him going around with a woman who was not his wife, a woman whose husband had been dead barely a year. He hadn't seemed to be the least bit worried, grinning fiercely from the stands. Whatever people might say behind his back, they likely weren't saying to his face, at least not yet; that was the extent of his power.

And I didn't tell Donny about what Mr. Todd had said to me. I thought that mentioning the conversation would give it more importance than it actually had, since I'd already decided not to do anything about it.

"Are you okay?" Donny asked. He rested his hand on the back of my neck.

"I'm okay," I said. Saying it made me feel better, not because I believed it, but because it was what we did, reassuring each other, checking for injuries. "Are you all right?" I said it again, leaned back into the warmth of his hand, and kissed him before I got out. I went to the front door, and I felt the drag on my body as he backed away, but I just waved as he drove off.

My mother was sitting on the couch in our otherwise empty living room, coffee cup steaming on our one remaining side table. Lamplight glowed in her lap; she'd changed out of the dress she'd worn to graduation and now wore jeans and a flowered blouse. She'd been reading, or wanted me to see that she'd been reading, some slim book with a reassuring-looking sunrise printed on the cover. Next to her was the New English Bible, with its cracked spine and dozens of little bookmarks sticking out along the sides and tops of the pages. I'd heard her comment with pride before on how beat up it was.

"I was going to give it a few more minutes and then go looking for you." She stood up with a tight smile, picking up her two books and holding them to her chest like a shield.

"I was—"

"I stopped by the lanes already and told Leo to call me if you showed up, so I'll just save you the trouble if you're going to tell me you were there."

"I was there earlier," I said, turning to go down the hall.

"So he covers for you now?"

I stopped and turned back around. My mother smiled again, her eyes steady on me but full of electricity. I hoped it was just the caffeine. "I thought we had dinner plans."

"I didn't know Pastor Jake was invited."

"Why wouldn't you want him to be?"

I looked at the floor to keep from rolling my eyes. "Well, for one thing, he's not family."

"Neither's Donny."

I snapped my chin up to meet her eyes again. "He is to me." *More than you.* The words came to me, but I knew I couldn't say them. I thought of Donny on that first day we'd met at the lanes, when he'd showed me how to work the soda dispenser. And the way Leo had introduced him, hands on his shoulders, holding him and yet easing him forward at the same time.

Now it was my mother's turn to look at the floor. She shook her head. "Tess," she said, "I am concerned about you. Jake is concerned about you. We need—you need—"

So now Pastor Jake was just Jake. "A father?"

"No." My mother held up her hand to stop me. "A friend."

It was funny to me how, when someone decided they were concerned about you, they could come up with all kinds of things you needed—to do, to think, to be. I swept my hand toward the mostly bare room. There were still dents in the carpet where the bookshelves had been. "Ask him why does he want us to give all our furniture away."

"Look." My mother leaned to drop the Bible and the other book on the couch, and something metallic swung out on a chain from her throat—a silver cross. This was a new thing. It was silver and flat and knuckle-length, and she caught it mid-swing and dropped it back into her blouse. She saw that I'd noticed.

"It's because I'm going to become a church elder," she said. She shrugged as if to say, *Who would've thought?* And I knew he'd given it to her. "So I'll have a graduation of sorts, too."

She seemed so proud, in spite of acting casual, that I didn't want to hold anything against her—Pastor Jake in the stands next to her instead of my father, the worn paths in our carpet tracing our empty rooms. She handed me an envelope.

"Here. From Pastor Jake." Back to the pastor title again, I noticed. She went into the kitchen to turn off the coffee pot and rinse out her mug. I could tell she was waiting for me to open it, so I pulled it out of the white envelope, which was marked on the back in big, square caps: TESS. The card—a photograph of a rainbow coming out of glowing clouds—and inside, the word "Inspiration" printed in script. Then, in Pastor Jake's block lettering:

TESS, ALL OF US AT THE EMMANUEL SEND YOU OUR PRYAERS AND CONGRATULATIONS.
PRAISED BE THE LORD!

He'd signed his name in even bigger caps. I looked up from reading to find my mother watching me from the kitchen doorway. I smiled the best I could. "Should I put this on the fridge?" I suggested, and I could tell that made her happy.

"Great idea," she said. She watched me tack it on the freezer door with the emergency 911 magnet which had come with the phone-book. I wished it had another number to call—not one for emergencies, specifically, but for a general sense of danger.

Then she said, "About the furniture." She said we needed to make room for our future, which we'd find waiting for us at the soon-to-be-built Savior Missionary in Marietta. She couldn't be specific as to how, but she said I could be certain that the Savior would give me real-life experience. "Millions are waiting for the Lord's word right here in Ohio," she said then, and I knew she was quoting Pastor Jake. I let her hug me and kiss me on the forehead. "Don't worry," she said. "I'll let you know when the time comes." Her promise made me shiver.

She checked the front door before heading upstairs. I went back to the living room to turn off the lamp and saw she'd left her tattered Bible and the cloud book on the couch. I figured I'd bring them up to her, but when I picked up the books, a single folded sheet of paper slipped from the cloud book and twirled to the floor. It looked like onion skin paper, the kind they give you in typing class. I picked it up to slip it back in. Then, in the lamplight, through the thin paper,

I saw some of the same chunky lettering that had been on my card. I turned it over.

PATIENCE. IT'S THE ONLY WAY WE'LL WIN HER OVER.

I slipped the paper back into the book. I felt dizzy as I put the book back where my mother had left it, trying to get its position just right and wondering what Jake's patience would look like, and how they planned to win me over. I turned off the lamp and walked down the dark hallway to my room, my parents' old room from that other life. I kept my hand on the wall because I didn't feel steady on my feet there in the dark. Somehow it seemed to me right then that if I lost my balance I wouldn't fall but float away.

18

ON THE MONDAY after July Fourth my mother and I both had to work. She left before I did. I went looking through the house for other notes from Pastor Jake. It hadn't occurred to me to do so until the induction ceremony, when it became clear that my mother had meant it when she'd said there was a plan, a reason for clearing out our house, making room for what would come next.

I found only one. All of two lines, written by Jake, but it was enough:

TIME TO GET READY. THE SAVIOR NEEDS US.

I found it in one of the Time-Life books stacked behind the couch, which my mother for some reason hadn't yet given away. It was tucked in a two-page spread showing the evolution of man from smallish monkey to ape to Neanderthal to modern man—all naked, right leg slung forward in stride to hide the equipment (wasn't it important to see how that had evolved too? Or had it just not changed much?). Somehow, Modern Man didn't seem very convincing leading that procession. But put a T-shirt and jeans on him and he could've been any guy walking down the street, rolling at the lanes, spouting angry prayers at the Emmanuel. All of them were perfect company for a letter from a guy like Pastor Jake, and I wondered if my mother had thought about that, or if it had just been chance. I wondered why she'd kept it, and how long we had left before it was time to leave.

I put the note back between the exact pages, tried to stack the books back just as I'd found them. I rode my bike to the lanes. It was one of those hot mornings when the sky was white with light off the lake. When I got there, Leo had already unlocked his closet office and gone in, and I left him alone. I went straight into putting on coffee at the bar because the old men who got there when the doors opened would be grumpy if it wasn't ready to pour. I unlocked the pro shop, plugged in the ball polisher. Over the parking lot outside I could see heat rippling the air. I set the snack bag trees on the bar next to the register, started the fryer, and got the first batch of fries in because the old men would start wanting lunch by eleven. It would be a busy day with the holiday, even with Cedar Point jammed with tourists, and the cars lining up for the Kelleys Island ferries. And there was a full lineup of kid's day camps and clinics ahead.

I flipped the sign to OPEN on the doors. A few minutes later, two guys who'd graduated a couple of years before me came in, trailed by their girlfriends or wives, both pregnant. They set up on Lane 3 and took drags on their cigarettes between rolls. The women sat in the plastic booth, staring at the balls going back and twirling their permed hair around their fingers. They looked too tired to talk.

The guys ordered drafts, so I had to fire up the compressor. This brought Leo out, because he never trusted me to get it going right. He stood next to me behind the bar, checking the lines. He was wearing his favorite Beers of the World shirt with all the labels in different languages, in honor of the holiday. He slapped open a catalog on the counter in front of me, pointed to a picture of a machine that looked like a large blender.

"What do you think, Wycheski?" he said. "You think I should order this?"

"What is it?" I asked.

"A smoothie machine. Wave of the future, apparently."

I shook my head. "I don't know," I said, pushing the catalog back toward him.

Leo frowned. "Hey, what's the problem?"

"I think my mother wants to sell the house for that church she belongs to."

Leo smoothed the catalog, folded down a corner of the page to mark it. "She ought to wait. The market's not good right now." He seemed unconcerned. He pointed to the smoothie machine picture again. "You can chop up candy bars in it. Donny will be proud."

As if he'd heard us talking about him, Donny called right then. Leo picked up; he was closer to the phone. "Galaxy," he said, and I wouldn't have thought anything of the call if it hadn't been for how quiet Leo was, standing there. Normally people were calling about league sign-ups or lesson costs, which he would hand off to me, or hours, which always pissed him off because he'd paid for a special ad in the phonebook that listed the hours, and people still called to ask.

Leo turned his back to me, looking out the plate glass doors toward the parking lot. He listened for a long time and then all he said was "Okay."

"What?" I said, and Leo handed me the phone, and I knew for sure then that it was Donny. I said his name rather than hello.

"My father," he said, his voice cracking.

I heard the jingle of keys and turned to see Leo patting his pockets.

"Wait a minute," I said, both to Donny and him. But Donny wasn't saying anything at that point, and I pictured him in the kitchen, where the phone was, his father maybe nearby, huge and white and shuffling, the dark red seam in his scalp gleaming. And the orange-sized tumor, not inside his skull but floating just off to one side.

"My father's been missing all night," Donny said then.

"Okay," I said, just like Leo had, who was right then heading for the door. "Wait!" I yelled, and the people turned to look at me from all the way over at Lane 3.

Leo stopped and looked at me like I was crazy.

"Don't hang up," I said to Donny. I held the receiver to my chest. "Please," I said to Leo.

"Family business, Tess," Leo said.

He could've slapped me and not shocked me more. What he thought made a family was beyond me. I pulled the phone cord as far as it would go past the counter and pressed the plastic receiver even harder into my chest, so hard it hurt, because I didn't want Donny to hear what I was going to say next.

"I know who you are in that family, Leo," I said. The fear of saying it quivered through my muscles, my jaw. I gritted my teeth to steady myself.

Leo stared at me. He stood absolutely still in front of the glass doors, hot sunlight streaming in behind him. I thought of my father, no older than I was and alone in the desert where Leo had left him. And Donny, whom Leo left as a baby. And his own brother. And the fact that I wouldn't have been born had things gone any other way, had my father not crawled away in disgrace, thinking he would never bowl again. The world came down to numbers, I thought, for as long as a score mattered.

The guys and their wives had gone back to rolling on Lane 3. The compressor was humming; the Lustre King ball polisher was glowing. Leo was a shadow in the middle of it all.

"Congratulations, Wycheski," he said. "You're fired." He turned to leave, and I put the phone back to my ear and looked away so I wouldn't have to see him walking out without me. I wanted to sit down on the floor right then, my legs felt so weak. I leaned against the counter instead. "Donny," I said.

I could hear him breathing. I said his name again. I imagined his mother standing off to one side in her navy pumps, hands clasped, waiting.

"I've been up all night looking for him," Donny said.

I leaned forward a bit because my stomach was hurting, like a cramp after running too hard. "You'll find him," I said. I looked at my father's picture on Leo's Wall of Fame, but I couldn't see it well because I was blinking away tears.

"It's my fault." Donny said, louder, but still shaky. I could hear him taking a deep breath, letting it out slowly.

I said no it isn't, and what are you talking about, and he said I didn't understand, and I wanted to punch the phone through the bar. "Don't tell me I don't understand!" I yelled, and the couples down at Lane 3 were not even trying to be low-key about watching me by then, the women leaning their teased hairdos close together and whispering.

"I'm coming to you," I said.

"Tess," Donny said, and his voice seemed calmer now. "Stay there, kay? Leo's on his way. Keep the lanes open, okay?"

I couldn't seem to get my breath. My face was wet. It seemed beside the point to mention that Leo had fired me. Jobs seemed to be part of another world.

"Tess?"

"I told Leo," I said. "I told him that you know." I could hear Donny breathing, taking this in. Then after a moment he said he had to go, and I said okay again and listened to him walk across floorboards, place the receiver on the metal cradle, the line clunking dead. I needed time to get the trembling in my legs under control, so it was fine to wait for a few minutes while the guys on Lane 3 finished their last set—or, as I explained to them over the PA, that this would have to be the last set. I told other people who'd come in that we'd be closing for a few hours, sorry for the inconvenience, league times would be rescheduled, just tell Leo they'd talked to me. I checked in the league book, too, and made a couple of calls, and shut down the deep fryer and the compressor, and the lights on the video games. I made sure the pro shop was locked. I stood there with my hand on the knob, looking at the drill machine, thinking of the ghost story Leo had told me once, when I could still turn my head and see my father waiting for me. I was thinking about ghosts and whether or not I believed in them now.

The last thing I checked was Leo's office, which was locked. I wondered if I'd ever see any of that cash he'd insisted I save all during this past year. On my way out, I taped a sign on the Galaxy door: CLOSED UNTIL FURTHER NOTICE.

Part Three

Leo Florida

19

THEY SAY THE dead haunt you worse when you fought them in life. I didn't believe that for a long time. By the time I'd heard about my old man, I'd left Wycheski in Vegas and made it to Minneapolis. Someone told me they'd seen a bit in the paper: "Roy Florida, 1930s local bowling hero who once ranked tenth in the nation in ten-pin match play . . ." None of that added up to much with him dead.

And what happened to Joe. No big deal in the scheme of things, I thought. The kid was green, he tried to go pro too early, he'd have other chances. Problem was I'd bet on him to lose. That wasn't exactly clean of me as his coach, not to mention illegal. But it happens all the time. My idea was to pick up a big enough wad of cash to make an offer to Bern on the lanes. I figured on coming back to Sandusky and being a good uncle, a father in any way I could, to Donny.

But I'd bet against Joe with a point spread, not a forfeit. This was the bigger problem. Not only had I lost what I'd put on the table, I was into the bookie for more. So I gave Joe my car and enough cash to get home and hitched a ride out of town that night. I figured I'd lay low for a year or so, maybe hustle here and there, raise enough funds to pay off the bookie—not that I gave a shit about my credit with him, but the boys behind him in Vegas were serious types. They would have made those bricks who showed up that night bullying my mother for grocery money look like schoolteachers.

Over the next couple of years, I stuck to the Northeast, familiar ground. I knew a lot of people in those places, so I had to check out places where the management had changed. One hustle, then out you go. For a while it was fine. Louise and the baby faded from my mind like a photo run through the wash. I was over her, I told myself. I was free.

But then I got to drinking, because what else do you do when you spend every night alone? A woman here and there. Otherwise you've got to get to sleep somehow. But the booze worked over my game and my mind. I spent the days sick and shaking, had to have a couple before going to the lanes. And I started to see Vegas types in every room. Then I heard about my father from that guy at those upstairs lanes in St. Louis where they were still hand oiling each lane every night. There'd been a clip about the records he'd held back in the thirties.

At the time I was glossed up enough not to feel it. But it didn't escape me that I had become my old man—not the guy I'd loved, cranking the competition down at the State, but the drunk who ran from his debts and left other people to answer the door.

When I got the news about him, I tried to sober up. I took it as a signal, a fork in the road, what have you. I could be an old drunk like him or not. I could figure out a way to pay off Vegas, if they didn't find me first, or keep running myself into the ground.

And this too—I had to quit wishing that my brother had gotten his head completely blown off instead of the job half-done.

Then I placed the call. Louise had gotten a phone after Walt got home in case of emergencies. I looked up the number in a library in Canton, Ohio, and I sat there for a long time with my finger right below my brother's name. Just the way Donny would do it, a few years down the line, tripping across me.

I made the call in a phone booth right outside the library. My heart was in my throat. But the woman who answered wasn't Louise. After the second hello I realized it was my mother.

Before I said a word, she knew it was me. She said my name. I heard the shake in her voice. She told me my father was dead. She asked me where I was. I told her something like Wyoming. Then she wanted to know why I was calling Louise and Walt but not her.

"I tried the house a few times," I said.

"Come home," she said. "Please."

I told her I was working my way back, and she said she was scared she would die before she saw me again. I took this to be the kind of thing you said when you'd just lost your husband. I told her I'd get home as soon as I could. And I should have left it at that, but then I asked about Donny. She said he was a beautiful baby, here he was two years old and already talking up a storm, dada this and dada that.

"How about Louise?" I said, and that was my mistake.

"You've been gone all this time and you can't let her go."

I leaned against the glass. Sun on my back but I might as well have been down in the belly of the State, listening for that dead kid cranking his first line. I'd heard that hollow rolling ball. Felt that jelly in the legs. There was nothing I could say, so I just listened to the air behind her voice. The air that was in the rooms where Louise lived. I'd played a sad joke on myself, thinking I didn't care about her anymore.

"Come home, Leo. You can see for yourself." She hung up, but I was still down there with that ghost. I was a ghost. I might as well have choked on my own tongue.

I went on for a while after that. Back to drinking at night, shaking through the days. Sometimes sleeping in a room, sometimes outside. Kids were everywhere by then. Long-haired, you couldn't tell the boys from the girls. Their dope smelled like burning shit.

Everywhere I went I saw faces of people I'd gone to school with, hustled, gone to bed with, rolled with. The man whose cheekbone I broke in Houston—I'd thought I'd seen him with the bookie in Vegas. He was following me, I was sure of it. Turned out he was a father of four, grew up in Jersey City, had never left his home state before, came down for work.

They sent me to the correctional facility outside of Sugarland. What a name for a place. Hot as hell, snakes in the fields where we grew cane, food that tasted like the metal trays. Other than that, it wasn't a hard life. Minimum security—we even got to work off-site after one year good behavior. I was there three, one year for every month that guy I'd hit was out of work—they did not like Yankees acting up in Texas. After I'd been there a year and was still alive, I figured anyone connected to my skipped bill in Vegas would have already taken his shot. I figured too that there was no point in going through my days scared of dying. That was what had gotten me in there in the first place.

So after that first year, I wrote Bern Schnipke. A month or two went by, and I figured he'd given up on me. That hurt worse than losing my father. Bern had shown me how to slice off my piece of life and be happy with it. Working the lanes in the town I was born in—before Bern, I would have told you I'd just shoot myself first. But he made it look good. Or at least not a defeat.

Then one day I got marched out for a visitor. There was Bern across the table from me. His hair had gone white. He kept his fingers laced, tapped his thumbs against each other when I sat down. "Your mother's dead," he said to me. He waited while I got my jaw straight.

He gave me the how and when—heart attack, a few months earlier. He said Walt and Louise had to sell my parents' house to pay for the funeral. "You know anything about that?" he asked, but I was gone. I was in my mother's kitchen, making coffee for Louise, I was in her bed, I was offering her sugar.

"I ought to beat you like you beat that guy," Bern said. "Maybe get the sense back in you."

I held my head in my hands, because I couldn't speak. Bern leaned forward. "You go ahead and cry. I was you, I would, too."

I choked out an excuse. "It was a loan. I was trying to turn it over."

"You were betting like a scum," Bern said.

"I was making an investment."

Bern's eyebrows went up his forehead. "I take that back. You are a scum." He shook his head. "I mean, what did you want? That you didn't already have?"

This I couldn't take. I knew when he left, there would be no one else. "To buy the lanes, Bern. That was the point."

It was Bern's turn to drop his head, stare at his hands. "Christ. Leo." When he looked up at me, his eyes were red at the rims. His face was a stack of wrinkles. He shook his head. "I would've given the place to you."

That was the winter of 1966. Three years after I'd left Joe in Vegas. A good coach would've helped him limp home, told him this was what came of rushing things. No, I take that back. A good coach wouldn't have let him go in the first place. There was a thread in me that could've gone that route. Come home to Bern and to my folks and gone on. Bern told me Joe had gotten married and had a baby girl. He told me he'd last seen Walt and Louise at my mother's funeral. "That boy of theirs ran around the whole time, couldn't get him to sit still."

"Donald," I said. I couldn't picture him running. He was still package-sized, fixing me with that infant stare. *He's mine*, I thought. But that seemed like something I'd made up.

"Donny, they call him." The guard walked over, and Bern stood up. "Your job's waiting when you come back," he said.

"I can't go back there," I said.

Bern looked down at me for a moment, pursed his lips, shook his head again. "Well, I'm not coming back here. I'm too old."

I nodded. Kept my eyes on the table so I wouldn't have to watch him walk out.

What happened was I wrote him when my time was close to up, and he wrote back and said if I wasn't coming back there I should call Sal Ventor in Atlantic City. I was a soda jerk and shoe boy at his lanes for three years. Almost married Sal's daughter, figured it was time. Then Bern called one day and said his wife was dead and if he had his way about it, he wouldn't be far behind.

When I got back to town, no one recognized me. It had been ten years since I left and I was forty years old. The apartment over Bern's garage had a tin mirror in the bathroom, and it took me a while not to be startled by what I saw in it. And unlike those drunk years, no one around me—on the street, in the lanes—looked familiar. *The Twilight Zone* would have been my favorite TV show if I'd had a TV. I was living it.

Bern was right, it turned out. Had a stroke not even a year after I came back. He hung around a few days, but the docs didn't have a chance. He'd stuck to the plan in other ways, too. He willed me the lanes and the house.

But before Bern died, Donny showed up. It was still cold but no snow on the ground. Kid woke me up on a Saturday morning. There he was at the bottom of the steps, a stick of a boy. I thought he was from the *Sandusky Register* hounding me again for a subscription.

"Didn't I tell you last week I didn't want any goddamn paper?" I yelled down at him.

He shook his head. "I don't have any papers."

"Well, I don't want anything else you've got then." I turned to close the door.

"I've got your last name," he said. His voice squeaked all over the place. He was scared.

"Wait a minute," I said. I went back inside, put on my pants. I got my coffee and a cigarette to settle my nerves. So this was it, I thought. This was Donny. I came out and took the stairs slow and sat down near the bottom, a few feet away from him. I flicked open a book of matches from the Galaxy and lit my cigarette.

"So what's your first name, then?" I said, like as if I didn't know.

"Donny." He was shivering, standing all stiff to hide it.

I took a drag to try to collect myself. "Your folks know you're here?"

He shook his head and then he glanced at his bike like as if he was judging the distance.

"Then who told you to come?"

"I saw you in the phone book."

"Well how'd you know to find me in the phone book if someone didn't tell you to look?"

"I wasn't looking for you," he said.

"You were looking yourself up, weren't you?" I said. He looked shocked that I'd put it together. Probably it didn't help that I started laughing then. But that calmed me down. "You wanted to make sure you exist," I said. I took another drag, waiting.

"I don't know," he said. He seemed to have settled down, too.

"Well, I know, even if you don't, Donny Florida," I said. "I've known about you since before you were born."

And then I told him who I was. I proved it by telling him his birth date, the family names, and the color of his mother's hair. I even told him how she wore it. I hadn't said her name in years. "Louise," I said again, just to hear it come out of my mouth.

Then I told him he could call me Leo. I told him I'd been gone for a while and hadn't been up to much good. I told him I was banned from most bowling establishments in Chicago, St. Louis, and the state of New Jersey for hustling. "I wasn't that great at it, is the bottom line," I said. "If you're good, you don't get caught." I couldn't tell what he thought of all that. But there he was. My son. I did the math. He was eleven, and he was almost as tall as I was. He could've caught on fire in front of me and I wouldn't have been more amazed.

I asked if he'd eaten, and he said he hadn't, so I invited him in. I gave him a seat at the kitchen table in one of the two chairs I had, and I fixed us a couple of pimiento sandwiches. I set out a jar of pickled eggs and gave him a Vernors. I sat down across from him and started eating.

He peeled open the sandwich to look at it. "What're those red things in it?" he asked.

"Pimiento peppers. That's what they call it," I said. "It's got a little bite. Try it."

He got through a mouthful. His eyes started watering and he threw the thing down.

"You oughtta try some of those jalapeño peppers those Mexicans cook with," I said. I'd gotten used to the stuff in Texas. I wanted to laugh just to settle my nerves again, but I didn't want to put him off. He wiped his nose on the back of his hand and then wiped it off on his jeans.

"Your mother saw you do that, she'd ring your bell," I said.

"My mother doesn't hit me," he said.

We sized each other up a minute. "Your father, then," I said.

He took in the scuffed floor. "They never talked about you," he said.

"I told you," I said. "I got in trouble." I got another bite, talked through my food. I had to tell him the truth. "I took some money off your grandparents and never paid it back. Your folks wrote me off, like they should've." I said that and thought of my mother at the door the night those goons had showed up. I was one of them now, that was a sad fact.

The boy got through a second swallow of sandwich and gulped the soda. "You could pay it back," he said.

I looked at his thin face. Had I ever looked like that? He thought anything could be fixed. He made me sorry to be in his line of sight.

"No, I can't," I said. He took a look around him, and I think he started to get it. I was living in a box over a garage. I had a toilet, a fold-out couch, and some pots and pans. I took a last swig of my cold coffee. "Anyway, even if I had the money, you can't pay back the dead," I said.

He pushed his plate away. "They don't know you're back."

"They'll find out soon enough."

We stared at each other. He didn't know me, and I didn't know him. But I did know where the fault was for that.

"Look," I said. "I don't care what you tell them." That was the truth. It didn't matter what he said. I was here, living over Bern Schnipke's garage. That's what I added up to.

"Here's my plan, Donny," I went on. "I'm going to rent shoes and oil lanes and say yessir and keep to myself otherwise. Down at the Galaxy. You want to come see me, you can. I'll give you free lessons if you want. I sure as hell know all the tricks, even if I flubbed a few."

Donny gave up on the sandwich, tossed it on his plate. He looked at me a beat. I'd dealt with some hard cases in my time, but I felt like as if he could take me apart with an eye blink.

He stood up then. "You were wrong about my mother," he said. "Her hair's short now. She cut it off a long time ago."

I stayed in my seat so I could catch my breath. I wondered if he knew who I was after all.

"See you around," he said, and maybe he sounded hopeful about it.

"Sure," I said. I listened to him clomp down the steps. It took me a while to get to my feet after he left.

Bern knew. I shouldn't have been surprised. He'd never missed much. I came out on the stoop for another cigarette after Donny left, and Bern came out the back door, leaned on the railing at the bottom of the steps. He looked me over while I smoked. I felt like as if my chest was on fire. Finally, he said, "He yours?" I nodded. I guess I was too thrown off to lie, or even act shocked. My whole idea had been to just keep to myself, get a feel for things back here again. My parents were dead, and Walt was halfway there, what Bern had heard. I did mean to go to Louise and ask forgiveness someday. And at least look like I cared what Walt thought. And Donny. Especially him. At any rate, Bern was the only person I ever outright told.

It took the boy a couple months to show up down at the lanes. It was spring by then and I'd about given up on him. I acted casual when I spotted him, but the truth is he scared me. Still I went about treating him like any customer. He looked to have grown about three inches since I saw him last. I set him up with a soda and a house ball and showed him how to roll that first day. He didn't have the sight but he could follow directions. He made a point of paying for the drink and the lane and the shoe rentals, said he had his own money mowing lawns.

He was taking off the rentals by the time I worked up the nerve to ask him about his mother. "You told her yet?" I said.

He looked up at me. "I thought you didn't care whether I told them or not."

I put his shoes the counter. "I don't want you sneaking over here."

"Why don't you tell them then?"

I had to hand it to him, he was sharp. I sat down on a bench near him. He stayed on the floor, fiddling with his shoes.

"I'm not the one—listen. Sneaking around on your folks is bad."

He laughed at this. He sounded delighted, actually. "Nobody notices where I go."

That I couldn't believe. He burned a hole in my vision every time I looked at him. "Don't come back if you're lying about it."

He got to his feet then. His jaw was tight. "You wouldn't know either way, would you?"

I looked at the lanes just to buy myself a second. He'd gotten to me again. "Okay. I don't care what you think about it," I said. "But I don't want your parents hearing about you hanging out here from anyone else but you. You want to come back here, you have to show me proof that your mother knows. She can come here, she can send a note, whatever."

This baby isn't yours, she'd said, standing there in the doorway, big with him. But I knew better. I wanted to get to her. I wanted her to know I was there.

"A note?" The kid looked pissed off enough to cry. "A note?"

"And I'll tell you something else, and this is probably more than I should say. I don't care what your father thinks, either."

He'd been waiting for that. "Your brother."

I let that pass. Walt had gotten rid of me a long time ago. No fault of mine for keeping the same tune. "All I care is that she approves," I said.

Donny didn't say a word, just headed for the door.

"Tell her I said hello," I said, but he kept going.

I didn't expect to see him again. Tried to make myself not hope. But he showed up one afternoon a few weeks later. I let him make his way to the counter.

"Help you?" I said. It was one of those early summer days that could break your heart. The sky blown through with blue. That light that didn't want to give up.

"I asked my mom," he said. His arms were tanned dark brown the way I used to get. I guessed his mowing concern was going strong.

I tried to picture what it'd been like when he'd told Louise I was back. There was a chance she'd known anyway—it was a small town. I wondered what she'd said to him. I waited for him to tell me, but he just stood there, thumbs in his belt loops. "So?" I said.

"She said she was gonna get new curtains."

"What?" It didn't even make sense at first. I thought he was cracking some kind of joke.

He just stared at me. He looked like he hadn't been getting much sleep. He scratched at his head and turned away like as if he was going to leave.

"Wait a minute." It was beginning to dawn on me what he'd said about the curtains. Those blue curtains I'd helped Louise hang. What do they say about your stomach dropping, all that? I felt like I'd been flung off a building. What did she mean by that, anyway? She was making a change, that was what. That was all. Maybe it didn't have anything to do with me. She just knew that I'd get it. Maybe even that was a good sign.

The boy was standing still, half-cocked for the door.

"What exactly did she say?"

He had that look again, like as if he was being chased. Maybe she'd told him the whole deal. I thought about just telling him myself. But what would that have gotten me? Maybe she'd keep him away then.

"Tell me the exact words," I said.

I could give up the story or not, it didn't matter. He knew. Maybe not the details, but he knew something was up.

"She said, 'Tell him I'm thinking of getting rid of these.'" He made a motion like she'd picked up the hem of one of them. I could see her in him then. The way she'd lift her hand.

I stared at him. I didn't want to think about what that all meant. But it was pretty clear. I'd hoped she'd warm up to the idea of me being back, maybe let me come over every once in a while. But she didn't want me there. He dropped his hand, shoved it in his jeans.

"Okay," I said. My ears felt stopped up. My head felt numb. "Fine. You can stay."

He walked past me, on his way to get a ball. "Listen here," I said. I was trying to get my voice back.

He stopped. I said, "Those jeans of yours are getting high on your ankles. You need money for another pair?"

He shook his head, started to turn again.

"Let me know if you change your mind," I said. "You can tell your mother I'll foot the bill for those curtains she needs, too. Tell her she ought to get a lighter color, let the sun in."

He turned full around then. "I never told you what color they were."

We took a good long look at each other. I could've tried to think of some way to explain. But I'd landed in that dining room, asking her. *Just tell me.* Windows up, those blue curtains folding back in the breeze. A day just like what was blowing in when Donny turned on his heel and walked out.

Bern had seen the whole thing. The man never missed much. He was a few months out from the stroke that would lay him down. Maybe he was getting to be a romantic, now that his wife was gone. Actually, that's not fair. He loved that woman, and maybe he was missing her. So that might've been why he gave me the one bad piece of advice of his career.

"Go see her," he said.

"What?" I said. I was hanging onto that counter like as if it was a cliff. I thought about my mother, hanging on for dear life at the kitchen sink when we first got the news about Walt. Now I knew why she'd had such a hard grip.

Bern dropped a rag on the counter. "You losing your hearing, Florida? I said, go see her."

"And what the hell will that do?" I said. I wasn't kidding. I really hoped he could tell me.

Bern leaned into me. "God, I worry for you, son. What're you going to do in this world when I'm gone?" He shook his head like as if he knew it was coming. "It'll show her you're serious. Don't dance around trying to get to her through that boy."

My boy. I put my head in my hands. Bern gave me a good knuckle or two on the skull.

"She's a married woman, right?" he said.

"To my brother."

Bern rolled his eyes. "Right. So, she's not going to send you an engraved invitation! Grow up, Florida. If you want her, you got to go see her. Tell her you're willing to wait."

"Willing to wait?" I said. Hell, it'd already been ten years and then some.

"Isn't it the truth?" He patted my cheek like as if I was a little kid. The way he looked at me—well, he felt bad for me. And he was right. It was the truth.

It took me a few trips to get myself to the door. By that time it was staying light pretty late. I wanted to get to her after Donny was asleep, not to mention Walt. How late did eleven-year-old kids stay up, anyway? Especially in summer. I had no way of knowing. So I sat in my car across the street like a stalker, waiting for the lights on the bedroom side of the house to go off. Just looking at the place made me nervous. I could see those blue curtains were still up, though. That gave me hope, whether it should've or not.

Finally I went up and knocked. Tapping like an old woman. If Walt had come to the door I would've just walked away. But there she was after a minute or so, leaning on the door edge in a blue robe. I looked at her through the blur of the screen, thought about what Bern said. I opened the screen, closed it quiet behind me. She didn't look a day older to me than when I'd first seen her. Just a more finished-off version of herself. Tougher.

So I went ahead and acted out the movie I had in my head. I pulled her to me, right there at the door. And she let me. She put her arms around me, pressed her face to my neck. She took my hand and led me into that front room. And there were those curtains again. I couldn't believe I was standing there. I hugged her again, kissed her. I was hoping I wouldn't make too much of a teenager out of myself.

She put her hands on either side of my face to stop me. She asked me did I want to sit. So we did, and we looked at each other. Seems like we did that a long time. In my memory, that's the way it runs.

"What did you say to him?" she whispered.

"I should ask you the same thing," I said. I was talking quiet, but she put her finger to her lips anyway.

She shook her head. "He thinks you don't want him there."

"That what he said?" There we were, sitting together. We were talking about our son. I could've gotten on my knees to thank Bern.

She nodded. She was beautiful. Her hair was like something liquid in the lamplight. Her blue eyes on me.

"Well, tell him he's wrong on that," I heard myself saying like as if I was floating over the scene. "Matter of fact, I'll tell him myself. I'll come by tomorrow."

She shook her head. "I don't want Walt to see you. He's still—"

"Louise," I said. "I'm sorry." I had whole speeches planned. I was going to tell her about all I'd done. Start with a clean slate. I was going to tell her how we could get some time together here and there. And how I'd be willing to wait. "Walt never liked me much," I said. "Maybe he's over it."

"No," she said. "He's not—it's not about Donny."

I looked down at her hands. "I'll pay the money back," I said, even though I knew what I'd said to Donny was true—it was too late for all that.

She shook her head again. "I'll apologize to him," I said. The thought of it made me want to chew my tongue off.

"I don't think so," she said.

"Well, what do you want me to do? Stay away forever?"

She looked at me. She wasn't shaking her head anymore. My guts turned over. "Come on, Louise. He's my brother. I can talk to him."

"He doesn't even know you're back," she said. "And that's the way I want it to stay. Okay?"

"Okay," I said. "But I can still see you, right? And Donny."

"You can see Donny. He'll come back to the lanes. But I can't leave Walt alone, and you can't come here," she said. I opened my mouth to stop her, but she patted my hand to shush me and kept going.

"I'm going to tell you this Leo, just once. Because I'm older now and I know my own mind." She took a breath. She was trying not to cry. "I love you. That is the truth."

She put her hands on my face, leaned her forehead to touch mine. I felt like as if my skin was peeled off, because I knew already. I knew she was going to tell me to go.

"Don't," I said.

"But I love him, too," she said. The tears were all down her face now. "And he—he forgave me, Leo. And he loves Donny. So I have to let him have this life. You understand?"

She didn't wait for me to answer. My answer didn't matter anyway. She kissed me and then started to stand, but I held onto her wrists. She got to her feet anyway, pulled her hands away. She started for the front door, but I caught her arm and pulled her to me. I turned her face to mine and kissed her hard. Then she had her hands on my chest and was pushing me away.

"It was easier when you were gone, Leo." She was steeling herself. I could see it.

"But I'm not gone. I'll do this any way you want to. I'll do anything."

I'd never begged anyone for anything like I was then. Or told the truth so clean. She hung her head. I just held her by the arms and let her cry. Her shoulders were shaking, but she was keeping it quiet so she wouldn't wake Walt or Donny. I could hear Walt back there, that whine in his breathing. I was still hoping somehow things would turn around.

Then I heard something in the hall. Maybe she didn't at first because of the crying. But she felt me look up. She knew I'd seen something.

"What?" she said. She turned around. But by then Donny was gone. She held her breath and listened but there wasn't another sound. She took a couple of steps and looked down the hall. She turned back to me.

"You have to go," she whispered.

"There's got to be sometime you can get out," I said. "I'll meet you at the grocery store. Help you get the shopping done."

She opened the door for me, pushed open the screen. I stood in the doorway. I was making a point of waiting for her answer.

"No, Leo. Please believe me. There's no way."

"Louise."

She started shutting the door. I made her do it right in my face. She did it quiet. Could've been closing a coffin lid on me.

I don't remember getting home that night. Bern pulled me off my couch after a couple of days. He had to let himself in.

"The kid came in looking for you."

I rolled over, faced the wall. Bern kicked at a couple bottles I'd left on the floor.

"I told him he could come back tomorrow."

It's a sad thing to think about the days out in front of you and have no interest in living them. But that's where I was.

"Open a window in here," Bern said. "Get a shower. I'll fix us something to eat."

I knew what that meant. Rolling the foil off a TV dinner. I groaned at the wall.

"Florida!" Bern shouted. I'm sure he saw me twitch at that. "I'll see you in twenty minutes or I'll come up here and knock you down the stairs myself."

"I wish you would," I said. But I waited until he slammed the door behind him, in case he wanted to take me up on it.

Donny came back after a few days. I never asked him about Louise again. I taught him straight up, textbook, and he was a good learner. If I told him to tuck his elbow or loosen up his grip, he did it. If I told him to speed up his approach, he did it. He didn't have the sight, though. Couldn't see inside and around the pins. But that was okay. He loved being there. That was good enough for me. When school started back, he came in the afternoons. I paid him a couple of bucks to sweep up around the place so he'd always have a reason to come.

Then Bern was gone. I knew it when I knocked on his back door that morning. The man had never slept past six, far as I knew. I found him in his bed. On the one hand, I was happy that was the way it went for him. But with him gone, I was alone. I sat on the bed with him for a while before I made the call. Tucked the covers around him nice. And—I'll say it—I kissed the man, right on his forehead, held his hand until the medics came.

Then I threw him a party at the lanes. Eddie Elias came, and Salvino stopped in—he was back on his game again after a long slump— and some guys on my dad's old team that were still doddering around. Of course Donny was there. And of course his mother wasn't.

Joe Wycheski came by. He didn't stay long. He just walked in and looked around. He walked over to his lucky lane, stood there a while. We didn't speak, and I didn't think he'd be back again. But then not long after that, there he was. Had Tess with him, just a skin-and-bones kid. He shook my hand like he'd just seen me yesterday, got out his gear, and rolled nine strikes. Said he hadn't touched a ball since Vegas. Still had a bit of the kid about him, too. I guess he wasn't thirty yet. I got the feeling he wanted me to know that he had a good life, maybe in spite of me. Wanted me to know he hadn't gone off the deep end. But I was the last one to hear from him the day he killed himself. People tried to say it was accidental, but Joe wasn't an error prone guy. Not even in his game. It was all or nothing. Perfect or froze up and couldn't roll at all. Maybe that's the reason. He couldn't compromise. The rest of us give in to stay alive.

What I couldn't figure out is why he didn't want to stay around for Tess. All those years he was with her, coaching her and going on about the Wycheski Plan. Tess could do pretty much anything he told her. It was like as if he just needed to say it, and then she could do it, like as if she'd been born to do it. That girl had the sight. It was obvious from Day One.

But he left her. I'm guilty of a lot of things, leaving included. But the look on her face after he was gone was about the saddest thing I ever saw. I did what I could to keep an eye on her while keeping a distance from her dotty mother. For instance, it was my idea about Donny mowing their lawn.

And then the next thing I know, Donny was with Tess. Never had asked a girl out before. Never talked about girls. He borrows my tractor, goes and mows her lawn like a middle-aged guy trapped in a teenager's body, sets himself up on a weekly plan. And that was that.

But he was the one who got her to come back to the lanes. From then on, if she was in the room, he was looking at her. In a way, that made me feel sorrier for him than when he'd had no one at all. Tess was a sweet girl, quiet and tough. She had her father's arm, but she also had his nerves, my opinion. And her mother—if she had any of that in her, she was in trouble. One thing I knew. She wouldn't stay anywhere long. So it wasn't a hard guess where that would leave Donny. Maybe he knew, too, but just didn't want to believe it. Just the way I'd been about Louise.

20

THEN THERE WAS that night Walt wandered off the first time. Donny and Tess were late for work, and on a heavy league night. She had twigs in her hair, and the back of his jacket was wet, if I needed any clues as to why.

They hadn't been there fifteen minutes when I got the call. Louise. It'd been, what, six or seven years since I'd seen her last, when she'd closed the door on me. Her voice put the bend in my knees. So when she told me Walt was missing, I just handed the phone to Donny and went to get my jacket. The temperature was going down fast out there. I wanted to save him and then I didn't.

I caught up with Donny driving slow past the mall with his windows down. I pulled up beside him at a light. "When's the last time you think he went to the movies?" I said. I waved at him to follow me.

Walt was in the very first place I thought to look. The woods right across from his own damn house. Same woods we'd run all through as kids. Made me think about that Halloween when he and his friends were Indians and I was a cowboy, how he'd scared the shit out of me. And then, of the night Louise told me about seeing that picture of us in our costumes. She and I in bed, and me still shaking from having her. Or no, that's not right. She'd had me, still did.

Donny and I found Walt on the trestle over the creek swinging his feet and talking to himself. He'd made the break in his pajamas.

At least he'd thought to put shoes on. That was a plus. Donny and I'd made a commotion getting to him through the snow and leaves, but he didn't look up.

"You go to him," I said to Donny. I figured it might go easier with someone he knew, and I didn't know if he'd even recognize me, all those years. Walt looked like as if he was some kind of ghost with that white hair.

Sure enough, he went with Donny, no fuss at all. I met them halfway down the bank. Donny was bringing up the rear, making sure he didn't slide back down. Walt grabbed my hand and smiled at me like this was a nice surprise, finding me there. I really don't think he had any idea who I was. His hand was ice cold. His pajamas were bunched up and stuck to his muddy shins. But he didn't seem to feel it. Donny and I were shivering hard by then.

"You picked a fine time for a walk," I said. He laughed at that.

We got back to the cars, and Donny wanted to drive him down the street. But Walt wanted to walk.

"Dad," Donny said, about to argue with him. It really rang my bell hearing Donny call him that. Any good feelings I had about helping with this rescue were gone.

"Let's just do what he wants," I said. I was thinking that's what he'd always gotten. I guess he didn't order up the dent in his head, but that didn't matter to me in the moment.

We staggered down the street.

I was about to help him make the last push to get Walt on his feet when I saw Louise in the doorway. I couldn't make out her face with the hall light behind her. She was hugging herself and shivering. I wasn't even feeling the cold myself, not by then. There was just her.

Louise reached up and touched his face, asked him why did he go and run off like that. It was almost more than I could take.

Walt straightened himself up. "How 'mout some coffee," he said.

Louise pretended not to hear this. She turned to me. "Thank you for tracking him down."

"He's alright," I said. "Needs to warm up." I didn't want to keep standing there, and then again I couldn't make myself leave.

"Come on, now," Walt said. "I'll make a pot." He sounded like as if he was sane as anyone right then. He was trying to be a good host. It was clear to me he had no idea who I was. I wished I could tell him. I wished I could explain why I was out in the cold.

Louise looked at Donny, then back at me. Donny edged past us into the hall.

"I'll run you a bath," Donny said to Walt.

"I want something to drink first," Walt said.

I had to take a chance. "You still drink it black?" I said to Louise.

She smiled, opened her mouth to say something, then stopped. "I don't drink it at all anymore," she finally said, and Donny looked at her, so I knew that wasn't the truth. She was just telling me no.

I had the feeling Donny was adding a thing or two up in his head. I decided to help him out. "You ever wonder why I'm never over here for Sunday dinner, Donny?"

"Leo," Louise said. She took a step to block my view, but I had some height on her. I craned my neck. Donny was staring hard at me now.

"It's not because I still have a thing for Sal Ventor's daughter, I'll tell you that."

"Who's Sal?" Walt said, pleasant as could be.

"You stop it, Leo," Louise said. "If you get him worked up again, I'll—"

"You'll what?" I said. I didn't need a shovel to dig my own grave. "Tell me."

Oh, she wanted to tear my throat out. And I wanted her to. Couldn't think of a better way to go. Even to have her mad at me was something.

Donny tugged on Walt's good arm, and Walt followed Donny down the hall, obedient as a dog. I heard the bathwater cut on. I didn't want to think about Louise sponging Walt down. I started for the front steps.

"You go ahead and run," Louise said to my back. "If I was you, I would, too."

I had to turn back to look at her. She was about to slam that door. I just stood there, waiting for her to do it. But she held back a second. Some of that hardness left her mouth. She felt sorry for me, she did. That was worse than anything. I knew she'd never have me in that house again after what I'd done. I headed down those steps before my knees gave out from under me. Didn't want to hear the sound of that lock turning.

Back at the lanes, Tess was waiting with a lot of questions. I told her maybe she didn't need to go asking Donny too much about what had happened with his dad. I figured I couldn't have told him any plainer who I was to him. Or at least set him to thinking. He was old enough now. But that night when I ran Tess home after we closed, when she told me you didn't keep secrets from people you loved, I wanted to sit her down and explain it all to her. Tell her how wrong she was.

* 21 *

THEN, SIX MONTHS later, there I was again. Fourth of July week-end, fireworks going off for three days straight, like as if people had nothing better to do. Donny had the day off. Tess and I were opening when he called. Walt had been gone all night.

The house looked pinched up, beaten. Not just because of those blue curtains pulled tight behind the windows, faded now. Maybe it was just me, feeling the way I did coming back there.

Donny met me at the door. He'd been up all night, looked like his head was going to snap off his neck. It wasn't right for a kid his age to look so worn out. How long did you have to be a good son? Not a question I had any real experience with.

And Louise. Even looking as caved in as Donny, she was that girl I remembered. It hurt to look at her. But there we were, the three of us, a family. What could've been.

"You here to save us?" she said.

The sound of her voice. Like sun on wood. Like a knife in me.

"Mom," Donny said.

"Call the police then," I said. "They'll find him."

She looked at me like as if I was in the way of something she really wanted to see. "I drove by the lanes. In case he was looking for you."

The thought of her coming so close, but not coming to me, cut me more than I wanted her to know. Outside, there was another round of firecrackers—*pop, pop, pop*. Louise flinched. I remembered that day on the back stoop, when Walt told me he couldn't do what husbands do. How that door slamming sent him over the edge.

"Do those things spook him?" I said to Donny.

He nodded. "He didn't even put on any shoes," he said.

Louise was looking toward the bedroom. I followed her down the hall. So there I was, in that room again with her. Twenty years, and I could still see her hanging my shirt over the back of that chair. The place smelled like the inside of a pill bottle.

"He took his gun," she said.

His trunk was in the corner of the room, standing open. "That why you think he was looking for me?"

She folded her arms tight against her chest. "I don't think he has any bullets."

"But you don't know."

She looked at me. I could see she was scared. Maybe she was thinking of her father right then. Those decisions that make everything go one way or another. She'd gone home from school with a friend one afternoon, so she lived. Maybe for the same reason her mother died.

"It's been years," she said.

"But you're okay with me finding out, right?" I didn't need to say it, because I knew it was true. Then again, I hoped it wasn't. I hoped she'd beg me not to risk it. So I'd been wrong about myself after all, see. I had all kinds of hope. Too much of it.

She smiled at me the way women do when they've had enough of you. "Not so sure you want to be a hero now, are you?" she said.

That knocked me down a notch. "Look, you called me."

"He called you," she said, nodding toward the hallway. "He believes you can fix things."

She looked me straight in the eye, like as if she was daring me to say different. But I wasn't sure myself anymore. I could look at Donny and try to find myself in his face. I could try to remember the feel of her. Or the way her hair smelled. I was sick of wanting her.

"I'll leave you to it, then." I stepped past her into the hallway. Donny was by the front door, stooped like an old man. I headed for him, but she wasn't done with me.

"Of course you will. That's always been the way, hasn't it? Where were you when he put his hand through that glass?" she said, and pointed to the windows next to the door. "Or when we nailed the windows shut or put in those deadbolts?"

I didn't even look where she was pointing. I knew that door. I'd rehung the damn thing. And watched it close in my face. Louise had her hands on her hips. "You know, he fought having a bedpan for a long time. But it got to where he just couldn't make it in time."

You want to give a man pause, let him picture not being able to point his own dick at the toilet. "I'll find him," I said.

"I'll go with you," Donny said.

"No," I said. But she had her hand on his arm before I'd gotten the word out. That was the difference, if I'd missed it. He would've had to kill her to get past her. But she could let me go. Maybe it wasn't fair to compare a mother's love to any other kind, but there were a lot of things in life that weren't fair. I'd tripped across enough of them to know.

"Your mother needs you here, I think," I said. "If I need help, I'll come get you, okay?"

Donny and I eyed each other there in the hallway. Louise was already walking back down the hall. She was through with me. Donny said something so quiet I couldn't get it.

"What?" Now that I was locked into my next step, I wanted to get out of there and get it over with. And knowing Walt was packing, and all those fireworks and people outside drinking beer on the holiday.

"Before I went to work yesterday," Donny said. "He was talking about sugar."

That stopped me. I dropped my hand from the doorknob. I saw Louise in my mother's kitchen, taking her coffee black. "What about it?" I said.

He looked at me with those tired eyes. "That you—that you gave it to her."

I put my hands on his shoulders. There was still so much boy in him, those stringy arms. What would a good father do? I had no idea. "I'll find him, Donny."

He turned away from me, and I let myself out the door. It was a fact, what people say about the truth hurting. The truth was I couldn't do any better than trying to drag my damaged brother home like a lost sock. Maybe I wanted him back in that house so Louise couldn't turn me away on my shortcomings alone.

I went straight to the lanes. When I pulled in the lot, there was Tess' sign in the window. Who could blame her? Hell, I'd fired her. I checked the door to make sure she'd locked it. Of course she had. I could've gone in and wandered around to burn a few minutes, made sure she'd shut everything down the way she was supposed to, but I knew she had. I shaded my eyes and looked at the place through the glass door. I didn't know why I was doing it. I hoped no one driving by saw me. But the roads were empty. Everyone was either at home sleeping it off or headed to the parade. And inside, everything was just as still. Like as if it was frozen. Like as if I'd never been there.

I went back to my car. No sense in putting off what was waiting for me. Then I heard a sound over by the trash bin. Kind of a whine, like an injured dog. But I knew better before I got to it. I knew that whine, all right. I'd sat there in Louise's living room with my father after Walt got home, both of us pretending not to hear it.

He was asleep next to the trash bin, pistol clutched to his chest. Probably like he'd been trained to do. Cuddling the damn thing with his good arm. Might help you survive in the moment, but it was no way to live. One of his legs jerked in that dog way, and I eased closer. I figured I'd try to slip that gun right out of the picture, put it in my trunk if he didn't wake up, or fling it in the woods if he made a fuss. Anyway, no question he'd been looking for me.

The smarter thing to do at that point would've been to get some help. But now that I'd found him, I wanted it over with. I was already running through the speech I'd give Louise when I got him home, about how this was the last time I was going to get sent on search patrol duty. If she wanted to keep a large, deranged man in her house, that was her business, and so forth.

But things didn't go like that. My arm wasn't even stretched out all the way for the gun before Walt had it pointed at me. He'd moved so fast I almost fell over. I froze.

I looked at my brother's smashed face. "Walt," I said.

Hearing his name seemed to snap his focus. He raised the gun, took better aim at my chest. The strange thing was, I wasn't scared. I felt quiet as those empty lanes.

"Mack off," he said. Still no good at that *b* sound. I straightened up, took a step back, then another. He looked calm as a judge, even on his back, hair standing on end. Donny was right, he'd left barefoot. His feet were caked with either mud or blood.

"Need a hand getting home?" I asked. I tried to sound like this was the kind of thing that happened to all of us sooner or later, waking up with a possibly loaded gun.

He kept quiet, kept the gun pointed at me. When I took another step back, he ticked it up. "Me still." Be still. He worked himself into a sitting position. His dead arm limp against his ribs.

"Look, I'm just trying to help," I said.

His mouth gaped open at this. He was laughing, but no sound. He talked slurred, but I heard him plain. "You wanna help me."

"Sure thing," I said. This was like a hustle going bad.

He got to his feet, never took the gun off me.

"I've got my car," I said. "Why don't you put that thing away and we'll go?"

He laughed again. This time a grunt. "You help enough, Leo."

My stomach turned to rock. He knew who I was. He'd known where to find me. I thought about Donny and the sugar. Had Louise told him about that? If I was going to die, I wanted to die seeing her in that blue dress, her hair down her back. I didn't need to think of making love to her, or anything that had happened since. The moment in my mother's kitchen was what counted. Everything led to and from it.

"You took her," Walt said, clear as day. "You got e'rything."

"She stayed with you."

"Out of guilt."

Whatever the reason, he was with her and I wasn't. He got to claim Donny as his son and I didn't. Now he was going to decide what to do with me. I'd spent so much time in my life lying, I figured it'd be best to end with the truth.

"Do what you want, Walt," I said.

He narrowed his eyes, and I thought I saw him start to squeeze the trigger. I waited for the blast to come. But then he lowered the gun, stumbled to the side a bit, like as if he'd put all his strength into holding me up, and now he was spent, too. He turned half away from me, the gun loose in his fingers. Then he rolled open the barrel, emptied the bullets. I felt the air slide out of me, watching that.

In the car, on the way back to the house, the gun in my trunk, Walt cried and didn't try to hide it. "I want to die." He cradled his dented forehead in his good hand "'Ut not killin' myself like a coward."

For my part, I was trying to get ready to say good-bye to Louise for the last time. *Your husband can still load a gun perfectly well*, I'd tell her. Word to the wise.

"We get to survive, Walt," I said. "That's our punishment."

And that was the truth. Living was the hard path. Living with what you couldn't have. I guess I had carried around a notion of how it would work out, all these years. With Louise. With Donny. All of it after Walt was gone. I'd had that idea so long it was like as if I'd already lived it. No one could call Walt a coward, no matter what he did. Me, now, that was another matter.

When we got to the house, I offered to get Donny to help me walk Walt in so he wouldn't have to put all his weight on his bloodied feet.

He shook his head, wiped his eyes. "I'll come in my own way," he said, clear as a bell.

I helped him out of the car and stayed close to him, just in case. I looked up and saw Tess in the front window. She knew about me and Donny knew. And it was a relief. All those years pretending, thinking I was protecting him. All those years of wanting her. Now all I wanted was some kind of forgiveness if I could get it.

Walt and I made our way up the walk. I helped him inside where Louise and Donny and Tess were waiting. I knew what people meant when you let something go, how you feel lighter. I hugged Walt before he went down the hall. It was the last time I saw him standing.

Tess Wycheski

* 22 *

THE GALAXY LANES reopened two days after Leo fired me. He hired me back the minute he got back with Mr. Florida.

"And I want you to get ready to work," he said, nodding in the direction of the lanes. Donny and Mrs. Florida were down the hall cleaning Mr. Florida up. "The women's qualifiers are in a month. We'll have just enough time to get you back in fighting form."

I stared at him. "You're kidding, right?"

Of course, I knew when the PBA qualifiers were, and that they'd be held in Toledo, at the Southwyck, which was newer than the Galaxy Lanes and almost three times as big, with sixty-four lanes. These were the qualifiers my father had been planning for. But I'd written them off when my father died, along with everything else in the Wycheski Plan.

Leo shrugged. "You've got the average, and you've got the stamina now," he said.

"But I won't be eighteen for four months," I said.

"Glad you can do simple math, Wycheski," Leo said. He stood up, rolled his shoulders back. "You make the grade, they'll let you in. I'll sign for you. You said you wanted to."

"But my mother—"

"But your father," Leo said. He pulled open a curtain, looked outside. "You also promised him."

I stood up. "You're a fine person to—" I started, but I stopped myself. I meant to say that he wasn't in any position to talk about my father, or what had been promised to him, or to talk about fathers or families at all. But then I saw his face. It might've been true he wanted me to qualify as a kind of payback for failing my dad. But I also knew he was talking about Donny, and about me. I was sure I saw something else in him just then. Some kind of need.

"Okay," I said.

Those last few weeks of the summer seemed to pass in a kind of dream, my eyes opening in the dark of my parents' old bedroom to Donny gently pulling the screen off the window and setting it against the house (a new step he'd had to take since mosquito weather set in, but he'd sprayed the screen frame during one of his mowing days so it wouldn't squeak), and the whisper of his undressing, our bodies moving against the sheets. There was a new thickness in his shoulders and arms. We were still growing, still that young, though at the time we felt old as anyone we'd ever known.

What we craved, other than each other, was routine: the rhythm of opening and closing the lanes, the short menu of customers' needs, the three of us working, me practicing for what had been, and still was, the Wycheski Plan. There was no need to think about anything changing.

But one afternoon I came home from the early shift to find my mother in the living room on the couch, holding a folder with a red-and-purple seal and *Savior Missionary* scripted in gold.

"Here you go," she said, smiling as if she'd just given me a prize. I took the folder from her and opened it. Inside were several forms, one titled "Injury Release" and another "Pledge Sheet" with a long list of things I would agree to do and not do, such as denouncing homosexuality or recognizing "Non-Christian" religions. There was a signature line next to a pair of floating hands pressed together in prayer. The application was titled "Foreign Missions Adventure Form."

"What's this?"

"It's a chance for you to do something truly great," my mother said, echoing a sentence in the brochure I'd just opened. I read the words as she said them. The AC came on and my mother shivered. "God has plans for us, Tess. But we have to win His love. Most people can't do it."

Like your father, she meant. I knew because this whole thing with the Emmanuel had started with him—when he couldn't go back to work and my mother started looking for something to pay the bills. It was just a part-time job! I wanted to shout. There'd been a time when she and I and my father had sat in this room. We'd watched television and eaten hamburgers. We'd never prayed. There hadn't been a need to. Or maybe there had been.

My mother saw the look on my face. "What is the best idea for you? Working for Leo?" she said. "Marrying Donny?" She pressed her lips together and waited.

I thought about the day I'd found her dressed for the interview at the Emmanuel. And how happy she'd seemed when she become an elder. Didn't she deserve to be?

My silence seemed to satisfy her. Maybe she thought she'd convinced me. Maybe it didn't matter to her whether she'd convinced me or not.

"I'm sorry." I said it without thinking, without knowing specifically what I was apologizing for. "But I can't do this."

My mother stood up. "We're leaving, Tess. I'm talking to a real estate agent tomorrow," she said.

She turned and headed for the stairs, and she seemed to be working hard to keep her balance. The reasons were different, but I knew how she felt. I went down the hall, pulled my father's Amflite from his bag, held its weight in my lap. There was only one person I didn't want to be without, and that was Donny. If I had to leave, then I wanted to leave with him.

And then the next week, a package came from State. Not to my house, but to Mr. Todd's. My mother, if I'd told her about it, would've said it was a sign. Mr. Todd called the lanes like he'd promised, and Leo gave the message to me.

Mr. Todd's summer school American Government class was just letting out when I rode my bike to the high school. The last of the students filed past us, all of them with bad cases of lecture face. They already looked like children to me. In fact, the whole place seemed smaller.

Mr. Todd pulled a brown envelope from his desk and handed it to me. "Open it."

The letter started with "We are pleased to inform you," and I saw the words "full tuition" and "work-study." There were several forms and a check made out to me for five hundred dollars. I brought the check, printed with an ocean scene, close to my face, studying Mr. Todd's leaning handwriting that I knew so well from the margins of my papers, where he'd written *Defend your pt. here* or *Don't leave me hanging.* "Ian and Leisl Todd," it said in the upper left hand corner. I looked at Mr. Todd, and he smiled down at me as if I were his daughter, the way I believed my father would have smiled at me.

"But I didn't go to any meeting," I said. I hadn't even bothered to type the application. I'd sent it in because I'd said I would, but I hadn't expected it to lead to anything.

"It's a new scholarship," he said, holding the envelope open for me so that I could slide the papers back inside. "Just for college bowlers. Isn't that great?"

I looked at him, and he smiled back at me. I waited for him to come clean, to tell me this was a deal he'd worked out somehow or another. Leo would've been proud, after all his speeches about everything being a deal struck. But what did Mr. Todd get on his end? Maybe the chance to save me. Maybe that was enough. Whatever the answer was, Mr. Todd wasn't cracking. He clasped the envelope, handed it back to me.

I thanked him, and he hugged me, and I heard his voice in his chest when he said congratulations. Then he said we should have lunch to celebrate. We headed outside and crossed the teachers' parking lot. A hot breeze bent the envelope forward in my hand, as if pushing me along. He put my bike in the back of his station wagon. But it was after two by then, and most of the restaurants in town were closed until dinner. That's the kind of town it was then. Mr. Todd had brought in a writer from the *New York Times* the year before to speak to our journalism class, a college buddy of his. He'd asked where a guy could get a late-night cup of coffee around here, and we'd all stared back at him as if he'd asked where he could get laid.

We ended up at Harry's. I hadn't been there since my father died. I wanted to say no, we couldn't go there, but I also wanted to have a reason to walk in again, to try to feel what might be left of him in the air. Mr. Todd bought a beer for himself and pop for me and two salami sandwiches from the cooler. He set my drink down and clinked the lip of his bottle against my can as he sat across from me. I peeled my legs up from the bench, settled them. We bit into our sandwiches. Mr. Todd drank half of his beer in two long gulps.

"So. How do you feel?"

"Nervous," I said. The salami made my eyes water. Mr. Todd noticed, misread it. He pulled a paper napkin out of the dispenser on our table and handed it to me.

"You okay?" he asked.

I dabbed at my eyes and nodded.

"And how about your mother?"

I understood that in addition to asking about her in general, he was also asking about whether I'd gotten around to telling my mother anything about school or not. I didn't want to admit that I hadn't. "She says she's selling the house," I answered.

Mr. Todd rubbed his eyes. "Oh."

"She's selling the house and giving all the money to the church. The Emmanuel."

"She said this?"

"No. But I know." I watched Mr. Todd pick at his beer bottle label and I could tell he thought I was probably wrong, or maybe he just wanted to believe I was wrong because he was an optimist, even though he'd said over and over again that journalists and thinkers couldn't be optimists. *It's a luxury the truth can't afford*, he'd said.

Mr. Todd took a swallow of beer, set the bottle down. "Tess." He pinched the bridge of his nose. "Some of those places are a—a front. For something else. Not all, but some. They set up shop, get members to sign over bank accounts, houses, and then they take off."

"I know," I said. "But I can't stop her."

"Your folks," he said then. He paused, opening his hands as if to catch the right words. "You just shoot down the middle and you'll be fine." He made the motion of rolling a bowling ball, and I wanted to explain that you actually didn't roll down the middle of a lane because the ball had to hook. But he wasn't a bowler, and so I just nodded and said I would.

Outside, Mr. Todd offered to take me home, but I told him I'd rather ride. I didn't have anything to put the envelope in, so I slipped it into the back of my shorts, pulled my T-shirt over it. Mr. Todd looked doubtful, watching this. "Do you have an account to put that money in?"

I nodded, even though it wasn't the truth. I told myself that if I didn't go to school, then I wouldn't cash the check. It seemed to be the fairest course.

He put his hands on my shoulders, squeezed, let go. "Don't forget about me, now," he said, sounding something like my father and Donny combined. I know he watched me ride away.

✳ 23 ✳

IN THE SECOND week of August, Leo drove me to the PBA women's qualifiers in Toledo while Donny stayed back to run the lanes. For the past month, Leo had kept true to the promise he'd made at Donny's house about working me hard to prepare. He'd insisted on double practices six days a week to build up my endurance. Donny set so many splits for me his back was sore, and Leo had gotten me a Dick Weber wrist brace because I was worried I'd strained it.

Leo watched my every move on the lanes. But he couldn't see everything. He didn't know I'd had Donny plug and redrill my father's sparkling red Amflite to fit my fingers. Or that I'd practiced with it while Leo was on lunch break. If he'd known, he would've gone through the roof, because you don't want to confuse your muscles when you're training. Plus the ball was heavier than what I was used to—that probably was the real reason my wrist was bothering me, not Leo's practice regimen.

Toledo wasn't the cross-country trip he'd taken with my father twenty years earlier, but I couldn't help feeling we were on more of a journey than a quick run up Route 6. I did exercises in the car to keep my wrist from getting stiff.

"How's it doing?" he asked me.

"Fine." I thought of what my father had said on that first day at the lanes, about my mother's weak wrists. Maybe he'd been talking about another weakness, one he couldn't describe to me at the time.

Maybe he was feeling the first aches of his own sickness even then and decided he shouldn't be one to point out any failings he'd seen in her.

"You're gonna roll right over them, Wycheski," Leo said.

I looked out the open window as we drove out of town. I could smell the lake, warm in the air. The heat was already drawing up from the street in waves, but there was a difference in the light over the lake, the sky a deeper blue, the shadows just a bit longer under the trees. My second summer without my father was coming to a close. I was aware of our movement in the car, and also our movement through time. I could feel the knowledge of what I was going to do down to my fingertips—my body was not resting but waiting. I was doing a balancing act in my head. On the one hand, I wanted my father with me. On the other, I wondered if the fears he'd suffered would freeze me up, too.

I fiddled with the radio knob. "You mind?" I asked Leo.

"Doesn't work," he said.

"No radio?" That surprised me. The first thing Leo did when he came in to the lanes was put on some music until people started feeding the jukebox. I'd heard every single from the latest Journey album a few more times than I cared for. Then again, Leo knew what customers liked. He'd listen to Bach if that's what they wanted.

Leo shrugged. "There's no new songs anyway."

"Give me a break," I said. But it was clear he wasn't kidding.

The qualifier was a combination event—stepladder elimination followed by match play. The Southwyck was a madhouse; we had to park at Egypt's ass, as Leo put it, and we threaded through trailers and news vans to the registration area inside the front door.

He was all business once we got to my assigned lane. "Take your time," he said, as I retaped my wrist and stretched. "Don't get cocky and forget the basics," he said.

"You're telling me not to get cocky?" I said. "Really?"

"All right, all right." He paced a tight line, back and forth. "You're going to go lane to lane. One wrong move and you're cut. So I mean it when I say take your time. Read the lane. Get down and commune with it if you have to, okay?"

I rolled my eyes. Leo said some more things to me while I warmed up, but I didn't really listen. What I was trying to do—what seemed particularly important that day—was to find my father in my roll. I could feel the ball's weight in my shoulder, not the elbow joint, which is where most people tend to hold it, which translated into weightlessness in my legs. *Imagine moving through water*—I knew I would explain it this way someday. I knew I looked like my father, and that I was feeling the things he felt—the light strain at the collar bone, the tightening of the muscles in the back of the arm, the turn of the bones in their sockets as the arm drops, swings back, then forward. I imagined my muscles were his muscles, and this was how I would keep him alive, in my roll and in my release.

We finished the stepladder, moved on to match play. I hardly looked at the other players. There came a point where the expanse of the place fell away and was replaced with something else. There was my breath inside my head. There was the blanketed sound of pinfall, the roll of polyurethane against wood, the announcer's voice. All of it a low thrum in the air, not unpleasant, but not relevant either. At one point there was a break, and they lowered the house lights and turned up the music, and I closed my eyes. It felt like Midnight Bowling at the Galaxy. It felt like my father might be standing right next to me, making fun of the disco ball. And so he would understand what I was about to do next.

We came down to the last matches. The winners would go on to qualify for the tour. I'd stuck with my Angle the whole time, which Leo had done adjustments on at least half a dozen times in the last few weeks to make it perfect for me. I'd told myself I'd just brought my father's ball to bring me luck. Getting it checked out and qualified while Leo worked the room was nothing more than a formality. I told myself people had prayed to all kinds of things over time, that there was no shame in what we loved.

It was down between me and a girl from Centerville, my mother's hometown. She looked like a nice girl, blond ponytail, athletic enough to play any number of sports. She probably wanted this as much as I did, maybe more.

So I understood the look on Leo's face when I came to my final roll and instead of pulling my Angle from the return, I went to my bag and lifted out my father's Amflite.

"What the hell are you doing, Wycheski?" He took a look at the ball and then at me. He looked at it again, recognized it. "Are you crazy?" he said.

I ignored him. There was nothing he could do, anyway. I walked past him to the foul line, found my point of origin. I wanted to soothe a certain seventeen-year-old boy's fear, meet him where he stood at the top of the Showboat. I wanted him to know that correct action could prevail. I lifted the ball to my chest and told him he was the best person I knew. I told him I missed him. My body felt warm and light, and I let myself believe what he'd said about how I could do anything with an arm like mine. I slid forward and let go.

I remember Leo shouting something, shaking his fist and smiling. I remember people clapping, patting me on the back. Everything I'd tuned out before came back—the sound in the room, the glow off the lanes, the throbbing in my wrist. I realized I was sweating and hungry.

We made our way out, and it was early evening, the sky still sunlit. I was so tired that after I ate the cheeseburger Leo bought me, I wanted to sleep in the car on the way back to Sandusky.

But Leo wanted to talk. "Nice work there, Wycheski." He was in coach mode.

I leaned my head back against the headrest and closed my eyes to let him know how excited I was about whatever he had to say.

Leo wasn't deterred. "That was quite a gesture back there, with the Amflite."

"I thought so," I said. In fact, I'd given it a lot of thought over those weeks of practice. I had imagined that moment, saving the Amflite for my final roll. I'd hoped it would be a winning roll, and that, at least, had worked out.

"You know I'm not much for speeches," Leo said.

I couldn't help myself. "But you're going to give me one now."

Leo cleared his throat. "Okay, I'll skip it and go straight to the bottom line. You're going to have to choose."

I looked at him, waited.

"What I'm saying here is that if you're going to be a pro, then you're not doing poetry out there. See? You practice so you can deliver a roll the same way, and win no matter what you are. You're not out there to have, I don't know, a beautiful moment. You're there to win."

I looked out the window while he went on about how going pro meant professional, which meant pro bowling was a job, and it just so happened that a lot of people wanted to have the job of being a pro bowler, so I couldn't mess around, etcetera. But I was hung up on what he'd said about the beautiful moment. I knew he was talking about my father. This was, if you were going to put a point on it, the thing that had ruined my father, in Leo's view. Wanting perfection.

Wanting to do something just for the joy of doing it beautifully. For the love of it.

And what did I love? I loved bowling—I loved it because my father had given it to me. He could've kept that part of his life locked away, but he had shared it with me. Everything about it—the practicing, the Wycheski Plan—had mattered to me because of him. But now Leo was saying I needed to choose. I had never thought about it that way before.

"Are you listening to me?" Leo said.

I nodded. "Sure. You're telling me I should be more like you. Right? Play hard, play to win. I get it."

Leo laughed. "I wouldn't wish being like me on anyone. I'm saying you have a chance. A real fighting chance. Okay? You're that good. So don't screw it up, is what I'm saying."

"That's some kind of congratulations, Florida," I said. Leo looked at me and back at the road. I'd surprised him, calling him by his last name the way he'd always done with me, and with my father. I was glad to have caught him off guard. I decided I wasn't done with that yet.

"You know what my father said about you one time?" I said then. We were coming back into town, the buildings blurred in evening light. Leo kept his eyes on the road. I remembered driving home that last night my father and I bowled together, and what he'd said about Leo, how much he'd loved Donny. And the ache of that—knowing all the love in the world might not make a difference. "He said that if it hadn't been for you letting him go to Vegas, he would never have had me. He said he should've thanked you."

I guess I was happy to see Leo's shoulders hunch up a bit, like he might be bracing for some kind of blow. *There's your beautiful moment*, I thought.

Leo turned onto my street and slowed at the end of my driveway. "Okay, pro," he said finally, when he came to a stop, but there was a strange tone in his voice. I turned to see where he was looking, and then I saw it, too. A "For Sale" sign—Wegman Realty and a phone number. I stared at it, a dark flag on our lawn that Donny had mowed the day before. I swallowed and swallowed again. My throat was dry. My wrist throbbed then like it was broken.

"You okay?" Leo said.

I nodded. I didn't want to look at him. I opened the car door, told him I'd leave my gear with him.

"Tess, if you need a place," he said. "There's always the apartment over my garage." He was maybe trying to make a joke. If I felt bad for myself right then, I felt worse for him. I shut the car door, but he reached across and rolled down the window.

"Look, why don't I just take you straight over to the lanes. Everyone's waiting for you." He wanted to save me, I knew, in spite of all of his tough talk. I was glad he wanted to.

"I've got to pick up some things," I said. "I'll be there in a little bit." I made my way up the front walk. He waited until I opened the front door before he backed out of the drive.

Upstairs, I heard a soothing male voice saying, "Think of Christ as your friend who walks with you when you push your cart down the grocery store aisles, even when you get the paper and go to work"— one of my mother's tapes on full blast. I'd noticed the tape recorder had made it through one of her last purges, during which she'd given away the last of my father's clothes from the attic. Our house looked like one of those model condos in magazines—just a couch and a side table to suggest the idea of furniture. Even the air felt different.

I heard my mother start the shower, and I wandered into her

room. Her dresses hung in a neat line in the closet, tapes stacked on her dresser. Then I saw a lavender duffle bag that had been mine, which I thought had been given away in a previous purge. It was wedged between the bed and the wall. It was unzipped and open, half-packed.

I went into the hallway, not sure what to do. Then I knocked on the bathroom door. "Hi Mom."

She peeked around the shower curtain, blinking. "You saw the sign, I guess?"

I told her I had. She asked how the tournament had gone, and I decided not to try to explain that it wasn't a tournament really—I told her I'd done fine.

"Well, that's good." She pulled the curtain closed again. I heard the top of the shampoo bottle click open and closed. I caught a glimpse of her in the gap between the shower curtain and the wall, eyes closed, face tilted up. I didn't underestimate how my leaving would hurt her.

"I'm going to work now," I said.

"Okay, honey. See you tonight."

"I love you," I said, and she said she loved me, too.

I went downstairs, pulled my hair into a ponytail, changed clothes. I grabbed my backpack from the back corner of my closet, and packed it with my father's bowling shirts, my photos, the envelope from Mr. Todd, and some jeans and T-shirts and underwear. I'd have to come back for my father's gear later.

By the time I locked my bike up in the rack at the lanes, the metal fan-shaped roof of the Galaxy was already reflecting the last pink tinge in the sky, and the white stones in the parking lot glowed a pale purple.

I could hear the hollow sound of pinfall even before Leo opened the doors, because of course he'd been watching for me. He yelled my name out to everyone there, and they yelled it back to me. "Wycheski!" they yelled, again and again. I stuck my backpack behind the counter. Donny was over at the control box, and I knew he'd been getting ready for the light show later. He was clapping for me and smiling, waiting for me to come to him, which I did, as soon as Leo finished taking my picture. Leo told me that by the time he got through that roll of film and got my picture printed and hung up in a frame, I'd be a pro for sure.

And there was my father on the Hall of Fame wall, smiling at me now, not as if he didn't know what the future held, but as if he did, and knew everything would be fine. It wasn't that I didn't ache anymore, looking at him. I'd just stopped willing myself not to.

That night, Donny did a great show for Midnight Bowling. You'd think it would be the same every night, but it never was. Sometimes the smoke rolled out evenly over the lanes like a piece of cloth, and the laser seemed to become different things—a spaceship, a man swimming, someone dancing. That night, the music was from *Close Encounters of the Third Kind*, and people leaned back in their booths, their faces open in the blue light. Donny made the laser disappear and then reappear in a sweep that washed over us all. He made it a knife, cutting light into the sky, then a layer of water that lifted above the lanes and spread itself so thin it was nearly invisible. The little spaceships and planets in the carpet glowed.

I closed my eyes and leaned my head back and wondered what we looked like from space. I saw my father leaning to read the lane, gliding forward to roll. *I just want to shoot down the middle*, I told him, knowing this would make him laugh. The music got louder until the laser broke apart over the lanes, coming back together into a single glowing point and then going dark. Everyone yelled and clapped.

At some point that night I went to the dimly lit back end of the lanes to get a new tub of conditioner for after we closed. This part of the lanes had always felt to me like the setting for some ghost story Leo would tell, all the machines doing their jobs with no one to watch them, funneling the pins into the right position every time— no crowding them like Leo used to do—each pin a blood cell, each belt a vein, pushing its cargo along. I tapped their warm, humming tops as I passed along the narrow walkway.

Later, I helped Leo serve up last beers and popcorns. In the control booth, Donny was shutting things down, the board lighting his face. He looked serious as an astronaut. He saw me and waved, and I waved back, and then he turned off the desk light, and I couldn't see him anymore.

Then it was cash-out time—I did change and Leo did bills. Donny was running the lane conditioner. I waited until Leo was done. He handed over the bills and watched me put them in the bag—he used a single ball bag rather than bank pouches; no sense, he said, in making yourself a target.

When we were done, I told him I had to ask him something. He knew something was up. He leaned back in his chair, lit a cigarette, considered me for a moment.

"Spill it, Wycheski."

I told him about State, and the scholarship, and the check Mr. Todd had given me. I told him the dorms were opening in a few days. Leo swiveled a bit in his chair, mulling this over.

"Well, you can always do college bowling, then go pro," he said. "Can't do it the other way around."

"I haven't talked to Donny about it yet."

"But you've decided." Leo took a long drag, let the smoke out slowly. "If you stay here, you can work when you're not on tour. Coaching, pro shop. Decent pay, benefits, for as long as we can keep the place running." He zipped the money into the bowling bag, shoved it to the side of his desk.

"And if I go?"

He tapped his cigarette, took a final drag, stubbed it out. "State's a lot further than two hours down the highway. I think you get what I'm saying."

I stared at the one photograph Leo had of himself in the whole place. It was tacked to the cork board on the wall. It looked like it had been printed on cardboard. He was a kid, maybe nine or ten, standing with his dad in front of the State. There was snow on the ground, and Leo had a pretty good-sized snowball in the palm of one hand. About the right size for duck pins. He looked like a happy kid. I thought about the ghost in the State Theatre, rolling lines of coiled smoke, how no one wanted to be the last one out. I thought about all he had ahead of him on the day that shot was taken. All that living, all that love and loss, still waiting for him.

"But I could come back, right? If I do go. In case things don't work out." I could've been asking Donny the same question. I wanted to know there was a place for me somewhere.

"Oh sure you can, Tess," Leo said. He reached across the desk and patted my cheek. "But you won't."

I felt as if something had broken loose in my ribs, and then I was crying into the brown polyester warmth of his shoulder, and he patted me. After a while he handed me some napkins to blow my nose.

"Breathe, sweetheart," he said. "Just breathe."

Once I calmed down, Leo reached into the bottom drawer of his desk for the cash box. He opened it up, pushed it toward me. "You better take this now."

I opened my mouth to say something, but Leo lifted a hand to stop me.

"You're going to need it," he said. He shoved his hand in his pocket, dug out a key on a string, handed it to me. "And this. This'll get you into my cabin on Kelleys. Not sure if I locked it, actually. You said you had a few days. Maybe you guys can take some time. Figure it out."

He stood up, stepped past me. I could hear him saying something to Donny outside the door. He was headed over to the bar to help Donny clean up. I pulled the cash out; the stack was so thick I couldn't fold it into my pocket. I went to my locker, shoved the money and the key in my bag, leaned my forehead against the cool metal door. Then I felt Donny's hands on my arms.

"Hey," he said. "Let's roll some."

I let him lead me into the dark lanes. We set up on Lane 3. Donny went up to his light board and started the stereo again, put the speakers on low. He turned on the disco ball, white lights in a slow swing, like stars in a planetarium. I sat down, switched my shoes, pulled my AMF out, and turned it in my hands. It was a little sparkling planet, all lakes and waves. I moved to the head of the lane, shoes slick like a pillow of air. I pulled in a deep breath, inhaling the place, which smelled like wood and oil and beer and my father. I balanced the ball and let its weight take my arm back, my body moving forward, my hand behind the ball, pushing it through the air. My thumb came free and my hand turned into an almost handshake, fingers flicking the skin of the ball as it left them, all this in a split second, like air leaving the lungs, like a kiss.

I shut my eyes and brought my father's face close to mine, skin around his eyes crinkling. *I'm leaving*, I told him, as the ball toppled the pins. I knew from the sound it was a strike.

By the time we got to my house it was very late. I made Donny go past it, down toward Mr. Ontero's, and turn off his lights. He'd seen the "For Sale" sign as we passed. We sat in the hollow car silence. I had my backpack and gear in his car, my bike lashed to the back.

"What are we doing?" Donny asked.

"Shh." I got out quietly, shivered in the cool air—a storm was coming, and the lake seemed to be throwing a chill from that deep layer that never warmed in summer.

"Just wait for me here, okay?"

Donny nodded and sat back. Every room was lit at my house, porch lights glowing over the sign in the front yard. My mother passed through the empty living room. I waited until I saw her walk upstairs and then I let myself in the front door. There was her lavender duffle bag on the floor, full and zipped, the keys on the bare kitchen counter.

I went first to get my father's Amflite from the closet. I heard my mother humming upstairs as I lifted her keys slowly and made my way quietly back to the front door. I looked back at the empty, brightly lit rooms. There was where I sat that morning my father asked me to come with him to the Galaxy that very first time. That moment seemed to have passed only minutes before. I whispered good-bye to the place, this ship my father had kept afloat as along as he'd been able, and then I pulled the door closed behind me.

I took the path around the side of the house to the edge of the trees behind our patio and set down my father's bag. The keys were cool in my hand. I held them up chin level, setting. My arm was trembling, tired but warm. I let it drop, fall back, my feet sliding with long, low strides, my arm swinging forward, fingers relaxing on the upswing, then releasing the keys, which flew upward for quite a ways, because they were lighter than what I was used to. They went a long way, even though my arm felt so weak. They landed somewhere in the dark trees with a muffled clink. I listened to the quiet air for a moment and then walked back to the car, where Donny was waiting for me.

Leo Florida

✳ 24 ✳

WALT DIED NOT long after Tess left. There was a small funeral at Pfeiffle's Funeral Home. Pfeiffle Junior had taken over, looked just like his daddy when we'd gone to see him the first time—same round face, same balding head with a few strings combed over. I wanted to tell him there were some things a man had to let go of. But I was one to talk.

After the funeral, which was just Louise, me and Donny, and a few old bones from the vets' home with their faded ribbons on their chests, I took Louise home. Donny had gone over to the lanes to check on things. We'd closed shop for the weekend, but I figured he was just trying to give us a few minutes.

I walked through the house while Louise put her coat away. I stood beside Walt's hospital bed. She still hadn't gotten rid of it, though he'd never come back from the vets' home once he went in. I remembered my mother's flowered sheets on the bed that had been there before. I felt like as if I could smell the candles Louise and I had lit all those years ago. There was that rocking chair still in the corner where she'd hung my pants. I didn't feel one bit sorry thinking about it. I'd lived with it long enough—in the end, I'd been right. The harder road was surviving.

I heard Louise in the kitchen. I headed in there, watched her fill the coffeepot and plug it in. It took me a minute to realize it was the one my parents had from all those years ago.

"That thing still work?"

She scooped coffee into the can at the top. "Works fine."

"Thought you didn't drink coffee anymore."

"I'm making it for you." Still with her back to me, getting down a cup and a spoon. The percolator coughed like an old car and started to churn. I saw that girl standing in my parents' kitchen in her blue dress, too tough for sugar. There was no point in waiting, far as I could see.

"When's the last time you been out to dinner?"

She turned around then, eyebrows raised. I'd surprised her. Her eyes were red from crying at the funeral, but she was spent now. She shook her head. "I wouldn't have thought you'd ask out a widow on the funeral day." Still that flat-land accent after all these years. *Widah.*

"Not even me."

"Not even you, Leo." The way she looked at me—nothing else to call it but gentle. Not put out, not amused. Just like as if she could see all the way into and through me. I had to hand it to her. To say I wasn't asking her out was a lie, and I knew she'd say she didn't need anyone carting her around out of sympathy.

"You pick the night," I said. "Once a week. We'll eat, and I'll take you home. I won't ask to come in, and I won't worry you any other time. I'll talk to Donny," I said.

"To ask permission?"

"Not permission," I said. "Just don't want to spring anything on the boy." *Our boy.*

"He's a grown-up now, Leo," she said. "But it's fine to spring things on me?"

She was fierce, chin up like that. And too quick for me. When had I started living in two times at once? I was with the girl in my mother's kitchen and the woman on her own ground. She wasn't giving up an inch of it. She'd stood by Walt. She'd loved him. Maybe she'd loved me once. Whether she could again was a question I didn't want to risk just yet.

She took a step toward me and put her hand on my face, just let it rest there. No woman had looked at me that close except my own mother.

"Why don't we sit together," she said. She turned then and got another cup out of the cabinet, set it next to the one she'd gotten down for me. She poured us two cups, black. She unlocked the deadbolt on the back door, and we sat on the back stoop, in the afternoon shade, sipping.

I told her everything I could think of. How I'd lost my folks' money, myself. Prison and Atlantic City and Bern calling me home. Donny at the bottom of my steps. And that second time Walt got out, when he came after me. How, after that, I'd figured out I had to show Tess she was a pro—maybe for her dad, sure. But also because of who she was.

"And I talked to Donny," I said. "After Tess left."

Louise turned her head then. She'd been letting me rattle on, elbows propped on her knees. We were on our last cup from the pot.

"He knew anyway, I think," she said. "All that time."

I couldn't look at her. I was still scared she'd put me out. I thought of her standing there pregnant on that spring day. There was no point in trying to explain why I wanted to get on my knees just then, in my sad, stiff, old man body, and hold her hands. But that's what I did. I rested my head on her lap. She let me stay that way until our coffees got cool.

Tess Wycheski

✳ 25 ✳

DONNY AND I were the first car on the first ferry out of Marblehead a few hours after he brought me by my house that one last time. We'd spent the night at his house, with Mrs. Florida's blessings. Before she went to bed, she made us sandwiches for our trip.

The ferry took the same route it had when my father first met my mother. The dawn sky was gold on our trip across the water to Kelleys Island, everything lit—our faces, our hair, the glowing signs of Cedar Point popping on and off as we passed—as if we'd made it happen.

We hadn't thought to bring sheets, but we had the blankets Donny kept in his car for our parking expeditions. We spent the day in bed in Leo's two-room cabin. Later, hunger drove us out; we went out to the Village Pump for dinner. That night we walked to a small, stony beach and looked out over the black glass of the lake. We sat thigh to thigh, leaning against each other. I wondered if it was the same spot my parents had sat almost twenty years earlier, and I said that to Donny. So maybe I shouldn't have been surprised by what Donny said then, but I was.

"What do you think about us getting a place together? You and me," he said.

I knew he was asking not just because he'd seen the "For Sale" sign in front of my house. But maybe he'd thought about it already. I certainly had—all those nights when he'd snuck in, and that one time when my mother was gone and we'd risked walking naked down the hallway to get a glass of water, and how I was shaking, afraid of getting caught—I'd thought how nice it would be to not have to sneak. When I'd imagined where Donny and I might live, I saw a small white cottage with flower boxes and a porch swing. Whether this house was in Sandusky or elsewhere was never a question I'd considered. And, oddly enough, I'd never put my hand on the doorknob and walked inside. I tried to picture the Turd parked in front. I tried to imagine us sitting in one of the sunny cheerful rooms I was sure would be inside, but I couldn't.

When I didn't say anything right away, Donny pressed his face against my neck. A patient, waiting kiss. Then he slid his hands back onto his lap, folding his fingers together, closing them carefully, as if it was important that he do it just right.

"I want to," I said then. "But just not right away."

I told him about the envelope I'd made sure to put in my backpack—the congratulations letter and forms from State. I'd been meaning to tell him since that lunch with Mr. Todd, but then again I also hadn't wanted to, because I believed I hadn't yet decided. When I imagined us living there, what always came to mind was a dorm room, not unlike the one in the college of Chelsea's and my girlhood fantasies. But I knew that sort of thing wasn't allowed on campus; we'd have to get an apartment.

I was saying these things and I watched Donny as I talked—his shoulders, the angle of his head, whether he was chewing the inside of his lip or not—and I tried to read his reaction. I got to the part about how maybe, if I took the scholarship money, I could go ahead and start, and he could follow when he was ready and get a job.

He looked at me, then over the water. "I have a job."

I realized then that I had to be careful of what I said next, and this was new between us. I looked over that same stretch of water and wondered what he was seeing. I could see my young father, emerging from those black waves as if being born into his new life. And my mother, afraid because she knew she was in love. And Leo, doing what he could for a son he couldn't claim. Even Chelsea—I could see her, too—the way she'd looked when I told her I didn't care about the things that mattered to her, how I'd felt I was standing on the edge of a huge expanse, the rest of the world on the other side. I turned to Donny. I was thinking about what Leo said in the car coming back from Toledo, about having to choose.

"We get to decide. Don't you think that's fair? They got to choose and now it's our turn."

He lifted his chin, a single nod. I thought maybe this was a good sign.

"We could have a life here," Donny said then, and I knew he meant back home. He wouldn't leave his parents—his mother, Mr. Florida, Leo. He would stay and take care of them. And this was what made him so good; this was part of what I loved about him. I wanted more than anything to feel the same. But in that moment I knew I didn't. I wanted to try another place, just for a while. At the time, I believed I would come back. I had not thought of living my life anywhere else. I closed my eyes and let myself in the front doors of the Galaxy Lanes. My home. The gleam off the returns, the warm light off the lanes. Leo opening for my father and me on those late nights when my father couldn't sleep, and there we were, in our skimming ship. I squeezed my eyes shut tighter, trying to fight down the ache in my chest. I wanted to force myself back in time, even only a few weeks, to when I hadn't had to ask myself that question: What next? I had lost my father, but I still had my life, the only one I'd ever considered. This was all Leo's fault—I decided—with his stupid speech. It was Mr. Todd's fault, too. They had turned me out of my own skin.

I watched Donny pull a weed from the stones, and its onion smell rose from his fingers as he stripped away each ribbon of green. His eyes were on the water, but his hands were busy with that slow work. I wanted them on me. This was, at least, something I still knew to be true. And it was a relief. I wanted him the same as always; my feelings hadn't changed. I said that we could take our time, that there was no harm in waiting.

He tossed the weed and leaned back on his hands. He smiled at me, shook his head, and there was something in his face that showed me what he would look like years from then. His shoulders would thicken more, but he wouldn't get a gut like Leo—he would stay slim like his mother, and his cheekbones would show a little more, and his brown hair would darken, then lighten slowly to gray.

He leaned to kiss me. "I used to believe all that, too, about getting to choose."

I know I cried at some point, trying to convince him. And then I tried to undress him, right there on that pile of stones, but he wouldn't let me. He said we just needed to go to sleep and when we woke up in the morning we'd feel better. He said whatever happened between us was up to me, which made me feel I'd already done something to him, something I couldn't fix.

But the next morning, when I tried to talk about it again, he didn't want to. "Let's just stay here as long as we want to stay here, okay?" he said, his voice still thick with sleep. We were naked in that old creaky bed, one blanket underneath us, one blanket on top. I remember the walls as single planks of wood with light streaming through the seams, but it must've been more finished than that.

"And then what?" I said.

"And then," he stopped, closed his eyes again, rested his forearm over his face. I traced with my finger a blue rope of vein running from his wrist to the inside of his elbow, where the skin was thin and pale. It was a man's arm, but delicate, and it made me ache.

"Donny, I'm—"

"You're leaving." He pulled his arm away, looking hard at me, though his face was still soft with sleep. We were thigh to thigh underneath our blanket, but there was a blur to him, as if he was drifting back from me, the air thickened with a distance I could feel rather than see. "You're leaving, and I'm staying, and we both know it, Tess."

We spent two more days there. We fried eggs in the morning on Leo's hot plate, took walks with picnics of bread, cheese, and apples in the afternoon, drank beer and ate pizza we bought by the slice in the evening. We probably walked the entire island. The only place I wanted to make sure to visit was the glacial grooves, because I remembered my father talking about them, how the rock looked like frozen waves. We didn't talk about what my mother might be doing to try to find me, or whether Leo was doing okay back at the lanes. In fact, I don't think we talked very much because any conversation would lead us to the one neither of us really wanted to have.

But the afternoon we left, I reached for Donny's hand in the car as we drove onto the ferry. "Are you going to visit me?"

He rolled his eyes. "I said I would. It's not that far."

This was true, but it did seem far. Donny parked and another car slid in behind us, and we got out and leaned against the railing. It was a hot day, the breeze off the water humid in our faces. We stood with arms around each other until we couldn't feel the pressure of each other's touch anymore. The land seemed to be easing toward us rather than the other way around. We'd decided that we'd give it a few weeks for me to get settled at school and then see what we wanted to do. It seemed a far cry from those nights we'd spent in my parents' old bedroom, planning trips out west. I wanted Donny to say he'd go with me that day, find a job, save money for him to go to school, too. I wanted to convince him that everyone would understand. Leo especially. But neither of us said anything about that.

After the ferry, we headed south on Route 2. What did we say on the way? What songs did we listen to? I don't know. I remember coming over a hill on a stretch of narrow farm road, the asphalt gleaming like a bright thread in the afternoon sun, a seam in the green all around us. And then we were coming into the city, turning where the big signs told us to on campus.

"Nothing's going to change," Donny said, maybe to himself, when we pulled into a parking space. I decided, because I wanted so much for it to be true, to believe him.

But a few days later, Chelsea was my first visitor at State, not Donny. We sat on my lumpy twin bed and drank beer until we were too sleepy to talk anymore. Chelsea yawned and stood up to climb in the top bunk, which was open because my roommate went home to Kent every weekend. I wondered why she hadn't just gone to Kent State instead; it would've been a lot cheaper than driving her laundry three hours each way.

At that point, I was drunk enough to risk asking if Chelsea had heard anything about my mother. Chelsea turned away from the bunk ladder then, wobbled over, and sat down next to me again.

"Didn't Donny tell you?" she said. "The house sold just a couple of days ago."

She put her hand on my arm. "I think she's already gone."

✳ 26 ✳

THAT LEO WAS dead was something I couldn't believe until I came back. Twenty-five years, and the town had changed and not changed, the way a place that lives inside you does.

The lot outside the Galaxy Lanes is now paved, and the spaceship-dotted carpet on the walls that glowed when Donny ran the light shows during Midnight Bowling has been replaced with solid blue. This Chelsea told me when she stopped in at the lanes after hearing the news about Leo. She wouldn't be caught dead in a bowling alley otherwise, she told me on the phone, not catching her own joke. Because that's exactly where Leo is—his ashes, at least—sitting on the front counter where I first met him more than thirty years ago.

It was a heart attack—he'd died in his sleep in the early morning hours in Bern's old house. Donny's mother called the ambulance that took Leo's body away. Chelsea got all of this from her second and soon-to-be former husband, the father of her three daughters, who is a doctor of some kind. He knew one of the EMTs who'd responded to the call.

Though Chelsea had left Sandusky as promised—marrying immediately after graduating from Bowling Green and moving to Phoenix, where she met her second husband—she and her family came back to Sandusky a couple of years ago, after Chelsea's father had his heart attack, the first of a series that eventually killed him.

"Go figure," Chelsea said over the phone after the news about Leo, moving briskly, as she always did, to her own concerns. "I said I'd never come back either, and here I am again, and now a single mother. You can imagine how well things are going with my mother."

I could see Mrs. Vickham—though as a woman younger than Chelsea and I are now—shimmering by the pool in her swingy pants, her highlighted hair piled on her head, her face bright with blush and lipstick. And then years before that, leaning on the counter in our kitchen, sipping on a can of Tab and chatting with my mother.

That old sorrow for my mother is like a window I can't bring myself to close—worse even than losing my father, because our separateness was a choice, at least at first. I learned later, long after Chelsea told me about our house being sold, that my mother had actually deeded it to the Emmanuel, and it was later sold to another family. Maybe this was why my mother never tried to contact me, because she knew I would have seen her decision as a betrayal. That and because of how I had left.

In those first few months of school, I wondered if I'd made a mistake, if I should ask Leo for that job he'd offered me. Donny came to visit a few times during that first year, and we sent letters. Eventually, I wrote one to break up with him, and I never heard from him again. I suppose he accepted it, the way he had accepted so much else in his life. I got summer jobs and sublets in Columbus when school wasn't in session. I never went back home. For a long time I couldn't bear to think of it even.

After I hung up with Chelsea, I looked at my calendar and was relieved to find there was a conflict. My older daughter had a championship tournament, and I wouldn't be able to go to that and Leo's funeral. Besides, I told my husband, I didn't see any point in going to

funerals. The person you love is already gone. If you hadn't kept up
with them in life, why start then?

My husband said the funeral I had to go to was the town. He said
I had to go to those places again and see them with the people gone,
or changed. "Drive by your old house," he said. "Visit your father's
grave. Go to the lanes and say goodbye to Leo."

My husband is an engineer. Through the eighties and nineties, he
installed automatic pinsetters in small towns and big towns turning
into cities all over the country—places where the latest setups hadn't
yet arrived. He'd urged me, over the years, to track down my mother.
In every town he worked in, he checked the local phone books for
me, looking for my mother's name. But by the time I was ready to
try on my own, it had been so long, and there was nothing about a
Pauline Wycheski online or anywhere. So I guess I shouldn't have
been surprised that he wanted me to go to Leo's funeral.

Even Chelsea hadn't ever been able to find my mother, and she
could find almost anything—for example, she'd found evidence convincing enough about her second husband's affair to secure excellent
terms for the divorce. Meanwhile, she began immersing herself again
in the town she'd always schemed to leave. She checked the *Sandusky
Register* for wedding and divorce and birth notices every day. She
called me when Mr. Todd got fired for having a relationship with a
just-graduated student. And she'd kept me informed on Donny.

She said he'd been cordial to her when she'd stopped in after seeing Leo's obit. He told her about the updates to the lanes—the new
carpet, digital scoreboards, new pinsetters, the ash trays taken out
now that the place is nonsmoking. He'd kept his hair, she reported,
and hadn't gotten fat. He'd bought his mother a condo out near the
mall a few years back. He still lived in the house on Pipe Street, which

he'd fixed up. And he still went once a year to Leo's cabin on Kelleys Island and fished. And—this I already knew, or she would've told me first thing—he'd never married.

After Chelsea's call, my older daughter, almost seventeen, said I shouldn't be afraid to go home. When I said that a lot of people believe you can never really go home, she gave me the same encouraging smile I've given to her all her life. She said if she could handle the championships, I could handle a day-trip. I'm her coach, the high school coach in fact, but I'm a mother first, and it's nice to see wisdom in your child. I've put all her trophies in the window, just like my father did. She takes them down, just like I did. My husband doesn't bowl very much, except to test his work. But he comes to every match and tourney.

And so I'm on the Miss America Highway, coming toward Sandusky from the west, which was the way Donny and I started out after leaving Kelleys Island. We took our time on Route 2 before going south because it was a pretty drive along the lake, and also because Donny wasn't in a big rush to deliver me to college and to a life that, he understood better than I did, wouldn't include him.

Maumee Bay. Camp Sabroske, Jerry's Ice Cream Parlor—still painted in pink polka dots—near the Turtle Creek RV Park. The Bait Barn, the Lake Erie Shiners. The Thomas Edison Bridge, the Angler's Inn. The lake on my left flashes between red-tinged leaves, and the sky is so blue it makes my throat ache. The roads are wider now, and better marked, and there are a lot more buildings and signs, all reassuring me that I'm going where I need to go, and that when I get there I can buy whatever I want. I feel lost anyway. But no matter what my daughter says, I'm not scared of the feeling anymore.

The airport where Donny and I drank beers and watched planes, the drive-in where we pretended to watch movies, still there. In daylight, it's hard to say if it's still open, what with restaurants that deliver and movies you can order online. It's hard to say why people leave their houses at all.

I have time, driving around before the funeral, to go by my old house. There's a late-model Ford in the driveway, plastic toys on the lawn. The house is freshly painted white with black shutters. The windows are open, and the early fall breeze off the lake carries the smell of leaves, boat fuel, cooling earth. A line of Canadian geese arrows across the sky. Someone's mowed a lawn nearby, and after all this time the green watery scent still makes me think of Donny, grass clinging to his forearms, standing at that front door, waiting for me. My father has been dead for twenty-six years, and I'm looking for myself in that house, where a child's voice rises and falls from somewhere inside, and there is the clatter of plates, the reasonable sounds of dinner. So I'm not too worried about idling in my car across the street, with my windows rolled down, until a car comes along behind me and turns into our driveway. I turn my car around at the dead end, and as I pass the house again, I see a young father walking purposefully to the door.

I did try to call my mother once, from a pay phone. The number she'd left with Leo was the front desk of the new Savior Missionary in Marietta. The woman who answered didn't sound like her, and I hung up without saying anything.

Now, I sit in my car in the parking lot in front of the Galaxy Lanes. It looks like tourney time with all the RV's in the lot, but it's just the old bowlers coming to pay their respects. My father said it was the same when Bern died in 1973, too. This was how my father had discovered Leo was back in town. My father had stepped inside, breathed in the air, told himself maybe it was time to come back.

It makes sense that Leo's funeral would be here, because this is

Leo's church. Before my father died, my mother would have rolled her eyes at such an idea. Afterward, she would have talked about the offense to God. Back at Bern's funeral, everyone said it was a good thing Bern's wife had gone first, God rest her, because she never would have allowed it.

It's embarrassing to me how shaky I feel, getting out of my car. I've got my gear in the trunk, but I take only my purse. I decide I'll only stay an hour—I'm having dinner with Chelsea and her daughters tonight. This is just a stop on the way. Leo would tell me to straighten my back. My father would, too. But maybe Leo felt the same shakiness when he made it back to Sandusky, and when Donny found him in that apartment behind Bern's house and stood his ground, not knowing at first what he was seeing. And my father, too, when he brought me to the Galaxy that first time, to show me how to be humble about what we love. The point is not that you get away from fear, but that you move along with it. You don't let it freeze you in place.

Above the aluminum arches of the Galaxy Lanes, the sky is that fragile violet of a late fall afternoon. I can smell the lake carried low in the air, and just above that, the leaves, turning in those cool, narrow breezes.

I'm at the glass doors, and there are a lot of people inside, and someone turns and I know I've been seen but maybe not recognized. I want to stop and close my eyes and see the place as it was before the way it is now takes over. My father walking in to find Leo that first day with me hanging onto his finger, and how I didn't know what it was for them to stand across the counter from each other again, two people who had crawled home. The spaceship-dotted carpet on the walls, Bern's promise that we were in a new age, already faded and smoke-dulled by then. The two pinball machines past the pro shop, the shoe racks, the chalk dust, the yeast smell of beer, the circulation of the balls down the lane, pins cradled in the setters, underneath and back up again, the air and blood moving through us. The old men I knew are gone, and there are new ones to take their places. I could walk up to them and throw my arms around any one of them, and tell them we were lucky, lucky for the time we had. I could say there was this time that I lived in, and I didn't know what it felt like until it was over. My father at the line, turning to me, telling me never to bowl with too much weight. Let the arm swing back—let gravity do its work. Never hold on too tight. I listened, and I'm sorry for it.

I walk toward the counter out of habit and then stop and turn back toward the lanes. People look at me and look away, and I'm relieved to not be recognized for now, while I get my bearings. I glance from face to face, almost start toward one man, thinking it's Mr. Todd. But, no, it's just a guy who looks like Mr. Todd might have if he hadn't aged and had decided mullets were still a good hairstyle for him. Then I see Mrs. Neidermeyer, whose son was my classmate and whose father had worked at Engineered Fittings with my father. She looks as if she's been trying for a long time to pull in air through a very small straw. Near her is Taft Peeler, partially turned away from me, but I recognize his height and blond hair, faded but still thick, the slab of one of his hands as he scratches under the collar of his shirt. I start over to him, even though I have no interest in talking to him, because I'm worried that if I don't talk to someone soon, I'll turn around and walk out the door. But just as I get close enough to tap him on the shoulder, he turns, and I see a white flash at his throat and realize his shirt is actually a priest's tunic. He smiles, ready to greet me, and I'm certain he doesn't know who I am, but I swerve anyway and walk into Mr. Todd himself.

"Tess," he says. He does not have a mullet; his hair is short and gray, and he wears small round glasses and a dark turtleneck—he seems to have evolved from the Jesus on those pamphlets my mother collected to a sad-eyed John Lennon. He takes my hands in his and I notice he's wearing no wedding ring, and he sees that I've noticed.

"Our son got a GED and a stock job at Cedar Point, so he's okay," he says. "But he took it out of us."

"I'm sorry," I say. But I want to weep with relief, that he is who he is, that he knows who I am. He looks at me, trying to decide something.

"Your mother came to me, you know, looking for you."

I look into his apologetic eyes. He shakes his head slowly. "I said I didn't know anything," he says.

"I've never found her." The words wedge in my throat. I cover my mouth and cough to have a reason for looking away.

"You will," he says. "I'll help you. I will if you want."

He takes me by the shoulders, and I'm afraid that if he hugs me I will not be able to keep my composure. But instead of pulling me to him, he is turning me toward the lanes. "Someone's over there you'll probably want to talk to."

Donny's mother. Her hair is gray-blond and short, and her freckles have faded. She's still thin and tall, but straighter in how she stands. I start toward her and she sees me, and she walks toward me and hugs me. It isn't until she pulls back that I can see the grief in her face. She is shivering with it, her skin papery and dry. She tells me how happy she is to see me. I bite the inside of my lip to steady myself.

"I'm sorry it's been so long," I hear myself saying. "Since I've been back."

She says, "When Leo coached he made the kids watch videos of you. 'Look at her delivery,' he'd say, or 'Watch how she releases. Excellent timing.'"

She smiles. And then, "He was proud of you."

I can't think of anything to say to this. Then, I'm not sure if she says she'll bring me to Donny, or if I just understand that's what she's doing when she takes my hand. I know I'll recognize him, would recognize him anywhere, even though the boy I remember is only a couple of years older than my daughter.

His back is turned, and I can see the long muscles in his arms, his hands at his sides. I know exactly the line of his shoulders. He's tilted his head to listen to a woman talking. She's telling him a story. She cups her hands and spreads them and cups them again, and she seems to be saying, *See what I mean?*

He nods and then I'm beside him, his mother saying my name. He turns and there is that long moment, though only a part of a second, when his eyes have met mine but the recognition hasn't quite reached his face. A neutral, kind expression. He's going to speak to this person his mother has brought to him. He's already opening his mouth to greet me when it hits him. His hair is darker and flecked with gray at his temples. He wears it very short, so the features of his face look larger than I remember, the bridge of his nose more pronounced, shadows under his brow and cheekbones and jaw.

Then he knows who I am and he presses his lips together and swallows. He's bracing himself. I take his hand—I don't see any sense in pretending a careful, friendly greeting. People are turning now, because they can feel a pull in the air.

"I didn't think you'd come," he says, and when he leans, as he'd always had to in the past, to hug me, I say, "I loved your father, Donny"—meaning both of them, meaning mine, too. And I feel that move through him. Over his shoulder I can see Leo's Hall of Fame wall. There are more pictures now, all faces I don't recognize. Except for my father, still in the middle of the top row; I can see that from across the room. Same gold-speckled frame; the newer ones are black. And mine next to it. Leo had put it up anyway, even though I left.

Donny sees where I'm looking. "You still can't have it," he says of my father's picture, and then he smiles and asks where my gear is.

I could explain that I left it in my car, but I just shake my head. The truth is I want to roll the way I did that first day. I don't want it to feel familiar.

The place is filled now only with the voices of people I remember; their faces come into focus for me now. The returns are still, the balls in quiet rows. Dead, Leo would say, and he'd laugh at how people think they're doing the right thing by not rolling at a time like this. Donny leads me by the hand to the counter, sets up Lane 3. I choose my weight while he gets the shoes. Leo reminds me there's no perfect strike. I follow Donny to the lane, and my father steps back from the line. Donny chalks his hand while I lace up. He asks if I have pictures of my kids. I turn to the bench where I've set my purse. I'm about to ask him if he remembers that year when he started Midnight Bowling, how Leo thought he was crazy. I want to tell him how it felt to me, the lanes starlit, the way you could close your eyes and believe you were anywhere. When I look up, he's already sliding forward, cradling the ball, letting it go.